Nigel McCrery worked as a dete[ctive] [...]
shire Constabulary, until he le[...]
Cambridge University. He has created and written some
of the most successful television series of the last ten
years. He is also the author of five internationally best-
selling Sam Ryan mysteries. Nigel lives in London.

Praise for the Lapslie series

'One of the most memorable monsters of modern crime
fiction'   *Daily Express*

'As repulsive and engaging a killer as any encountered in
recent memory'   *Los Angeles Times*

'A fast-moving, original and often genuinely frightening
novel. The main character is a brilliantly horrible creation'
                                            Mike Ripley

'Nigel McCrery introduces an excellent new detective . . .
highly original'   *Daily Mail*

'Gripping new series . . . a very sadistic murderer'
                                            Daily Mirror

SCREAM

Nigel McCrery

Quercus

First published in Great Britain in 2010
This paperback edition published in 2011 by

Quercus
21 Bloomsbury Square
London
WC1A 2NS

A CIP catalogue reference for this book is available
from the British Library

ISBN 978 1 84916 117 6

10 9 8 7 6 5 4 3 2

Printed and bound in Great Britain by Clays Ltd, St Ives plc.

For my Aunty Pat and Uncle Derek,
for stepping in when I needed them most.
With all my love.

PROLOGUE

The girl was sobbing uncontrollably now. It was the mask that had started her off – the macabre metal face looming suddenly out of the darkness of the cellar – but now, seeing the drill with its glinting brass bit coming towards her, she was on the verge of hysteria. Her upper lip and chin glistened with a combination of mucus, tears and saliva, and her jeans were soaked around her crotch where in terror she had voided her bladder.

Her captor's hand hefted the weight of the cordless electric drill. The battery pack was fully charged. It would run for an hour at least, which should be more than enough time.

The girl's jeans had been ripped across at the knees, exposing both kneecaps, and her legs were fastened to the metal chair with cable ties. There was no give in those ties. She wouldn't be able to move her legs, even when her captor started drilling, no matter how hard she tried.

And she would try, that much was certain. She wouldn't be able to stop trying. Within a few minutes she would be struggling so hard she would be tearing her muscle fibres in her attempts to get her legs out of the way of that drill bit. And she would be screaming so loudly that she would drown out the noise of the motor.

'I'm going to start drilling in a minute,' her captor whispered, feeling the tickle of breath hitting the inside of the mask and bouncing back to caress lips and chin. 'I'm going to drill slowly and horizontally through your left kneecap and into your femur, right into the marrow. The pain will be phenomenal. Absolutely phenomenal. You will never have felt pain like it in your life. I want you to know two things. Firstly, there's nothing you can do to stop it – nothing you can tell me, nothing you can offer me. Only I can stop it, and I'm only going to stop when the chuck holding the drill bit is grinding against your kneecap. Secondly, when that happens, when I've got as far up inside your bone as I possibly can, I'm going to repeat the entire process with your right knee. And after *that*, I'll start work on your elbows and your humerus.'

Her breath was coming in short gasps now, and her pupils were dilated so wide there was virtually no iris visible: just black, terrified holes into the raging fear inside her head. She tried to say something, but she couldn't force the words out past her choking sobs. Not that there was any point. Her words weren't important.

Only her screams were important now.

CHAPTER ONE

A bright-red insect was hovering outside Mark Lapslie's hotel room window. It was small and spindly, with a bulbous abdomen that doubled back underneath itself until it pointed in the same direction as its head. It was about an inch long, and it moved in short spurts so quickly that it almost disappeared from one spot and reappeared instantaneously in another, consciously or unconsciously dodging the fat drops of rain that fell monotonously past the window. Lapslie had never seen anything like it before. It looked to him like the insect equivalent of a hummingbird. He wondered idly if it was poisonous.

Beyond the insect lay the sprawling, low-rise buildings of Islamabad, capital city of Pakistan. Off to the left lay the diplomatic enclave, with its security guards and barriers. On his arrival in Pakistan Lapslie had visited the 1960s vintage concrete edifice of the British High

Commission to get a briefing on the security situation and the 'do's' and 'don'ts' of staying in a country which was about as close to the Taliban and Al-Qaeda heartlands as it was possible to get without actually being in a war zone – although the several bomb explosions that had occurred at various Army barracks in nearby Rawalpindi and Peshawar since his arrival made him wonder if the war had in fact actually moved to Pakistan without anyone admitting it. Almost straight ahead, on the horizon, he could see a triangular mosque, white with an inlay of coloured tiles, stark against the ominously low grey morning sky.

A street ran past the hotel's main entrance. Despite the rain it was full to bursting with dusty cars of uncertain age, weaving mopeds, small buses that could take only six or seven people inside, with another two holding on to the outside, and the ever-present 'jinglies' – lorries whose back ends had been enclosed with wooden panels painted with landscapes, abstract designs, jet fighters, tigers and anything that caught the painters' fancy with the obvious exception of people's faces, the artistic representation of which was forbidden by Islam on the basis that it verged on idolatry. And then, of course, there was the reason the lorries were called 'jinglies' – the curtains of chains and pewter discs that hung from any available edge and swung back and forth as the lorries stopped and started in the heavy traffic. According to the security officer in the High Commission, the 'jinglies' had nothing to do with religious custom – they were the Pakistani equivalent of fluffy dice hanging from the rear-view mirror or a stuffed toy pressed against the back window.

And everywhere there were men and boys dressed in the standard *salwar kameez* – baggy trousers worn under a tunic, invariably in brown or cream – along with jarringly Western black leather shoes, highly polished. Some of them were strolling in a particular direction, but many of them were just standing on corners or on the strips of grass that ran down the centre of the roads, singly or in small groups, despite the rain. It didn't look to Lapslie as if they were waiting for anything in particular. They were just . . . standing. Passing time.

According to the security officer at the High Commission, some of those loiterers were almost certainly working for the ISI, the Pakistan intelligence service, and were 'dicking' Westerners who arrived and left – making a note of who they were and where they were going. Looking at them Lapslie was convinced that they were either particularly naturalistic actors or they were taking the opportunity to just stand around and star vacantly at the passing traffic like their brethren.

The Serena Hotel was one of the only two hotels whose security was rated by the British High Commission as high enough for diplomats and government-sponsored visitors to stay at; as the other was the Marriott, which had been seriously damaged by a car bomb a year or two back, the Serena was where Lapslie had been put. He was taking part in a symposium involving law enforcement officials from the UK and America and their Pakistani equivalents, discussing ways of making the country safer. It had been Chief Commissioner Rouse's idea to send Lapslie, despite his medical history, but Lapslie had been surprised to find that he was enjoying himself. The Serena was like something out of the Arabian Nights, with marble floors and stairs, pointed arches, intricately carved wooden screens, musicians playing traditional instruments and men who would appear by your side with pots of green tea if you stood still for more than ten seconds. And it was quiet. No piped background music coming out of speakers everywhere, no raised voices. Even the musicians, with their *tablas* and *sitars* and *dholaks*, caused his synaesthesia to make his brain taste a subtle pistachio flavour rather than anything more intrusive, although that may have had more to do with the thorazitol he was taking to control it and the workshop that he had started back in the UK than anything intrinsic to the music.

Now, standing in his thickly carpeted hotel room, looking out of the double-glazed and probably blast-resistant window, Lapslie could hardly hear anything. It was as if he were cocooned inside a bubble of silence. And he loved it. For the first time in ages he felt completely at peace with the world and with himself. And, strangely, he felt at home.

There was something familiar about the bits of Pakistan that he had seen since he had arrived. On the first day of the symposium the delegates had been taken by minibus on a tour of the capital, taking in the Faisal Mosque, Parliament House and the Pakistan Monument and finishing with a buffet reception at a Pakistan Army base in Rawalpindi. Lapslie had been to a number of British Army bases back in England, either on duty or attending a ball at the invitation of a friend, and the base in Rawalpindi seemed to him to be modelled exactly on the English design, down to the regimental regalia and the photographs on the walls. He had mentioned this to one of his hosts, who had said: 'What you have to remember is that you British built all this for us. We took it over when you left, and we kept the traditions going.' He paused, smiling. 'Even when you abandoned most of them yourself.'

On the way back, looking out of the grimy minibus window, Lapslie had seen children on almost every street playing impromptu games of cricket, just as he imagined it had been like in England in the 1950s.

A swathe of green grass edged with flagstone walkways led away from the base of the hotel towards the security barriers separating it from the road. Guards in loose white two-piece uniforms walked around the perimeter of the hotel, keeping to the walkways, their shoulders and backs dark from the rain. Each of them held a rifle or a shotgun. As a police officer the thought that a country was so lawless that even the hotels had to be protected by armed guards horrified him, but as a Westerner staying in one of those hotels, he found it reassuring.

A marquee was being erected on the grass. One of the doormen had told Lapslie that a wedding was being held the next day. Lapslie had a strong feeling that, no matter how innocuous it was, even the wedding would be guarded by armed men.

Even the wedding? he thought wryly. In the topsy-turvy world of national terrorism, perhaps it should be *especially* the wedding. A high-profile gathering of important people at a hotel associated with Western visitors . . . in some twisted way, it was an obvious target, one guaranteed to cause headlines around the world if it were disrupted.

Down on the road, on the other side of the security

barriers, a car went past towing a flatbed trailer. A donkey stood on the trailer, idly looking around as if being driven through traffic were an everyday occurrence. And that, Lapslie thought, summed up Islamabad to him: unusual sights taken for granted everywhere you looked.

The insect flickered and then vanished, presumably having relocated itself somewhere outside of Lapslie's line of sight. He made a note to email Charlotte about it. She had the same kind of mind that Lapslie had: interested in passing oddities. She would probably have time to search on Google and find out what kind of insect it was: how rare, how poisonous.

They'd met at Braintree Hospital, where Lapslie was briefly being cared for having passed out very publicly during a press conference: a side-effect of the synaes-thesia that was increasingly controlling his life at that point. The cross-wiring of his senses that led to things that he heard manifesting themselves as tastes in his mouth – or, rather, in his mind – had led to him becoming a virtual recluse. The most innocuous sounds – the wind in the leaves, passing traffic, the murmuring of people in a restaurant – would sometimes cause Lapslie to taste things so nauseating that he would be sick, or collapse. It had been getting worse, to the point where he was failing in his duties as a police officer, but meeting Charlotte – a resident doctor specialising in anaesthesiology – was a turning point in his life. She had persuaded him to join a cognitive behavioural therapy group at the hospital in an attempt to develop what she called 'coping strategies'. She had also researched some drugs that were undergoing clinical trials and managed to get him allocated to one of the test groups. Between them the CBT and the drugs had suppressed his synaesthesia to a point where he could function almost as a normal human being. To celebrate, he had bought her dinner – the first time he'd been able to stand being in a crowded restaurant with other people for more than a few moments. One thing had led to another and now they were a couple, much to Lapslie's wonderment. He hadn't expected, at this time in his life, to find love again.

It was a shame that Charlotte hadn't been able to take time off from her hospital routine and join him in Pakistan. She would have loved the combination of exotic and familiar, despite having to cover herself up with a thin scarf and long-sleeved blouses. He'd felt alone, disconnected from humanity, for longer than he cared to remember, but loneliness was a new and uncomfortable feeling for him.

Still, Charlotte had said in her last email that she had a surprise for him when he returned: tickets for a concert. The thought made him nervous – all those people, all that noise – but he trusted her. And the nervousness was tinged with expectation: it was like being a teenager again, exposed to new sounds, new experiences.

Lapslie had bought her some presents during an escorted trip to a local flea market: a couple of pashminas and a necklace that the vendor said was jade, but was probably something less unusual. It didn't matter: it was the look that Charlotte loved, not the knowledge that whatever it was he had bought her was expensive or rare. She was sensual in the literal sense of the word: she had a direct connection to her senses in a way that other people seemed to have backed away from. Perhaps that's why he had fallen for her. Perhaps that's why she had initially been interested in him. No matter – now they were a couple for all the complex reasons that pulled people together, not just one.

The flea market had been fascinating for Lapslie. He'd been brought up in East London during the 1960s and 1970s, a stone's throw from West Ham United football ground, and there was something about the arrangement of the stalls in the market, the way it was squeezed between the walls of nearby buildings, the combination of exotic fruits and household items like light bulbs for sale, and the Urdu language that was in use everywhere, that reminded him with a bizarre but unexpected jab of nostalgia of the Queen's Market, just outside Upton

Park tube station. He'd often wandered through the Queen's Market as a child, initially with his mother as she shopped for food, and then later by himself. The smells were imprinted in his mind: rotting vegetables, sawdust, incense. And now, thousands of miles and tens of years from home, he'd found it again.

Back in the 1970s, the Queen's Market had been located on the border of three different gang areas. South of the market had been the largely white area dominated by football thugs and the National Front. Northeast up to Stratford had been the preserve of the Pakistani and Indian immigrants to the East End, some of whom had been around for several generations; indivisible to the outsider but riven by political and tribal affiliations internally. North-west to East Ham had been African-Caribbean territory: with the sound of reggae music drifting from windows and parties that seemed to go on for days. The Queen's Market had been a neutral meeting point, a fulcrum around which the area revolved.

It was all different now. The Urdu and Punjabi lettering on the shop-fronts in his old stamping grounds had been replaced by Cyrillic: the Pakistanis, Indians and African-Caribbeans supplanted by Poles, Chechens, Balkans and Russians. And every second shop was selling codes to unlock mobile phones.

Lapslie remembered patrolling the Queen's Market, back in the early 1980s, and passing a dozing West Indian boy with dreadlocks emerging from beneath a towering leather cap. He was slumped against a stall selling Scotch bonnet peppers and chunks of goat. Partially aware of something passing in front of him, he jerked awake, saw Lapslie and performed a perfect double-take, then jumped to his feet and raced off, presumably to warn his brethren that the police were around. Almost exactly the same thing had happened in the Islamabad market. The Western policemen, shepherded by their Pakistani bodyguards, had passed by a stall selling chunks of chicken and fresh mangoes. A local man, small and unshaven with a random scattering of teeth in his mouth, sleeping with his head on his knees, had suddenly jerked awake and seen the parade of Westerners passing by. He too took off, the difference being that he had been pulling a mobile phone from his *kameez* as he ran. ISI or Taliban? Lapslie didn't know, but the tour of the market was abruptly cut short and they were bussed back to the Serena. Strange how things at opposite ends of the world could be so similar.

Thoughts of his past, and of the East End, reminded him of Dom McGinley. The two of them had first met in the warren of back streets between Plaistow and East Ham tube stations: in pubs like the Green Man, the

Boleyn and the Black Prince. Pubs where tough men in leather jackets and women with Essex facelifts – hair scraped back into ponytails so severe that their skin was stretched – drank for hours on end, and the smell of stale urine from the toilets drifted out to mix with the spilled beer and the cigarette smoke in the bars. Lapslie had been a police constable, McGinley a runner for the Clerkenwell Syndicate, run by the legendary Adams family. And now Lapslie was a detective chief inspector, McGinley was emotionally involved with his sergeant, Emma Bradbury, and the Adams family still controlled half the crime in London. It was, as someone had once observed, a funny old world.

Which reminded him: in the time since they'd caught the serial killer Carl Whittley, Emma had avoided being alone with him for more than a few moments at a time. Lapslie had promised her that they would talk about her new relationship, but she had made sure that the chance had never presented itself.

That would change, when Lapslie got back.

The symposium was scheduled to run for another two days, and Lapslie was down to give a presentation on the Braintree Parkway bomb and the subsequent forensic investigation. He hated public speaking – a feeling that had multiplied exponentially since his collapse at the news conference a few months back – and he wasn't looking forward to it. The problem was that Inspector Dain Morritt – a supercilious police officer in a sharp suit and Masonic cufflinks who had taken a dislike verging on hatred to Lapslie – would be in the audience. He was giving a presentation on how computer profiling could separate dangerously extremist Muslims from the broad sweep of perfectly innocuous ones. Lapslie knew that he would be able to feel Morritt's eyes on him all the time, just waiting for him to falter, to fall. It wasn't a pleasant thought.

Lapslie's police laptop, open on the bed and connected to the Serena's broadband internet service by a bright blue cable, went 'ping', indicating that he had an email. Turning away from the window, and the endlessly fascinating vista of Islamabad, he crossed to the bed to check on who was trying to communicate with him. The odds were that it was either spam offering to help him satisfy his partner in bed by the use of various herbal concoctions or a Nigerian criminal gang pretending to be an innocent banking official who had control of some money from the estate of a recently deceased long-lost relative to send to him once they had received a goodwill payment of £100; but there was always the chance that it might be Charlotte, making contact. He did a quick calculation in his head, subtracting five hours and getting to some ungodly time in the morning in the UK, but Charlotte kept doctors' hours, and therefore could be awake at any time. Much like a policeman.

The subject line wasn't encouraging: *You Need To Listen To This*; and the sender's address was an anonymous Hotmail account consisting of a hash of numbers and letters. Lapslie nearly deleted it unread, but decided at the last moment to take a quick look. He was bored, and there was always the chance that it was a communication from one of the various informants that he had kept with him over the years. And his computer was installed with the latest anti-virus software and internet firewalls.

He opened the email.

There was no message, no signature; just an attached file. Judging by the .wav file extension it was a sound file. A recording.

Who would be sending him a sound file? And why?

He double-clicked on the icon representing the sound file.

The Microsoft Sound Recorder program opened up in a separate window and started to play the sound file, representing its volume graphically as a series of green mountain peaks against a black background. For a few moments the file was silent, and then the sound started.

It was someone screaming.

Lapslie flinched at the raw agony in the sound. Shocked, his synaesthesic brain pushed back against the drugs and the coping strategies to flood his mouth with beetroot and salt. He almost vomited. Swallowing hard, he hit the pause button on the laptop screen.

The sound cut out. Peace and quiet filled the hotel room.

Lapslie took a deep breath, settling himself. He used the laptop's touchpad to move the slider showing the progress of the sound file back to the beginning.

This wasn't spam, and it wasn't a casual message from a friend or a colleague. It sounded like someone being tortured.

Sliding the volume control down to a lower level, he pressed the 'Play' button on the Sound Recorder window. The file began mindlessly to play again.

Now he was concentrating, he heard something in the opening seconds: the ones he thought had been silent on first hearing. Behind the hiss of the recording process, almost hidden, was the sound of someone breathing. Ragged, hoarse, on the verge of panic. And sobbing, muffled as if the person didn't want anyone to hear them, or to know how close to complete nervous collapse they were. Then there was a scuffling, as someone moved. Footsteps, dragging on a dusty surface.

Then the screaming. First a sudden, shocked sound, as if the person had run into something hard, or sharp and quickly pulled themselves away. Then another scream, followed by rapid scuffling. Whoever was making the noise wasn't moving carefully any more; they were running. Running fast. More screaming, continuous now, driven by fear rather than pain, but punctuated by occasional sharper screams. Something was happening, but it was impossible to tell what it was.

The screams were getting weaker now, more desperate, and there was a sense from the scuffling noise that whoever was there was blundering around blindly and hitting things, or getting caught by things.

And then there was another scream, sharp and shocked.

Then sobbing, as heartfelt as if it was being pulled from a soul who had just found out that God did not exist, salvation was a joke and all was darkness.

A low, indistinguishable noise, over as soon as it began.

Then silence. No sobbing, no breathing, no scuffling. Nothing.

The sound of someone who had just died.

Lapslie leaned back until he was lying on the bed, staring up at the ceiling.

It could be a con: an actor making noises to convince the listener that they were being killed. But why the mystery? Why not make the cause of death obvious: the repeated sounds of stabbing, a gunshot, the choking as they were strangled? Or it could have been an extract taken from the soundtrack of a horror movie; one of the so-called 'torture porn' movies: *Saw* and its six-odd sequels, *Hostel* and its two sequels, plus various others with one- or two-word titles and stark posters. But didn't films usually have some kind of soundtrack music to emphasise what was on the screen: ominous chords or heavy rock? No, Lapslie kept coming back to the same thing. This was real. Someone had died, and their death was recorded in that sound file.

A 'snuff' recording.

But why send it to him? Did they expect him to do something about it? Then why not send something more obvious: something pointing him to where the death occurred, or who it was that had died?

He rubbed his eyes and sat up again, the taste of beetroot and salt still spiking his tongue. Questions like that would just lead him around in circles. There was an obvious course of action. Either other clues would fall out of that course of action, or they wouldn't. He could only take one step at a time.

Working quickly, Lapslie composed a quick email to Emma Bradbury asking her to forward the sound file on to the Essex Police Forensics Laboratory for analysis, and also to notify the hierarchy within the police that a new incident needed to be recorded and a team formed up to investigate it. He hesitated before pressing 'send', wondering how quickly Emma would get it. If she was on leave for a few days, or engaged on a case, it might just hang around in cyberspace like a lonely orphan. He copied in Sean Burrows, the Head of Forensics, on the email and changed the text slightly to reflect the new instructions. Then, having finally consigned the email to its electronic fate, he phoned British Airways to check whether his flight could be brought forward to that evening. It turned out that it could: he had an open ticket, and there were empty seats on the flight.

He quickly packed his suit carrier and his carry-on bag – taking one of his thorazitol tablets before he packed his toiletry bag away – and headed down to the lobby with a new spring in his step. He had a purpose in life, and a reason not to give his presentation. And by the time Assistant Chief Superintendent Rouse found out about it, he would be on an aircraft and heading home. And who could fault him: he had a murder to solve. An apparent murder, at least.

'I'm afraid I have to check out early,' he told the desk clerk, sliding the chunky brass key across the marble counter to her.

Her gaze slid down to the computer screen beneath the counter. 'That's fine, Mr Lapslie. Your room is pre-payed. Thank you for staying at the Serena Hotel.'

'Can I get a taxi to the airport?'

She smiled and nodded. 'I'll organise that. If you would care to wait in the lobby, I'll make sure you are called.' She glanced towards the revolving doors that led outside. 'Assuming the rain doesn't get much worse.'

'Is that likely?'

She shrugged: a graceful movement of her shoulders and neck. 'Who knows?'

Lapslie found a comfortable chair and waved away the ever-present green tea. Delving into his carry-on bag, he found a brown A4 envelope. Inside was a USB stick containing his PowerPoint presentation and a copy of his script. He crossed back to the desk.

'Could you make sure these get to another of your guests – a Mr Dain Morritt?'

'Of course. Is there a message?'

'Just tell him . . .' Lapslie paused. 'Tell him: "It's over to you. I have some real work to do."'

She nodded, looking serious. 'I'll make sure he gets the message.'

It was a good twenty minutes later that he looked up to find the clerk standing in front of him. 'Your taxi is waiting just outside the security checkpoint,' she said. 'Would you like me to have your luggage taken down?'

'Thanks, but I'll carry it myself.'

Leaving the hotel, he was amazed to find that in the time since he had been in his room, gazing out of his window, the rain had intensified to a continuous torrent, and the road outside was awash. Passing cars were up to their hubcaps in water.

'Is that normal?' he asked the doorman: a seven-foot-tall and stick-thin Pashtun whose peaked white head-wear made him look even taller.

The man shrugged. 'Ground is dry and hard,' he said in good English. 'Water hits it and rolls off. Comes down from the foothills. Turns the roads into rivers. Not good for traffic.'

He was right. By the time the beaten-up BMW taxi had made a couple of turns and made it onto the Islamabad Highway, leading out towards Rawalpindi, where the airport was located, it really was as if they were driving down the centre of a river. The sides of the highway were lined with concrete blocks which served only to funnel the water, and the ground was indeed baked so hard that it wouldn't absorb a spilled bottle of Evian, let alone a full-scale rainstorm.

Lapslie gazed incredulously at the passing cars, most of which were submerged up to their door handles and pushing water ahead of them so that a v-shaped wake led back from an aqueous bulge ahead of their bonnets. He couldn't work out how they kept moving without their engines flooding. And incredibly, nobody batted an eyelid. He'd only ever seen flooding on this scale in the UK in news broadcasts about Cornish villages, but there it counted as a national emergency. Here it was apparently just a fact of life. Drivers kept on driving in conditions where, if they opened their doors, water would swamp the inside of their cars. And he could swear that there were people still standing around on corners and on the central reservation, waiting patiently for something that might never come.

What a country.

He was flying Club, which meant that he could slip inside the executive lounge after he had cleared the various levels of security at the airport. He had been pre-warned by the Security Officer at the British High Commission that leaving Pakistan required collecting various stamps on tags and documents which were variously attached to his hand luggage or left to him to carry, and if he didn't have all of these stamps intact when he got to the steps of the aircraft then he would be sent back to start the process all over again, and never mind the fact that the aircraft would be leaving soon.

The main advantages of the executive lounge appeared to be actual seating, internet access and the absence of milling crowds of toothless tribesmen who, as far as Lapslie could see, were one step away from leading camels through the terminal. Lapslie connected his laptop to the internet, just to see whether there had been any replies to his email, but there was nothing. Perhaps Emma Bradbury wasn't in the office. Perhaps she was on leave. Perhaps she just wasn't taking his email seriously.

He boarded the flight without incident, and sank back into the comfortable leather seats, fishing inside his jacket pocket for his ear plugs. Despite the CBT and the drugs, he didn't want to subject his quiescent synaesthesia to the stress of a full take-off and a five-hour flight.

Flicking through the Club Class magazine, he discovered that one of the films available for viewing by customers on personal DVD players was *Saw VII*: another episode in a continuing story about a serial killer and his protégés who tortured members of the public in various ironic ways depending on the sins they had committed in their lives and the bad choices they had made.

Remembering the sound file, he didn't think that was funny.

The flight back to the UK took six hours. Lapslie slept for most of it, but he woke abruptly three times, hearing the screams echoing in his head.

CHAPTER TWO

The sound of a text message arriving on her mobile phone dragged Emma Bradbury from a deep, dreamless sleep. Beside her, Dom McGinley's bulk made a small mountain range out of the duvet. He didn't react to the sound of the text.

The sun was shining horizontally through the window of McGinley's bedroom, casting an orange light across the far wall. His house was in Chigwell; just about on the boundary between the Metropolitan Police and the Essex Constabulary. He often joked that he'd chosen it deliberately, just to increase the paper-work burden if he was ever arrested and to make sure that if he ever had to he could make a run for it into two different administrative areas, depending on who was battering the front door down. She suspected he was thinking more about American-style state lines, and sheriffs skidding to a halt on the interstate before they infringed someone else's territory, but she hated to disillusion him. For a man who'd seen more than his fair share of the seamy side of life, he had a romantic streak a mile wide.

Listening to McGinley snore, Emma wondered yet again what it was that she saw in him. Was it a father thing? He was nearly twice her age, and had the authority of a man who was used to being listened to. Was it a rebellion thing? The last person a detective sergeant ought to choose as a lover was a man who had been involved with half the criminal activity in London over the past four decades, although to be fair he'd never been convicted for anything. Or was it just that he was the most *alive* man she'd ever known: a man who had experienced more than any of the callow, hair-gelled guys who regularly chatted her up in nightclubs and still wanted more?

And he was a fantastically imaginative lover as well. That helped.

She rolled out of bed without disturbing him and padded naked towards the bathroom, retrieving her mobile phone from the dresser as she went. She checked the message, guessing as she waited for the phone to display it that it might be from Mark Lapslie. He was in Pakistan, at a conference, but he'd texted or emailed a couple of times since he'd flown out, about various cases they had that were either stalled or wending their way towards trial. The Whittley case was causing problems, for instance, with the psychiatric community saying that Carl Whittley was obviously insane and the Crown Prosecution Service, backed by Carl's mother Eleanor, maintaining that his actions were complex and covert, and thus showed obvious evidence that he was sane enough to make careful plans and cover his tracks. Lapslie, as far as Emma could tell, was on the sidelines; he just wanted the bastard punished for what he'd done.

The text wasn't from Lapslie. It was from the incident room at Chelmsford Police Station. *Body discovered on Canvey Island. Foul play suspected. Local police request assistance from murder squad. You are the senior officer until you establish that a more senior officer should take charge.* There followed a postcode which Emma could type straight into her satnav in order to get her straight there, then the words *Please confirm receipt*. She quickly typed a response and sent it off.

It was the new way of doing things. Rather than phone up and give her instructions, the Chelmsford Police HQ computer could send her a text with all the salient details. It was a cost-saving measure, apparently; one brought in by the management accountants who were convinced that millions of pounds could be saved each year by shaving small amounts off lots of separate budgets and doubling the price of the coffee in the machines. Emma favoured the opinion that the easiest way to save millions of pounds each year would be to sack the management accountants, but nobody had asked her.

She dressed quickly. Canvey Island could get cold, she'd heard, so she pulled on tights and then jeans, and then topped the ensemble off with a T-shirt covered with a sweatshirt and a Napa leather jacket. Screw the fact that she'd probably be the most casually dressed person there; she could be there for a while and she wanted to be comfortable. The first time she'd worn a pencil skirt and high heels to a murder scene in the middle of a field she'd vowed that practicality had to win over style every time.

Which was probably why she'd failed her Inspector's Exam last time she'd taken it. And the time before.

She debated writing a note for Dom, but he'd never read it. He'd ring her if he wanted to know where she was.

Actually, if he really wanted to know where she was he'd probably get some criminal crony to trace which mobile phone mast her mobile was currently registered with. He'd done it before.

She slipped out of the house and started up her Vauxhall Tigra: a present from Dom to replace the Audi that she'd previously owned and lost in a motorway crash which had left her shaken but uninjured but which had totalled the car and several others. Punching the postcode in, she pulled away, peppering Dom's Jaguar with gravel.

The drive took just over an hour, including a pit-stop for a pee and a takeaway coffee at a Starbucks, and she spent the time trying to remember what she'd picked up about Canvey Island during the course of her time stationed in Essex. It turned out to be virtually nothing, with the exception that there was a track called 'Canvey Island' on an album by British Sea Power: one of her current favourite indie bands.

Dom didn't like British Sea Power. He didn't like her taste in music full stop. He was stuck back in the 1970s, with Jethro Tull, Tangerine Dream and Yes. The only band that sat in the area where their tastes overlapped was the Ozric Tentacles.

Eventually, Emma found herself on a long, curving, elevated causeway that led across a landscape of creeks, fields and banks of mud. Off in the distance to her right was a series of thin metal chimneys and fat storage tanks – an oil refinery looming like some science fiction cityscape over the tiny houses that surrounded it.

By the time she left the causeway she was part of a steady stream of commuter traffic and school-run people-carriers on the roads. Canvey Island looked just like any of the more modern conurbations in Essex: tacky 1970s houses all based on the same design, built with the same bricks and tiled with the same red tiles.

With less than half a mile to go she found herself driving through a small industrial estate. The satnav directed her to turn into what appeared to be a disused petrol station; the lack of an obvious police presence caused her to keep driving until she saw the collection of police cars, unmarked vans and people standing around aimlessly that generally marked a focus of police activity. She parked in the shadow of a strangely shaped yellow plastic box on a grey metal pole, about ten feet above the ground. The box looked a bit like a beehive: slatted, with openings all around.

'DS Bradbury,' she said to a young constable who approached her car with the obvious intent of shooing her away with as much condescension as his twenty-two-year-old frame could muster. He nodded, as if he'd known that all along, and gestured her towards an open gate in a ten-foot-high wire fence that led into a car park.

The building in whose shadow she left her car was large, warehouse-shaped, made out of metal and painted in bright pink with large yellow spots: the kind of thing she expected to see at three a.m. on a Saturday after an evening drinking a combination of absinthe and Red Bull, not at nine a.m. on a weekday. Stuck to the front of the building was a large cut-out sign featuring a meerkat-like creature wearing a waistcoat in the same colours and winking at any passers-by. A sign to one side of the meerkat proclaimed: 'Marty Meerkat's Maniac Playground!'

'What the hell?' she said, getting out of the car.

A passing constable nodded at her, probably thinking that she was with Forensics, rather than the ranking officer. 'Psychedelic, isn't it?' he said chummily.

'Disturbingly so. What is it?'

'Children's play area. Place for the mums to bring their kids and sit around having coffee and cake while the carpet-crawlers tire themselves out. It's filled with padded climbing frames and slides and stuff. All perfectly safe.'

'What's wrong with a patch of waste ground and a rusty bicycle?' Emma wondered.

'Or a street corner and a vial of crack cocaine?' the constable replied with a smile.

'Point taken. If you don't provide them with somewhere to go, they'll make their own entertainment.'

'Can I help?' he said, emboldened and changing direction towards her. She'd seen that smile, and that body language, so many times before.

'DS Bradbury,' she said wearily, flashing her badge. 'Apparently I'm taking over.'

He came to a dead stop and bounced back a step, a mask of professionalism slipping rapidly across the thinly disguised wolfish interest. 'I think the Sarge would appreciate that. We don't normally get anything like this around here.'

He nodded to her, and moved away, presumably to tell everyone that an outsider had arrived and was pulling rank. There was probably a word for 'outsiders' in the Canvey Island slang. 'Grockles' was the favoured term on the Isle of Wight, where she had grown up

She pushed open the entrance doors and went in.

The interior of the building was floored with rubber gymnasium matting and filled, floor to ceiling, with what appeared to be a massive structure constructed out of scaffolding poles covered with foam rubber which itself was coated in brightly coloured wipe-clean plastic, all attached to the scaffolding with plastic builders' ties. The scaffolding divided the structure into cells of various sizes and shapes which were walled with nylon netting and interconnected by holes, tubes, tunnels, gates, slides and ladders. Some of the cells were nearly filled by inflated spheres which the kids presumably had to manoeuvre their way past if they wanted to get from the entrance on one side to the exit on the other. A slide that must have been ten feet wide ran from a platform at the very top of the structure to a pit at the bottom which was filled with foam rubber balls, intended to cushion the impact of landing. On the other side a series of ropes allowed the kids to swing themselves safely from one end of the structure to the other. The overall effect was something like a kids' board game – *KerPlunk* or *Mouse Trap*, perhaps – blown up to giant size.

'Dear God,' Emma murmured to herself. 'You don't even realise these places exist if you don't have kids.'

She looked around, trying to work out who was in charge. Or at least, who had been in charge until her arrival. Uniformed policemen and Crime Scene Investigators in white papery coveralls were dotted around the place. The CSIs were dusting for fingerprints, taking photographs or generally taking a close interest in things too small for the human eye to see. The uniformed police were standing around looking lost. Over to one side was a coffee bar area, with round tables and metal chairs, presumably for the parents to sit at. The chairs didn't look particularly comfortable. Presumably that was so that the parents didn't settle down for the day, and to guarantee a degree of turnover in the clientele. 'Churn' – wasn't that the term? She headed over there, if for no other reason than the best place to find a senior officer was where bacon baps and coffee were available.

A harassed-looking uniformed sergeant was trying to deal with three subordinates at once. He saw Emma and broke off what he was doing.

'DS Bradbury?'

'The very same. And you are . . .?'

'Sergeant Murrell. Keith Murrell.' He stuck his hand out. Emma took it, surprised at his friendliness. His grip was firm.

'Sorry,' she found herself saying, 'but I was told to report here and take over. That's about the extent of my knowledge.'

'Not a problem,' he replied. 'I'm out of my depth here. Yeah, Canvey Island gets deaths like any other area, but most of them are fights in pub car parks that get out of hand or domestic disturbances that have been brewing for years. Cold-blooded murder is something else.'

Emma glanced around. 'I feel embarrassed asking, but where's the body?'

'Follow me.'

He led the way over to the ball pit at the base of the slide, which was accessible via an archway in the padded scaffolding. One CSI was taking photographs while two others were carefully picking out foam rubber balls and sealing them individually in plastic bags, numbering them, then placing them carefully in a storage box. Each one was about the size of a tennis ball, made from foam rubber and coloured red, blue, yellow and green, although there seemed to be a larger preponderance of red than Emma would have expected.

And then she realised that some of the red balls weren't originally red.

They were covered in blood.

Sergeant Murrell nodded to one of the CSIs. 'Can you show us the body without disturbing it any more than it has been already?'

One of the CSIs looked up, nodded, then reached into the ball pit. She fished around for a few moments, then took hold of something and pulled it carefully up.

Emerging from the ball pit like a whale surfacing from the depths of the ocean came what looked initially to Emma like something from a butcher's shop window. Pale skin with slices taken off to reveal white bone and yellow fat. An eye, isolated in raw flesh. Meat, raw and bloody.

It was only when the CSI's hand emerged from the balls supporting a gore-streaked mane of blonde hair that the individual parts came together to form a complete picture, and Emma realised that she was gazing at a woman's head that appeared to have been repeatedly slashed by someone with a long knife or a sword.

'Good God,' Emma murmured.

'Not based on this evidence,' Sergeant Murrell responded softly.

'Is the rest of her in there?'

'As far as we can tell, the body is intact – with the exception of those slices of flesh that appear to have been removed.'

'Naked?'

'Oh yes.'

'And those cuts – are they confined to the head or do they extend over the whole of the body?'

He grimaced. 'We've not conducted a full visual examination as yet, but there are certainly cuts to the hands, arms, shoulders and chest. One breast has been completely sliced off. The legs have some shallow cuts to them, and the feet appear to be untouched.'

Emma tried to visualise what she was being told. 'The cuts to the arms and hands: do they look defensive?'

Murrell shrugged. 'That's a valid interpretation.'

'So – someone hacked away at her while she was standing or crouching, and she defended herself until the blood loss was too great.'

Again, he shrugged. 'I can't argue with that interpretation, but I've never seen anything like this before.'

'Forensics and the post-mortem should be able to confirm or deny it.' Emma thought for a moment. 'The flesh that appears to have been sliced off – have you found it?'

'There's no indications of another crime scene within

the building, and with that amount of blood loss I'm sure we would have spotted it. The bits that have been removed might be buried underneath the balls, they might have been taken by the killer or they might have been left at the place where she was killed, wherever that was.'

Emma nodded. 'So there's likely to be another crime scene that we haven't discovered.'

'That's the way my thoughts are going.' Murrell swallowed, and looked away. 'Some of the men are talking about . . . cannibalism. Is that a viable theory?'

'At this stage,' Emma said, 'anything is a viable theory, but try to discourage too much speculation. We don't want to get so focused on one path that we miss evidence for another.'

'Understood.' He nodded. 'So, what's next? What do you want us to do?'

'You've got the CSIs here already, which is good. They'll process the evidence and document everything photographically. I presume the pathologist is on the way?'

'Expected within the hour.'

'Who discovered the body?'

'The manager of this place. His name is Gareth MacFarlane. He said he arrived at around eight o'clock to open up, and found that the door had been forced. He called the police straight away, assuming that the cash register had been raided. When the initial response team got here they found the cash register was intact, but looking around they spotted traces of blood on the rubber mats, as if something had been dragged. They followed the drag marks to this ball pit. They were debating whether to call it in or wade into the pit and see what was there when one of them saw a hand sticking out. So they called it in.'

'Wise move.' Emma suddenly realised that the CSI was still patiently holding the slashed head up for her investigation. 'Okay, you can settle that thing back down now.' She looked at Sergeant Murrell again. 'It looks like you've got a grip on the processing of the scene. This manager bloke – Gareth MacFarlane? – is an obvious initial suspect, so let's get him down to the local nick and take his statement. The next thing we need to do is to identify the victim, so let's get someone checking missing persons reports, especially ones from yesterday, and let's also see if we can go through her pockets for identification. A driving licence would be good.'

'She's naked,' Sergeant Murrell said patiently. 'No clothes.'

'Clearly,' Emma replied, feeling a blush spread across her cheeks but recovering ground quickly, 'but her clothes or her handbag might be buried under the balls as well. Let's have a fish around, eh? Oh, and make sure the door and the lock are processed. At the moment that's the only thing we know for sure that the murderer touched apart from the body.' She glanced around. 'No chance of security cameras?'

'Not inside. There's all kinds of regulations about recording pictures of children. The argument is that it gives paedophiles carte blanche to snap away if there's no valid reason to stop them. Outside is a different matter, but the manager informs me that they're just for show. They're not connected to anything.'

'Okay.' She quickly ran through a mental checklist, in case she'd missed anything. 'I think it's all sewn up. Make sure the constables on the perimeter keep any journalists out – the moment they get a sniff of this they'll be trying to sneak in through the back door or take photographs through the windows. I'd rather not see this splashed all over the front pages – even if it's just the front page of the local freebie newspaper.'

'Understood.' He glanced at the gore-smeared foam rubber balls that hid the body. 'I've ... never seen anything like this before. I'm not sure how to react.'

'I've seen too many things like it,' Emma said soberly. 'And I still don't know how to react. I think if you ever get to the point where you can take it in your stride then you need to find another job, and quickly.'

'I guess,' he said quietly, 'if you can look at a body

like this one and not feel something, then you're only one step away from looking at your wife or girlfriend in the same way.'

Emma left Murrell supervising the CSIs in the ball pit and spent the next hour prowling around the building. At one stage someone came up and handed her a polystyrene cup of coffee, which she took gratefully. In the back of her mind she could hear the voices of children playing: screams, laughs, the occasional frustrated yell or triumphant shout. The ghosts of previous customers, still haunting the premises.

Would any parents bring their children here again, knowing that a mutilated body had been discovered there? Would any mother or father let their children roll around in the ball pit ever again? She suspected not. And despite what she'd said about photographers, it wasn't the police's job to suppress straight reportage. The place would go out of business, slowly or quickly.

By the time she'd got back around to the ball pit most of the balls had been removed and catalogued as evidence and the pathologist was supervising the removal of the woman's naked body. Emma moved alongside her.

'Doctor Catherall.'

Jane Catherall glanced up at Emma. 'Detective Sergeant Bradbury, how pleasant to see you here, at the edge of the known world. Is DCI Lapslie also around?'

Emma gazed down fondly at the pathologist. She knew, from what Lapslie had told her, that Jane Catherall was one of the last people in the UK to have suffered badly from polio as a child. As a result, her back was twisted, her torso malformed and her eyes protuberant. And she was simultaneously the sweetest person and the most fastidious pathologist that Emma had ever met.

'No, the DCI is sampling the local food in Pakistan under the pretence that he's attending a conference on law enforcement and counter-terrorism.'

'And they've let you out alone?' Her eyes twinkled. 'How lovely for Mark. I do hope the sound of the jet engines won't set his synaesthesia off.'

'He's actually being treated for it at the moment. He's happier than I've ever seen him.'

Jane Catherall smiled, and her face transformed. 'Good for him,' she said.

Emma watched as the body was carefully transferred into a black bag and from there onto a wheeled stretcher. 'When can you get around to doing the post-mortem?'

'I've actually got a space now. I'll start straight away when we get back.'

'In that case, I'll come with you.'

She crossed over to where Sergeant Murrell was standing and told him that she would be back later, and that he was in charge while she was gone. 'Get all the balls from the ball pit individually sealed in plastic bags, tagged and sent to Forensics,' she added.

'Are you joking?' he asked, looking at the thousands of balls. Noticing the look on her face, he added, 'No, you're not.'

Following the stretcher outside to where the unmarked pathology van was parked, she watched it pull away, then got into her Tigra and followed.

The drive back to Braintree took over an hour. Emma resisted the temptation to overtake and zoom ahead at speed; all that she would accomplish would be to guarantee herself an hour's wait in the mortuary car park. As she trailed the van through traffic, past people-carriers and white vans, down streets lined with neat, semi-detached houses and past rows of local shops, she was struck by the fact that nobody they passed knew how close they were to a mutilated dead body. And after half an hour of thinking that, she started wondering what other secrets were lying in the vans and the houses that she was passing, and she shivered.

At the mortuary, Doctor Catherall's assistants laid the body carefully on one of the massive, lipped, stainless-steel tables. After they had washed it and catalogued it with a series of photographs, Jane stepped forward, moving slowly around the table and examining each wound, each slash, each exposed area of muscle, tissue and bone with equal care, murmuring all the time into a digital voice recorder. It occurred to Emma that it was like some strange modern dance, with all the partici-pants knowing their motions but where the audience had to interpret the meaning of what was being done on stage.

After opening up the body she cut through the ribs with a pair of medical shears, then moved forward again and lifted the breast bone free. The remnants of the ribs hung down from her hand like the legs of some stark, white spider. Putting the breast bone to one side, she proceeded to remove every organ from the body cavity, meticulously weighed it and then put it to one side for later analysis.

She paused when she came to the liver. At least, Emma assumed it was the woman's liver. Whatever it was, it was dark red and glistening, and it flopped over both of Jane Catherall's hands. The pathologist gazed at it for a few moments, weighing it in her hands before placing it to one side. She spoke quietly into the digital recorder for a minute or so before continuing with the autopsy.

After finishing with the organs in the chest cavity she moved to the head and made a cut all the way around the back of the skull, following the hairline, and then with a grotesque crackling sound she pulled the scalp forward, exposing the bony, bloody plates of the skull and leaving the flesh resting on the face like an eyeless, mouthless mask of raw meat. Cutting through the skull, she eased the brain free of its bony confines, lifting it up so she could cut through the spinal cord. The brain went with the rest of the internal organs, and Jane stepped back, examining her handiwork.

Jane glanced at her watch. 'Fancy some lunch?' she said to Emma. 'It's getting late. There's a decent little bistro just across the road.''

'Thanks,' Emma said, dry-mouthed, 'but I don't really fancy anything at the moment. I'm happy to have a glass of water while you eat, though, if you promise not to have anything with beef or pork it in.'

'Just pasta,' said Jane, 'I promise.' She turned to where her assistant, Dan, was standing against the far wall, waiting. 'Close this lady up,' she said, 'and then take samples from the organs and send them to Mr Burrows for analysis. And see if you can reconstruct what her face looked like before the cuts were made, based on the photographs and the remaining skin and subcutaneous fat. I'll be back in an hour or so.'

Emma and Jane left the mortuary and walked across to the Italian restaurant. Emma found herself having to slow down, just like she'd done in the car, to make sure that she stayed with the pathologist.

Sitting down with a bottle of sparkling mineral water in front of them and Jane's order being prepared, Emma voiced the question she'd been wanting to ask for hours.

'What happened to her?'

'Difficult to say at the moment,' Jane replied judiciously. 'There are traces of chafing on the wrists and the ankles, so I suspect that she was bound tightly for a period of time. The skin is bruised but not broken, suggesting that whatever was used to restrain her was soft and flexible, not hard and unyielding. My initial findings are that there is some chafing over chafing, which leads me to believe that she was unbound and then bound again several times—'

'—Suggesting that she was tied up for a while.'

'Yes.' Jane Catherall paused for a moment, thinking. 'At the risk of being indelicate, the area around the anus and the perineum shows signs of staining and blistering.'

'I don't like where this is going,' Emma sighed, feeling her stomach briefly clench.

'She has been forced to sit in her own bodily waste for some time before being cleaned up, poor child. Part and parcel of the process of restraint, I would venture.'

'All of this is sounding more and more like sexual perversion,' Emma said grimly.

Jane made a *tch* sound through her teeth. 'Perhaps, but my initial examination of her labial area showed no obvious tears or bruises. The sexual assault tests will tell us more.'

'And what about the obvious wounds on the body?'

'At first sight, I thought the various cuts and slices were inflicted by some sharp-edged instrument such as a machete or a samurai sword, but if that were true then you would expect some directionality to the cuts.' She took her knife off the table and leaned over towards Emma, tracing cuts across her face, shoulders and chest. 'If the killer had been standing in front of her then cuts on one shoulder should have been pointing in a different direction to the cuts on the other shoulder, and I should have been able to trace all the cuts back to a point directly in front of her – ' she tapped her right shoulder with her left hand – 'like so.' She heaved herself back to her seat, and started hacking at the white tablecloth instead. 'Or if the perpetrator had been standing over the victim, if she was tied to a table perhaps, being tortured, then the cuts should have been similarly traceable back to a different point, off to one side, like this.' She stopped, frowning. 'But the cuts appear to me to be inflicted from random directions – from the sides, from the top, from the back, but not as far as I can tell from below.' She sighed. 'I've never seen anything quite like this before. I can't yet tell what kind of weapon was involved. I'm not even sure it was a bladed instrument, in the classic sense.'

'Were the wounds inflicted before death?'

Jane nodded. 'Oh yes. But not long before.'

'And they were the cause of death?'

'I'll have to wait for the results to come back on the organs and tissues, but a few of these cuts intersected arteries. The poor girl would have bled to death.' She shook her head. 'It would have been painful, and it would have been slow, but it would have been certain. This was not an accident. This was deliberate and sadistic murder.'

'Anything else I need to know?'

Jane put her head on one side for a long moment. 'The liver was unusually large. Hepatomegaly is the technical term. I will need to do some further tests to identify the reason.'

A waiter appeared to one side and slid a plate of pasta in front of Doctor Catherall. It was coated in a red, creamy sauce that glistened just like the liver that she had been holding in her hands just an hour or so earlier. The pathologist hesitated, her fork poised. She glanced, bird-like, at Emma.

'Go ahead,' Emma said. 'If I wasn't hungry before, I'm definitely not hungry now.'

CHAPTER THREE

Landing at Heathrow in the middle of the afternoon, Lapslie felt strangely displaced in time. He'd slept on the flight, and his body wasn't sure what it should be doing: eating, sleeping or moving around.

The light from outside was grey, and England was surprisingly noisy, smelly and dirty compared with Islamabad. The terminal at Heathrow, which had once looked so clean and cutting-edge, was dirty and frayed around the edges, and the walk from the disembarkation point to the luggage claim area was a long trek past threadbare seating, faded signs and stationary moving walkways. The place had an air of uncertainty and anxiety about it, absorbed into the walls and furniture from the millions of passengers who passed through every year. It didn't advertise Britain well.

The general low murmur of voices would normally

have provided Lapslie with a running trickle of blood in his mouth, shot through with spikes of caramel when the tannoy announcements cut across everything, but the drugs and the coping strategies he was employing pushed everything to the edge of his awareness so that it was only there if he thought about it. He still wasn't quite used to the freedom of being able to experience noise.

He'd left his Saab in the long-term parking. While he waited in a dank concrete underpass for the coach to arrive to take him on the five-minute journey to where it sat, he turned his mobile phone on. No messages from Emma, but one from Charlotte saying she was working unexpectedly until early the next morning, and a text from Sean Burrows at the forensics laboratory asking him to pop in when he had a moment. He made a flash decision to head across straight away. With Charlotte working he had little reason to go home. He had a Synaesthesia Therapy Group meeting that afternoon at Chelmsford Hospital which he'd already said that he couldn't attend, but now he might just be able to make it after seeing Sean Burrows.

From Heathrow he drove counter-clockwise around the M25 towards Dartford. He briefly considered diverting to visit his old stamping grounds in Tower Hamlets and East Ham, but the flight and the wait at

Heathrow had depressed his spirits and he didn't want to lower them any more by seeing all the changes that time and the local council had wrought. Instead he kept driving towards the wooded and secluded location of the Essex Forensics Laboratory. By the time he parked his car outside the perimeter fence at around four-thirty he had a low-grade buzz in the back of his head that told him his body needed food and sleep in order to reset itself.

The police officers on the gate were armed with Heckler and Koch semi-automatic carbines. They watched him as he crossed to the reception cabin; muzzles pointed at the ground, left hands locked around the stock, right hands protectively caressing the grip. He wondered briefly when, if ever, they had last fired those guns for real. It was something like an insurance policy, he supposed. You armed your guards in case of terrorist attack, hoping that the attack would never come.

There used to be a joke, he recalled, that the armed police on gate duty at these establishments were issued with guns if the alert level went up to 'Amber', and then given the bullets if it went up to 'Red'. That was before the Al-Qaeda bombs in London in 2005. Now, Lapslie suspected, those guns were fully loaded at all times.

Despite the fact that he was a familiar face to the ladies on reception, he still had to be given a plastic pass incorporating his photograph, taken by a webcam above the head of the receptionist. He left his car in the external car park and walked through the trees towards the single-storey blocks that housed Sean Burrows' team.

The forensics laboratory was built on the site of an old Napoleonic fort, and Lapslie soon found himself passing a grassy mound to his left that he'd been told had once been the location of a local militia armed with flintlock rifles, eager to give Napoleon a bloody nose if he dared invade. As he walked he considered the ironic counterpoint between the original explosives in use on the site – gunpowder – and the kind of high-tech experimental explosives being developed by terrorist groups and tested here on site by Burrows' people.

He found Burrows sitting in his office, sleeves rolled up, reading something off his computer screen. He refocused his eyes on Lapslie and smiled.

'Detective Chief Inspector,' he said in his warm Irish brogue. Previously it had tasted of blackcurrant wine, but now Lapslie could detect no taste within the words. 'Most people wait until they come back from a foreign trip before they give out their presents. You sent me one while you were still away.'

'I thought you probably wouldn't appreciate a pashmina, which is about all they had at Islamabad Airport.'

'Quite right too. How was Pakistan?'

'An odd combination of the very familiar and the rather unusual. Have you ever been?'

'Not as yet. There's a possibility that I might fly out later in the year to set up a training course on forensic examination of bomb debris. A recurrent problem, if the media reports are to be believed.' He shook his head. 'A friend of mine in the Army was over there last year to evaluate their bomb disposal methods. He told me over a couple of pints one night that they picked him up at the airport and drove him straight to a Pakistan Army base where they'd proudly laid out on the parade ground all the fragments of terrorist bombs they'd collected over the past year, and all the material they'd recovered in raids. He said he stood there looking at live packs of explosive with fuses hanging out and drums of what appeared to be unstable ammonium nitrate, while Pakistan Army personnel wandered past him with cigarettes hanging out of their mouths and small children played in an Army nursery across the road. He didn't know whether to laugh or cry. In the end he spent an hour rendering safe everything he could see.'

'Lovely. We didn't get that far, although I did get the impression that their evidence collection technique was little better than picking stuff up and having a close look at it.'

'And how are you feeling now? Jet-lagged?

Lapslie smiled. '"The enormous wheels of will drove me cold-eyed on tired and sleepless feet,"' he quoted. 'That about sums it up, I think.'

Burrows looked at Lapslie over the top of his glasses. 'Meanwhile, that sound file you sent me. How did you get hold of it?'

'It was sent to me,' Lapslie said. 'I have no idea who by.'

'An anonymous gift. Beware of strings attached.'

'So what can you tell me about it?'

Burrows stood up. 'Take a walk with me,' he said. 'We'll head down to the audio lab.'

The building, one of many scattered across the site, took the form of a central spine corridor from which spur corridors radiated at right angles. Burrows led Lapslie down the main corridor and then diverted off, having to type a four-figure code into a keypad before the door would unlock for him. Doorways to either side gave access to white-painted laboratories lined with wooden benches and computer screens. Burrows led the way into one such laboratory which looked to Lapslie little different from the others.

'Sara,' he said to the blonde-haired girl who was sitting at a bench wearing a white coat. 'Do you have that sound file up?'

'Just working on it now,' she said, glancing from

Burrows to Lapslie and back. She looked barely older than Lapslie's sons.

'Mark, this is Sara Hawkins. Sara, this is DCI Lapslie. Can you give him an update on where we are?'

'Sure.' She thought for a moment, then indicated the computer sitting on the bench in front of her. It was flanked by two large speakers, and the screen indicated what looked to Lapslie like images of two long, white mountain ranges reflected in lakes, one above the other. 'This is a pictorial representation of the amplitude of the sound file over time,' she started. 'As you can see, it's a stereo signal – two channels, slightly different from one another – so it was recorded with two microphones. The sampling rate is 44.1 kilohertz, with 16-bit resolution for each channel, which means that the sound is sampled 44,100 times per second. That's CD-level quality.'

She smiled at Lapslie's blank expression. 'It's okay. Look, any sound that's been recorded and then translated into digital format exists as a series of numbers. The numbers represent the characteristics of the sound, like volume and frequency – taken a number of times per second. If you think of the original sound as a smooth curve then the digital representation is a series of steps which try to match the curve. The more steps you have per second, the smoother the resulting profile looks. So, 44,100 samples per second, with 16 bits per channel, and two channels, will result in a bit-rate of 1,411,200 bits per second. That's almost perfect sound quality. A sample recorded at a rate of, say, 320,000 bits per second is listenable. Even 190,000 bits per second is more than acceptable for most purposes. By the time you get down to 128,000 bits per second then you can hear a noticeable degradation in quality, something like a radio broadcast, and 64,000 bits per second is more like listening to something over a phone than anything else. Clear?'

'I have no idea what you're talking about,' Lapslie said in a heartfelt voice.

She smiled. 'Don't worry. If you take one thing away from this, take away the fact that the sound file was recorded to preserve as much information from the source as possible, given the constraints of data storage.' She paused, and fixed him with a piercing gaze. 'Whoever recorded it wanted it to sound good. They *cared* about the sound quality.'

Lapslie thought for a moment. 'You've indicated that there's a trade-off at work there – sound quality versus size of file. Would it be possible to record it in a way that preserved as much of the sound as was technically possible?'

'Oh yes,' she said. 'But that would take up a huge amount of hard disk space, assuming it was being stored on a computer.'

'So why would this person compromise on the sound quality?'

'So they could store more sound files,' she said brightly. Her face fell. 'Oh. That means—'

Lapslie finished the thought for her. 'That means whoever recorded this sound file probably has so many files that they have problems with the storage, so they have to compromise the sound quality.'

'So whoever is doing the screaming—?'

'—is either not the only screamer—'

'—or they've done a lot more screaming than just this.'

The lab was silent for a while as the three of them absorbed the implications of what they had just worked out.

'What else can you tell me?' Lapslie asked quietly.

Sara was considerably less bubbly now than when Lapslie and Burrows had come in. 'I ran the file through a series of filters to reduce hum and static and to enhance the audio frequencies. First, judging by the slight echo on the screams, she's in a large and relatively open space.'

'She?' Lapslie asked.

'It's definitely a woman's voice. Analysis of timbre confirms that. Whatever it is that's happening to her to cause her pain happens twenty-seven times. That's the number of cries there are. And thanks to the fact that it's a stereo recording we know that either she was moving around while the recording was being made or the person that made the recording was moving around.'

'Either way,' Burrows interjected, 'it suggests that whatever is going on is not straight torture, with the victim restrained and the torturer standing over them. This was mobile.'

'The recording is original and unedited,' Sara added. 'What's there is what actually happened, from the moment the "Record" button was pressed to the moment the "Stop" button was pressed.'

'How do you know?' Lapslie asked.

'We use a specialised piece of software to detect signs that a file has been edited. It was originally developed for use by the KGB, but it's available on the open market now. It analyses any recording for signs of tampering, like changes in background noise, artefacts left by stopping and starting recording, and a whole load of other signatures that can be electronically detected.' Her face darkened. 'And I'm pretty sure that she dies at the end.'

'Because . . .?'

'Because of the very last sound.' She turned to the computer and, using the mouse, highlighted a particular mountain peak at the end of the graphical representation. She pressed the 'Play' button on the screen.

Lapslie drew his breath in sharply as the final moments of the sound file played: a low, indeterminate noise that still managed to chill the spine, despite its ambiguity.

'That could be anything,' he said.

'It's a death rattle,' she replied. 'The last breath catching on mucal secretions in the back of the throat. I've—' She stopped, swallowed – 'I've heard it on recordings before.'

He raised an eyebrow questioningly.

'Usually last confessions from someone in hospital, recorded by a police witness,' she added. 'Not one of the more pleasant aspects of the job, but we have to be able to prove that they are genuine for the courts.'

'"Life, like a child, laughs, shaking its rattle of death as it runs,"' Lapslie murmured softly.

Burrows frowned. 'What?'

'Nothing. Just a phrase.'

'Oh,' Sara said after a few moments, 'I almost forgot. The file was recorded in the UK, probably in Essex.'

'How do you know?'

'Electrical Network Analysis. ENA.'

Lapslie looked at her blankly.

'If the recording device was connected to a mains supply then there's going to be a modulation of the audio signal due to electrical network frequency fundamentals, their harmonics and sub-harmonics. We use specialist forensic software to detect the number and relative amplitudes of electrical network frequency components, detect what type they are – mains, uninterruptible power supplies, etcetera – and compare them to a database of various national mains supplies that's been compiled by acoustic forensic experts across the world. This allows us to identify the grid that generated the components – continental Europe, UK, USA and so on. We can also, if we're lucky, narrow the components down to a particular generator or substation, which is what we did in this case.'

She sighed. 'I wouldn't want you to think that it's easy. We have to ensure that our own equipment housings, equipment, cabling and so on is properly screened, that the equipment which we've connected together for recording and analysis purposes is connected in a way that avoids earth loops that would give rise to an induced local electrical network frequency and that safeguards are in place to avoid radio frequency interference from mobile phones which could bleed into the recording and analysis equipment.'

'And that,' Burrows said, 'is why I keep asking for a larger and larger budget. Remember that, when you're Chief Constable.'

'I will, I will,' he promised, deeply impressed by the technician's grasp of her subject. He turned back to Sara. 'Anything else?'

She shrugged. 'I'm still analysing the file for back-ground noises – anything extraneous to the woman's actual voice. I'll be able to tell you more in a day or two.'

Lapslie nodded. 'Okay, I'll be back then.' He hesitated. 'Good work,' he added awkwardly.

On the way out, something occurred to him. He turned to Burrows. 'Wait,' he said urgently, 'I forgot to ask where the email was sent from.'

'Different lab,' Burrows said succinctly, and kept walking.

Back to the main spine corridor, down two spurs (liter-ally, as the building appeared to be built on a hill and the spine corridor dropped two steps every few hundred yards) and through another security door, and Burrows led Lapslie into a lab that looked to all intents and purposes like the exact twin of the one he had just left. Even the girl sitting at the computer was the same age and build, except this one was a brunette rather than a blonde.

'Lucy, this is DCI Lapslie. Mark, this is Lucy Whiteman.'

Lapslie nodded at her. 'Pleased to meet you.'

'That email with the attached sound file,' Burrows continued. 'Any joy on tracing the email address?'

She nodded. 'The address is a dead end,' she said. 'It's a Hotmail account, set up anonymously. There's no way of tracing it back to a particular person.'

'What about the location it was sent from?' Lapslie asked.

'Don't let me get you bogged down in detail—' she started.

'Oh, please don't,' Lapslie said.

'—but the IP address is one of the new Internet Protocol version 6 addresses. An IP address is a unique identifying number which identifies a particular computer. They can be reassigned, which means that a single IP address might, over time, refer to many different computers, but only one at a time. Not that many of the version 6 addresses have been assigned as yet. This one is part of a set that are dynamically assigned static IP addresses; what we refer to as sticky IP addresses. That means that if the computers that they point to are powered-on for extended periods of time, the address leases are usually set to long periods and simply renewed upon expiration.'

She leaned back and gazed at Lapslie expectantly.

'Which means?' he prompted.

'Which means that there's a good chance that the IP address from which this email originated is still in use by the same physical computer. If not, it's likely to be one in the same locality.'

'Okay,' Lapslie said after a pause. 'And that locality is . . .?'

'Oh,' she said. 'Yes.' She leaned forward and typed something into her keyboard. 'It's located in a hospital in Chelmsford. I've got the address here. It looks like it's one of a set associated with an internet café based in the hospital.'

'What's the hospital's name?' Lapslie asked grimly.

'Chelmsford General,' she said.

Lapslie felt his stomach clench into a hard ball.

Burrows looked at Lapslie, detecting something in his stance. 'Familiar to you?'

'You could say that,' Lapslie snapped. 'I'm being treated there. I know it well.'

'And someone there knows you well,' Burrows said simply.

That thought echoed around Mark Lapslie's mind as he walked down the hill from the forensics lab towards the main gate and the car park. And as he walked, concern began to bubble up within his chest like a dark, corrosive liquid. He'd not spoken to Charlotte since he'd got back. She'd texted him, but that might have been days ago. Or it might not have been her, but someone pretending to be her.

He knew he was panicking but he couldn't help it. He was being targeted. The sound file had been intended for him, and sent by someone who knew him. There was no doubt about it. Knowing that the person who had sent the email obviously knew about him and details of his life, didn't that make it more likely that the target was someone he knew? Such as his girlfriend? By the time he'd got to his car he could feel his pulse racing, the blood pounding in his neck and his temples, and he was sweating. He pulled his mobile phone out and called Charlotte, but it went straight to her voicemail.

'It's Mark,' he said. 'I'm back. Can you call me?' He knew his voice sounded shaky, but he couldn't help himself. He needed to know she was safe.

He hardly saw the Essex countryside flashing past as he drove from the forensics lab to Chelmsford. Pulling into the hospital's pay car park, he found himself staring up at the blank windows balefully, wondering which one of them hid the person who had sent him the email. If, of course, the person actually worked at the hospital or was a patient there. Perhaps they'd been visiting someone, or attending an outpatients' clinic. Perhaps they had just slipped in to use the internet café and then left again. There was no way to know.

He headed straight for the office Charlotte shared with another doctor, but the door was locked. He debated sticking a note on it, but if she was okay, if she was still alive and not the subject of some serial killer who wanted to taunt Lapslie, then she would think he was getting desperate, and he didn't want her to think that. He could come back later. He *would* come back later.

He glanced at his watch as he entered the hospital. He had twenty minutes before the synaesthesia workshop started at 6.30 – timed so people could get there after work. Enough time to take a look at the internet café.

It was located on the ground floor, just off the main hall and next to the real café. Twelve computer terminals were lined up along two benches, their cables carefully hidden away from fidgeting hands. Patients or visitors could access them for 50p per half-hour, paid to a young man who sat behind a counter and presumably provided some level of tech support. Useful, Lapslie assumed, for checking emails, keeping up to date with eBay bids or finding out what had happened on *EastEnders* the previous night, if they'd missed it because they were giving birth or something. The screens all faced into the central aisle, preventing people from obviously accessing pornography unless they were particularly shameless. Lapslie assumed that there were firewalls set up anyway, to block access to dubious sites. Tiny blue LEDs glowed in the centre of the plastic border around the screens. Half of the terminals were occupied: three by patients in dressing gowns and pyjamas, one by a doctor in a white coat and one by someone dressed casually in jeans and T-shirt.

Lapslie looked around, hoping to see a security camera pointing into the centre of the internet café, but there was nothing. No chance to access CCTV footage of his mysterious interlocutor.

He kept watching for a while, not sure what he was watching for, then abruptly turned and left. Resisting the urge to go back to Charlotte's office, he headed up to the fourth floor.

The synaesthesia workshop was held every week, under the auspices of the Neurology Department. Approaching the disinfectant-tinged quiet of the central waiting area, he found that six chairs had been arranged in a half-circle around a seventh. Five of the six chairs in the half-circle were occupied by people who were chatting in desultory fashion or just looking around blankly, waiting for something to happen. Lapslie recognised four of them from the last workshop. The fifth – a man of about Lapslie's age – was presumably a newcomer. The sixth chair was obviously set out for Lapslie and, as usual, he was last to arrive. The seventh chair, the one set at the focus of the other six, was also empty. That was where the man leading the workshop – Doctor Garland – would sit.

Lapslie took his place in the half-circle, nodding to the others but not engaging in their conversations. He was too worried about Charlotte to want to chat, but even on a good day he knew he came over as stand-offish. He couldn't help it. He found small-talk to be a chore. If he talked about something, he wanted it to have meaning, otherwise he was just wasting his breath.

Was that where it had gone wrong with Sonia? he wondered. Even before the synaesthesia had hit home, she'd been the one who wanted to chat while he wanted to talk, and she didn't realise there was a difference.

A door on the far side of the room opened and Doctor Garland walked in purposefully, almost as if he had been waiting for Lapslie to appear. His face was dominated by a bristling moustache, beneath which his skin always seemed slightly flushed, as if he'd had a couple of glasses of wine. Maybe he had. Apart from a band of bristles around the back of his scalp, he was bald.

'Good afternoon,' he said as he entered the half-ring and sat down. He was holding a clipboard. His voice had once tasted to Lapslie like the rubber that children's balloons were made out of, but that was before his synaesthesia had become quiescent. Now, however, Lapslie found that looking at Doctor Garland made him think of a red balloon, floating in the air, with a moustache drawn on it in felt-tip pen. 'Thank you all for making the effort to be here today. Glad you could all attend.'

The people sitting around him murmured their greetings.

'We've got a new member of the group today,' Garland continued, 'so I'd like you all to introduce yourselves. Give us a quick résumé of the particular form of synaesthesia you suffer from.' He glanced good-humouredly at Lapslie. 'Starting with the last one in.'

Lapslie glared at Doctor Garland. 'Mark Lapslie,' he said, still trying not to let his thoughts turn back to Charlotte. 'My brain turns sounds into tastes.'

The person next to Lapslie was a man in his forties. He was wearing a corduroy jacket over a blue denim shirt and chino trousers. His hair was long at the back, but his hairline was receding at the front. 'I'm, uh, Steve Stottart,' he said in a voice tinged with a Mancunian accent. 'I'm the new bloke, although you'd probably already worked that out. Like Mark, I hear sounds and I can taste them.' He glanced sideways at Lapslie. 'We ought to compare notes – see if we taste the same things when we hear the same noises. Might be interesting for the researchers here.'

Lapslie shrugged. 'What do you taste when the good doctor here talks?'

Stottart frowned. 'Coffee grounds,' he replied. 'Old coffee grounds. Bitter.'

'Ah,' Lapslie said. 'Not the same then'

'Why – what do you taste?'

'Squeaky rubber balloons.' Lapslie smiled at Doctor Garland. 'No offence.'

'None taken,' Garland sad, smiling tolerantly back. He switched his gaze to the girl sitting beside Stottart, a teenager whose cheeks were flushed and who couldn't meet anyone else's eyes. 'Arlene – you next.'

'Arlene Waverley. I . . . hear things. Like someone is whistling, but it's really high pitched. It happens when I see bright colours and bright lights. Only then.'

'Thank you,' Garland said, reassuring her. 'And you, Jeanette?'

A middle-aged black woman, whose hair was plaited in a complex pattern, followed on. 'Jeanette Sanderson. I . . . I see colours when I hear . . . musical notes. Boring, I know. Sorry.'

The man on her left was in his thirties, with a leather jacket and jeans. He had a ponytail. 'Hi, everyone. I'm Chris. Chris Furlong. If I taste something in my mouth I can also feel it like shapes on my skin. Like, chicken makes me feel sharp spikes, and coffee makes me feel round, warm, soft things like –' he blushed – 'well, you know. Like . . . skin. Women's skin.'

Garland glanced at the person in the last chair. 'And finally . . .'

'Dave Ferbrack,' the last man said. He looked like a truck driver, somewhere indeterminate between thirty and fifty. 'I smell shapes. I mean, when I touch things, like rough surfaces or smooth surfaces and stuff, I smell things that aren't there, like cigar smoke and perfume and stuff. You know.'

'Great. Thank you. You're all here, of course, because you are looking for ways to control your synaesthesia. Rare condition. You six are the only people in Essex who suffer from it enough that it affects your lives, so far as I know. The most frequent occurrence is people who associate colours with words, or numbers, but that doesn't work to the detriment of their lives. In fact, they quite like it.'

'There are artists and musicians who depended on their synaesthesia as their muse,' Arlene said quietly. 'Oliver Messiaen and Alexander Scriabin are the best known composers, and Wassily Kandinsky the best known artist.' She looked around nervously, as if afraid someone was going to contradict her, then continued. 'Beethoven called B minor the black key and D major the orange key, but he might just have been being metaphorical. Same with Schubert, who said that E minor was "a maiden robed in white with a rose-red bow on her chest".' She blushed. 'When I found out I had synaesthesia I spent a long time on the internet, learning all about it.'

'Very good,' Garland said warmly. 'You've obviously done your homework, Arlene. Yes, some artists depended on synaesthesia, but with you, it's different. You've all lost jobs, or had accidents, or suffered some form of nervous collapse because of it.'

'I crashed me car,' Steve Stottart muttered to Lapslie, but loud enough for the others to hear. 'I were driving and someone was singing out of tune on the radio. I suddenly tasted something like rotting fish. I swerved and crashed into a parked car.'

Arlene shivered, and a couple of others grimaced in sympathy. Lapslie just nodded. He'd had much the same experience a few times.

'Last time,' Garland continued, 'we discussed the history and the possible causes of synaesthesia. I'll quickly go over what we said then, just to remind you – and for the benefit of Stephen.'

He paused, glanced around, then continued: 'You'll recall that it's been generally accepted that the condition arises when extra connections in the brain cross between regions responsible for separate senses, but researchers at the University of Oxford have pinned down four chromosomal regions where gene variations seem to be linked to the condition. All of which means that it may be caused genetically, rather than by a problem in the brain's wiring. One of those regions has also been associated with autism, so there may be a common genetic mechanism underlying the two. For that reason there's unlikely to be a cure, but there are ways of reducing the symptoms. Most of you are already taking a new drug called thorazitol, which was originally developed as an antidote to LSD but which is believed to help suppress the cross-wiring in the brain, but it's best used in conjunction with techniques such as cognitive behavioural therapy, neuro-linguistic programming or good old-fashioned meditation. That's what this group is here to do – learn some of these techniques so that you can at least live with your synaesthesia, if not actually beat it.'

He paused again, and smiled beneath his huge moustache. 'And today we'll be learning about cognitive behavioural therapy.'

'Brilliant,' Steve Stottart murmured to Lapslie. 'We're going to have a buzz!'

CHAPTER FOUR

On her way back from lunch with Jane Catherall to set up her incident room in Canvey Island, Emma Bradbury took the opportunity to drive around the various streets, roads and avenues of the area, familiarising herself with the locality. After all, she might be there a while, depending on how the investigation went.

If she was being honest with herself – which frankly didn't happen very often – then Emma was nervous. She'd never really handled a big murder investigation before. Stabbings outside nightclubs, yes; bottles suddenly smashed over the heads of wives or girlfriends in the kitchen after a domestic row, yes; but premeditated and sadistic murder – not with her in charge. She'd worked on that scale of investigation before, of course, but playing second fiddle to a more senior officer. In the past year or so that officer had been Mark Lapslie, and she'd learned a lot from him about how to project authority without making it look like you were doing so. Now she had to put those lessons into practice.

Canvey Island, she thought as she drove around, was one of those places that you had to be deliberately going to in order to find it – you couldn't just drive through on your way somewhere else – and for that reason Emma had managed to inadvertently avoid it for her entire time in Essex. She realised, as she cruised around, that she had actually missed something rather special. It was charming, in its own 1950s way. Isolated, but thriving and full of energy. Something about it reminded her of the early *Carry On* films, although she couldn't quite place what it was.

Part of her brain was flagging street names as she drove – a habit she'd got into years ago, before satnavs, so that she always knew roughly where she was if she had to check a street map. After five or six strange names her conscious mind picked up on the anomaly, and she found herself reviewing the names without quite knowing why. Paahl Road, Waarem Road, Vaagen Road, Delfzul Road . . . she decided that there must have been some kind of Dutch influence in Canvey Island, years ago. Passing Cornelius Vermuyden School a few minutes later she was pretty much convinced about it.

She passed a church as she was driving: a squat, white tower with an oddly styled roof, set behind a black ranch-style fence. The church was attached to what looked like a hall and a house – perhaps the vicarage – both of them white-plastered as if they had all come as part of a job lot. The tower had a massive cross set into it, large enough to crucify a giant. Emma's hand crept up to cross herself, shoulder to shoulder and forehead to chest and she had to repress a twist of guilt within her heart.

The board outside the church named it as 'Our Lady of Canvey and the English Martyrs'. There had to be a story behind that, she thought, and made a note to look into it. Who could possibly have been martyred at Canvey Island, and for what?

A little further on, she passed a pub with the appealing name of the Lobster Smack. It was freshly painted a gleaming white, but beneath the paint it looked old, as if it dated back hundreds of years. It sat in the shadow of one of the concrete sea walls that appeared to line the island, protecting it against high tidal floods. A row of wooden cottages sat beside it, looking equally venerable. She wondered briefly if the pub had rooms. This case might require her to stay around for a while, and it wasn't as if she'd passed a Travelodge or a Premier Inn while she was driving.

She kept going alongside the sea wall for a while, then got bored and turned around, taking a different route back and passing a surprisingly modernistic building looking out onto the Thames Estuary that appeared to have been designed to mimic the bridge of some ocean-going liner, with a curved central portion and wings to either side. In contrast to the Lobster Smack, which looked Victorian, this place was built in a style reminiscent of the 1930s. Again, it was a stark white against the leaden sky. White seemed to be a favoured colour around Canvey Island. Perhaps all the other colours kept getting used up by the time the deliveries got this far. Signs attached to the central drum-shaped portion identified it as a restaurant and bistro, and Emma made a note to check it out. Chances were, this close to the Thames fishing grounds, she might be able to get a decent seafood linguine. Well, seafood at least. Linguine, like coloured paint, might not have got this far.

Finally, she found Canvey Island Police Station. It was a two-storey red-brick building – thankfully, not white-washed – although it did have white-framed windows. Two police cars and what looked like several cars belonging to the staff were parked outside the front. Security appeared to Emma Bradbury to be non-existent. She was used to sealed-off parking areas around the back of the nick, accessible only with a security code or a swipe card. This was almost civilised.

She parked up and looked around. Gulls wheeled

overhead, crying out like abandoned babies, their eyes scanning for rubbish bins and discarded chip packets. She could swear that their eyes tracked the back of her neck as she walked towards the front door of the police station.

'DS Bradbury to see Sergeant Murrell,' she said, flashing her warrant card. The youth on the front desk – Police Community Support Officer, rather than a *'real'* police constable – visibly gulped, tried not to look at her chest and said, 'Certainly, ma'am. Would you like to come inside?' He buzzed her in through the door – the only sign of security that she'd noticed so far – and led her down a short corridor to a small office.

Sergeant Murrell was scanning what looked, upside down, like staff reports. He turned the top one over and stood up as she entered.

'DS Bradbury. I wasn't expecting you so soon.'

'Please, call me Emma,' she said. 'I've got the preliminary results of the autopsy. We've confirmed that it's a murder, so I need to set up an incident room and get going on the investigation. How many staff can you spare?'

'And I'm Keith. I've got five full-time PCs and nine PCSOs,' he replied, 'and although they're not exactly overworked, they're not sitting around with their thumbs up their arses either. We don't get a lot of murders here, but there's a fair amount of antisocial behaviour and domestics. Something about being at the far edge of the country brings out an almost Scandinavian moroseness in people, I find. I can probably spring a PC and two PCSOs for a while – anything else would compromise the visible patrolling that we like to do here.'

She debated briefly whether to push for another PC, but she didn't want to alienate Murrell – not just yet, anyway. She nodded. 'That'll be fine for now. Where can I set up an incident room?'

'We've got a crew room, where the team can grab a cup of tea and read the paper during their breaks. If necessary, we can turn it into an incident room.'

'Again, it'll have to do. Apologise to your team for me for taking their crew room away.'

'Don't worry – there's a café across the road.' He paused. 'Talking of which, can I get you a coffee?'

'Please. Black, no sugar.'

'Chris,' he said, turning to the PCSO in the doorway who had been trying to steal glances down her T-shirt; 'A Whoopie Goldberg for the DS, please. And a Julie Andrews for me.' He gestured to a seat in front of his desk. 'Take the weight off your feet. Is there anything I can tell you before we start setting your incident room up?'

'I'm a bit unsighted on the area,' Emma said, sitting

down. 'Can you tell me something about Canvey Island?'

He shrugged. 'What's to say? It's a reclaimed island in the Thames Estuary, separated from the rest of Essex by a network of creeks. At various times in the past it's been known as Counus Island and Convennon Island. It lies about three metres below sea level, on average, which probably makes it the closest thing that England has to Holland. That means it's prone to flooding on occasion. Last time that happened was 1953, before I was born. Fifty-eight people died then, and it's still a scar on the local psyche. That flooding led to the building of fifteen miles of concrete sea wall around the edge of the island, which provides a level of protection against all but the worst tides.'

He paused, brow furrowed. 'What else? Originally the place was a source of salt for the Roman invaders, although they switched to Maldon, further up the coast, where the salt is purer. It was then turned over to sheep farming for a long time. More recently the petro-chemical industry built a large oil refinery down in the Hole Haven area, and the island was the site of the first delivery in the world of liquefied natural gas by container ship, which makes us feel like we've contributed something to history. Of course, the whole thing is disused and partially dismantled now, and it's a nature reserve.'

'What's the population?'

'Nearly 38,000 people, 30,000 of whom moved in since the Second World War. For a while it was one of the fastest-growing seaside areas in the UK, although it's stabilised somewhat now.'

'What about you – are you local, or were you posted here? You said "we've contributed something to history" just now.'

'Well spotted. I'm a local, born and bred,' he said. 'My family go back to the eighteen hundreds. Best way to be taken seriously around here is to have a name that's familiar from the tombstones in the cemetery.'

'How nice.' She paused, remembering. 'I saw a building on the way here – looked like it was a restaurant of some kind. What's that all about?'

'You mean the Labworth Café?'

'Is that what it is?'

He nodded. 'Designed by some famous engineer – I can't remember his name. It's the most notable land-mark we have.'

'Why "Labworth"? Was that the guy who designed it?'

'No, apparently there used to be a Labworth farm there, before the café was built. I remember my nan, God rest her soul, telling me that the name came from two Old English words: *lobb*, meaning spider, and *werda*, meaning a low-lying marsh. Easy – ask me another.'

Emma grinned. 'Where's the best place to get a seafood linguine around here?'

'Chelmsford.'

She laughed, unforced. 'Yeah, I was afraid of that. Oh – something else I meant to ask about that I saw when I was driving around. There's a church called "Our Lady of Canvey and the English Martyrs". What's that all about then?'

'Ah, now my nan used to wax lyrical about that as well. Back when she was a girl, there were a fair few Roman Catholics on the island, but no Roman Catholic church. This was before the bridges were built, so if they wanted to go to Mass they had to walk to the ferry and take a trip over to the mainland – or if the tide was out, walk across the stones in the creeks – and then take a train from Benfleet to the nearest town with a church, then do the whole thing in reverse to come back. Apparently, permission was given for Mass to be said in a local house belonging to a Mr Levi—'

'Doesn't sound particularly RC.'

'No, he was Jewish, but his wife was RC. He converted after a while. They built a shed in the back garden for Mass, and then later, just before the Second World War, a church was built. It was named "Our Lady of Canvey" after a navigation beacon erected at Deadman's Point around the turn of the century.'

'I assumed it was a reference to the Virgin Mary. A kind of wish-fulfilment that she had some special interest in Canvey Island.'

'No, it was this beacon. Apparently it looked like a woman, with a ball for a head, her hands on her hips and wearing a triangular skirt. The beacon's gone now, sadly, but the church remains.'

'And the English Martyrs?'

'You've got me there. I think that was some kind of sop to the bishop. They'd snuck this local joke past him, naming the church after a shipping beacon, so they threw in the English martyrs to compensate.'

'Clever.'

'Right,' he said, standing up, 'enough of the history and geography lesson. Let's go and get that incident room set up.'

The room was large, whitewashed and lined with pinboards which were covered with posters highlighting Essex Constabulary's position on sexism and racism in the workplace (they were against it, Emma was pleased to see) and with fliers advertising meetings of the Police Federation. A couple of trestle tables were scattered around, with plastic chairs pulled up to them. Another table, set against one wall, formed the base for a filter coffee machine which, judging by the nose-wrinkling smell, had been continuously keeping its coffee warm for several weeks. Two constables and a Community Support Officer were sitting together and talking. They looked up when Keith Murrell and Emma Bradbury entered. Murrell caught their eye, and they quickly drained the dregs of their coffees and left.

'Will this suffice?' he asked. Emma looked around. She'd seen worse. 'It'll do nicely,' she said diplomatically. 'The pinboards will come in useful. What are the chances of getting some whiteboards, a couple of computers and a couple of local maps?'

He pursed his lips. 'The maps we can get straight away from stores. The whiteboards I could order for you, but you'd have to wait a couple of weeks until they arrived. Or I could send a PC across to the mainland with a handful of cash and get him not to come back until he's found a Staples, or something similar. The computers could be a problem. Any chance you could get some spares from a bigger police station – Braintree or Chelmsford or even Southend-on-Sea? If they've got the PCs then I can get a police van sent across to collect them.'

'I'll make some calls,' Emma said. 'Oh, phone lines. We'll need to get some phone lines in here.'

He grimaced. 'I'll have to talk to Christine on the switchboard. She can tell me how to go about doing that.'

'Appreciated.'

He glanced around the room. 'Give it a day or so and you won't recognise this place. You'll have your own little kingdom.'

'Just what every girl wants,' Emma replied drily, 'after a My Little Pony and a fairy dressing-up costume – the chance to be a princess.'

Murrell smiled. 'Don't worry,' he said, indicating the anti-sexism poster on the wall, 'you won't have to fight for respect here. The men will be bowled over by your brusque charm and the women will envy your stylish plainclothes shoes.'

He left her there to think about how she was going to arrange her incident room. Ten minutes later, her phone rang. She expected it to be Mark Lapslie, but it wasn't his number flashing up on her screen. It wasn't Dom McGinley either.

'Emma Bradbury,' she said.

'DS Bradbury. This is Jane Catherall.'

'Doctor Catherall. What can I do for you?'

Typically, the pathologist didn't answer the question directly. 'Where are you? I remember you said you were heading over to Canvey Island when you left the restaurant.'

'I'm there now, setting up my incident room.'

'*Your* incident room. How very possessive.'

'Don't you start. What's up?'

Emma heard what sounded like a snort from the other end of the line, as if Doctor Catherall was exasperated at the lack of witty banter. Too bad. 'I've got the preliminary results back on the dead girl.'

Emma's interest was suddenly piqued. 'Go ahead.'

'Well, firstly the sexual assault kit was negative. She had not been raped, and if there was any sexual activity then it was some days ago.'

'Okay. That rules out one motive, I guess. Anything else?'

'Indeed. You may remember that we took samples from beneath the girl's fingernails. There was something there: a powdery, white substance which we sent off for analysis. The results are now in.'

'Cocaine?' Emma asked, feeling a sudden rush of excitement. A drug connection might lead to a whole set of new leads and a whole load of arrests.

'No, sodium chloride.'

And her interest subsided again. 'Salt. Just salt.'

'Don't be so dismissive of salt, my dear. This is not your common or garden table salt. There are no anticaking agents, such as sodium silicoaluminate or magnesium carbonate, and no iodising additives such as potassium iodide, sodium iodide or sodium iodate. There are, however, significant mineral additions: sulphate ions, magnesium, calcium, potassium, bromine and minute traces of boron and strontium.'

'Contaminants?'

'More like something naturally occurring as part of the chemical formulation. I think you will find it is sea salt: salt that has been created by the natural evaporation of sea water in large, flat pans.'

'Sea salt.' She remembered something that Sergeant Murrell had said earlier, and her excitement quickened. 'They used to make salt on Canvey Island. They made it for the Romans. Apparently.'

'This isn't from Canvey Island,' the voice on the other end of the phone said.

'How can you tell?'

'Gas chromatography. There is a distinct difference between the chemical composition of sea salts from different coastal regions, even if they are only a few tens of miles apart. Tidal patterns create unique chemical signatures.'

'So where is this salt from?'

'Maldon, if the particular percentages of the various ions are to be believed.'

'Anything else on the samples?'

Jane hesitated for a moment. 'Let me see if I can get this confounded computer thing to cooperate.'

There was silence for a moment, then the sound of keys being hesitantly tapped. Silence again.

'Actually, I do have an email from the chemical analysis laboratory. It came in a few minutes ago, shortly after the one about the salt sample. Yes, they have apparently also analysed the blood and the various organs I sent them, which is quite unusual considering the timescales to which they usually work. Perhaps they are under-employed at the moment. Perhaps the rate of serious crime in Essex has gone through an unusual statistical blip. No matter.'

She paused for a moment, and Emma imagined her peering through bifocals, trying to focus on the words on the screen. 'Yes . . . let me see. They have found traces of an anaesthetic in the blood of the corpse. It's a variant water-soluble form of propofol known as fospropofol. I believe it is marketed under the name Lusedra. It is a quick-acting anaesthetic which is injected into the blood-stream.' She hesitated again, then continued as if talking to herself. 'Interesting, because I did not notice any marks from a hypodermic syringe. Any injection point may have been hidden in the area of the nipple, or the armpit – it's a relatively common trick.'

'Yes, thanks for that. So, she was drugged.'

'Indeed. Presumably to prevent her struggling when she was abducted.'

'And this propofol . . .'

'Fospropofol.'

'Fospropofol. How easy is it to obtain?'

'Easy enough if you are a doctor or have some kind of medical reason for using it; more difficult if you are a member of the general public. Remember, the singer Michael Jackson died from a mixture of propofol and the benzodiazepine drug lorazepam.'

'Doctor Catherall, I'm amazed you even know who Michael Jackson is – was.'

The Doctor had the good grace to laugh – a sweet sound, like the tinkling of bells. 'After that case we had involving the TV presenter whose arm was stripped of its flesh I decided that I needed to find out more about popular culture. I am now a proud subscriber to various popular magazines, including *OK*, *Hello* and *Bella*.'

'I don't know what to say. I think you're scaring me.'

'I'm scaring myself. I've become an avid fan of *Britain's Got Talent* and *The X Factor*. I never miss an episode.'

'DCI Lapslie's not going to recognise you when he gets back. Whenever that is.'

'Actually, Mr Burrows at the forensics laboratory mentioned that Mark was already back in the country. Apparently he's got a case on. Someone has sent him a "sound file", whatever that is, of a person being murdered in a particularly protracted and horrible manner.'

Emma was stunned. 'And he flew back just for that?'

'The file was emailed specifically to him. He's been singled out for some reason. He felt it best to return.'

'Meaning that he never wanted to give a presentation in the first place and he's offloaded it to some other poor bugger.' She shook her head. 'Rouse isn't going to like that.'

'Yes,' Jane said shrewdly, 'another good reason for Mark to have done it.'

'You said that the lab had analysed the organs as well. There was something about the liver, wasn't there? I think you said it was larger than normal.'

'I did, and well done for remembering. Yes, the analysis showed that the woman suffered from galactosemia, which sounds like some kind of science fiction film but actually is a genetically inherited disease that prevents the sufferer from digesting sugars such as lactose and galactose properly. It is usually diagnosed in infancy, but if left untreated it can lead to various symptoms such as an enlarged liver, cirrhosis, cataracts, renal failure, brain damage and ovarian failure. Without treatment, mortality in infants with galactosemia is about seventy-five per cent. This woman obviously survived, and I found no obvious damage to her kidneys or her ovaries, and no cataracts, but she must have been living on a diet that had a high level of sugar to cause the liver engorgement.'

'Does the galacto-thingie help us at all?'

'Funny you should ask,' the pathologist replied, 'but galactosemia is much more prevalent in Travellers than in the ordinary population.'

'Travellers? You mean Pikeys?'

'I mean *an Lucht Siúil*, or the Pavee,' Jane said firmly. 'They are a recognised ethnic group in English law. Terms such as Pikey or Gyppo or Diddycoy are considered derogatory. You should know that, Sergeant.'

'I apologise,' Emma said, chastened by the fierceness of the pathologist's response. 'So she was a member of the . . . Pavee, then?'

'Quite probably.'

'Hmm. What about the girl's face? Have you managed to do a reconstruction of what she looked like when she was alive?'

'I've had Dan working on that. He's a dab hand with an HB pencil and a pad.' She paused. 'Of course he's always on at me to get him some computer-aided design package with facial modelling software, but I keep telling him that when civilisation collapses into barbarism and the electricity generators fall silent an HB pencil is all he will have left.'

'Doctor Catherall, when civilisation collapses into barbarism and the electricity generators fall silent, I think Dan will have bigger issues to contend with than reconstructing the faces of murder victims. Such as, just staying alive.'

'Hmm.' She sounded unconvinced. 'He's still better off with an HB pencil, in that case. He can always jab it through someone's eye socket and into their brain. It's an instantaneous way of either killing someone or at the very least rendering them unable to retaliate.'

'I'm revising my opinion. Maybe you and Dan *are* the best people to be with if civilization collapses.' She paused, bringing herself back to the case. 'If he's got a good facial reconstruction can you get him to scan it in and email it through to me? I should be able to pick it up on the system here.'

'I'll ask him how far he's got.'

'Thanks.'

Emma spent the next hour or so moving furniture in her new incident room until she got it into the right shape, and using the opportunity to get to know the names and faces of the people who popped in to get coffee, paused to ask her what she was doing and ended up staying to help. Having got about as far as she could without whiteboards, computers or phone lines, she set off to find a spare terminal and check her emails. Still nothing from Mark Lapslie to say he was back in the country, but Dan at the mortuary had emailed through several GIF files containing a number of pictures of the dead woman's face, taken before the autopsy, and a high-resolution scan of his drawing. Emma had to admit, he was a pretty good artist. She had no idea of how accurate a representation the drawing was, but he'd apparently taken the underlying bone structure of the skull and extrapolated layers of fat and muscle on top, using what had remained of the girl's face as a guide. What he had ended up with was a pretty, vivacious blonde with a rather pointed chin and prominent cheek bones. He'd even put a smile on her face and a twinkle in her eye. It should be good enough for someone to identify her, if she'd been reported missing.

Remembering the Maldon salt beneath the dead girl's fingernails, Emma forwarded the picture straight on to the Maldon Police, asking if it matched the photographs of any missing people in the area, especially those of Traveller origin. If that didn't pan out then she would circulate it to all the other Police Stations in Essex, and then to all the other Constabularies in the UK, but it might take weeks for someone to come up with a match. At the moment, Maldon was her best bet.

She popped her head around the door of Keith Murrell's office.

'I've done about as much as I can here for now. I'm going to book myself into a hotel. Any recommendations?'

He thought for a moment. 'If you want something big where you can be anonymous, come and go as you like and can get reasonable food at all hours, I'd go for the Cocklecatcher. It's independently owned, not part of a chain. I'll draw you a map.'

'The Cocklecatcher? You're kidding me.'

'No, I swear it's true.' He nodded in emphasis. 'Cockles are very popular in these parts. They're delicious on toast, with butter. And black pepper.'

'Anything to disguise the taste.' She grimaced. 'I can just see the remarks back at Chelmsford when I put in a claim form for something called the Cocklecatcher. Still, if it makes them happy . . .'

Leaving Canvey Island Police Station, she drove back out along the main road, following Murrell's directions, until she found the hotel. She had been imagining something out of a Dickens novel, but it turned out to be a pub that also had a restaurant attached, along with a small number of rooms. They had some spare and she had an emergency bag in the boot of her car with two changes of clothes and a toiletries bag, so it seemed like a done deal. She dumped the bag in her room and quickly splashed some cold water on her face to freshen up. The room was surprisingly large and decorated in beiges and browns in order to offend as few people as possible, but it did have two large beds, side by side. For a crazy moment she considered phoning Dom and getting him to drive down and join her. That way they could be together but he could get to sleep in a bed to himself which, considering his size, would give her the chance of a better night's sleep, but she quickly quelled the idea. Mixing business and pleasure was never a good idea. And Lapslie, if he ever found out about it, would never forgive her. He and Dom McGinley had some kind of history that neither of them particularly wanted to talk about. Sometimes, in an obscure kind of way, it made her feel jealous.

She drove back to the police station, having become familiar enough with the roads around there that she was already able to navigate on autopilot. As she entered the station, receiving a cheery nod from the PCSO on the front desk, Murrell popped his head around his doorframe.

'Ah,' he said, 'I thought I heard your car pull up.'

'You can tell people by the sound of their cars?'

'I can tell from the engine noise that it's not one of the regular cars that pulls up here. And you need to get your exhaust looked at – it's got a slight rattle.'

'Will do. What's up?'

'I've got a detective sergeant from Maldon on the phone. He thinks he recognises the sketch of the body you sent through.'

She nodded, impressed. 'That was quick.'

'Ditto. You got that sketch out pretty rapidly as well.'

He led the way back into his office. Emma followed. The phone receiver lay on the desk, and Murrell reached out to press a button on the phone itself.

'I've put you on speakerphone,' he said loudly. 'In the office here you have me, Sergeant Murrell, and you have Detective Sergeant Emma Bradbury.'

'And I'm Sergeant Rossmore, Maldon Police,' said a deep voice with a Scottish accent, distorted by the speaker on the phone. 'Thanks for the sketch you sent through. Good work there. We think it's a woman who went missing in this area about a month ago. Name of Catriona Dooley. She's part of an extended Pikey family that's been rehoused on a council estate in the Maldon area.'

'Not Pikeys,' Emma corrected. 'Travellers. They're a recognised ethnic group with a distinctive culture.'

'Whatever,' Rossmore grunted, obviously unimpressed.

'You say she's been missing for a *month*?' Emma questioned. 'According to the autopsy she's only been dead for a day or two.'

'Then she must have been kept somewhere,' Murrell said. 'Imprisoned.'

'Probably by someone in her extended family,' Rossmore said. 'There's all kinds of familial feuds and tensions in Pi— in *Traveller* families. Rape and abuse are common within marriage. You try telling the women that these things are illegal and they just won't believe you. That's their "distinctive culture" for you.'

'There were indications that she had been tied up,' Emma added. 'Restrained. And for long enough that –' Emma swallowed – 'that she had soiled herself.'

Murrell sucked his breath in. Rossmore was quiet on the other end of the phone for a few moments.

'Signs of sexual interference?' Rossmore asked eventually.

Emma shook her head automatically, although the Scottish sergeant couldn't see her. 'Nothing obvious. No signs of forcible sexual activity, at least.'

'So she was abducted, imprisoned for several weeks *without* being raped, and then, what?' Murrell asked. 'Just killed? Why? What was the trigger?'

'Unknown, as yet,' Emma replied. 'We need more evidence.'

'If she was kept prisoner,' Rossmore said, sounding as if he was thinking as he was talking, 'then she must have been fed, or at least given water. Either that or the body would have shown distinct signs of malnutrition.'

'Not that I saw,' Emma said. 'She looked normal.' She

caught herself. 'As normal as possible considering what had happened to her, I mean. At least, she didn't look like she had starved to death or died of dehydration.'

'What about stomach contents?' Rossmore continued.

Emma silently cursed herself. She hadn't asked Jane Catherall that question, although, to be fair, the pathologist hadn't volunteered the information either. 'Tests are still under way,' she said guardedly.

'Any suspects?' Rossmore asked.

'Only the manager of the kids' play area where she was found,' Murrell responded, 'and I can't seriously see him in the frame for this.' He glanced at Emma to check that she agreed. She nodded. 'What about the missing girl's friends and family?' he went on. 'Husband, boyfriend, any romantic triangles?'

'We've covered the family fairly extensively,' Rossmore said. 'No obvious motives there. They all seemed appropriately distraught at her disappearance.' He sighed. 'I'll have to go and give them the news. And then I assume there'll have to be a formal identification.'

'We'll arrange to hold that at the mortuary,' Emma said. 'Let's do it tomorrow – it's getting late, and rushing isn't going to bring her back to life now.' She glanced across at Murrell. 'If we arrange for the identification tomorrow, that will give us a chance to re-interview the family, given what we now know. One of them may have kept her captive for a month, done God knows what to her, psychologically and physically tortured her and then killed her in a particularly grisly way. And distraught or not, I'm going to make sure they pay for that.'

CHAPTER FIVE

The scream rang out around the office: raw and filled with anguish and surprise. Lapslie flinched. It didn't matter how often he heard it since it had arrived the day before; the sound went through him like a stiletto, making his heart stutter and his breath catch in his lungs.

Was it Charlotte? He just couldn't tell.

He clicked the 'Back' button on the computer screen to reset the file back to the beginning. And then he pressed 'Play' again. A moment of silence, and then that first scream, filling the office, pushing against the walls and the window.

The door burst open. A uniformed policewoman stood framed in the doorway, framed by the early morning light spilling through the windows behind her, face white and shocked. She took in the scene – Lapslie sitting in front of a computer screen – and halted, face crumpling into puzzlement.

'Sir . . .'

'It's a recording, Constable,' he said wearily, pressing 'Pause'. 'Not an interrogation. Don't worry about it.'

She frowned, still unsure. 'But – Sir . . .'

'It's an ongoing investigation. A murder, although we don't have a body yet.' He paused, waiting for her to leave. 'Shut the door on your way out.'

'Yes, Sir.' Habit overcame curiosity, and she closed the door, leaving him alone in the small office. He could hear her voice outside, explaining to a colleague what was going on. A middle-aged detective chief inspector was sat alone in an office listening to a woman screaming. Yes, of course. Happened every day.

He pressed 'Back' again, and then 'Play'.

The scream. Familiar now, but still shocking, not so much because of the sound itself but because of the overtones and undertones of disbelief, horror, confusion, pain and a hundred other half-formed emotions that had accreted around it. Thinking about his own synaesthesia, Lapslie had once likened it to flavours: various combinations of salt and sweet, bitter and sour making a thousand different tastes in the same way that simple combinations of red, blue and yellow paint could make millions of subtly different hues. He realised now that the same was true of sound. A simple electronic sine wave, of the kind he remembered from physics lessons at school, was the simplest, purest, least emotive sound there was, but combinations of sine waves at different frequencies, added together and interfering with each other, made the sounds more and more complicated: piano strings, violin strings, guitar strings, vibrating columns of air in trumpets and tubas and bassoons. And with that complication came emotion and meaning.

He hit 'Pause' again. He knew he was obsessing about the noise, playing it again and again in the hope that he could hear something within it that told him it wasn't Charlotte, but there was nothing. His mind kept getting hooked on that raw agony.

Twenty-seven screams. He had listened to them all now, one after another, classifying them into categories based on length, volume, level of shock, level of tiredness and level of pain. He had played them forwards and backwards; he had played them at normal speed, speeded up until they sounded like birds twittering in the trees and slowed down until they sounded like whales lazily talking across the immensity of the ocean. No revelations leaped out at him. They were the screams of a woman being slowly killed. That was it. That was the meaning.

He leaned back in his chair and massaged his eyes, grinding them into his head with the heels of his hands.

This was madness. All he had was an electronic file a few megabytes in size; a cluster of electrons on a hard disk, a set of binary pulses existing as information somewhere in cyberspace. Nothing else. And yet the implications were huge and horrendous. Somewhere out there a life had ended – maybe someone he knew, maybe not – and he didn't know where.

His mobile rang. He checked the display, and the world seemed to tilt beneath him as he saw the name 'Charlotte' on the screen. *Thank God*, was his first thought, *she's alive!* Within a second his brain reminded him that sometimes the first thing a policeman did on discovering a dead body was look for a mobile phone and check the contacts list and the received messages, and given the sound of his voice the last time he'd left a message for Charlotte they would want to talk to him.

'Hello?' he said, dreading the next few seconds.

'Mark?'

His world tilted again, then righted itself. It was her. She was alive.

'Hi,' he said. 'How are you?'

'Fine. You sounded strange on your message. Everything okay?'

'Yeah, just . . . jet-lagged.'

'Good. Can't stop on – I'm in surgery in fifteen minutes. I just wanted to check everything was all right.'

'No problem. Talk soon.'

'Bye.' She hung up.

He leaned back in his chair and let his breath return to normal.

The dead woman wasn't Charlotte. Which left the question; who *was* it?

Knowing that the file had been sent directly to him, Lapslie had done a quick phone-around of the few friends and relatives he had left, on the off-chance the case was more targeted against him than he had thought. His parents were dead but he still had a sister with whom he exchanged phone calls twice a year and Christmas cards in December. She was alive and well, and surprised to hear from him out of sequence. He'd texted Jane Catherall, his favourite pathologist, and received a response, so she was fine, and she'd told him that she was working on a case with Emma Bradbury, so she was okay too. Sonia, his ex-wife, was happy in her new relationship, and the kids were fine. A female colleague with whom he had once had a short and intense affair was also in good health – now a detective superintendent in the north of England. She had been icy and distant on the phone, and it was only during the call that Lapslie remembered that the break-up had been brutal and unpleasant. Presumably that was all buried now, and she didn't want to be reminded of it.

He'd also checked the records of any bodies of women who had died in acts of violence and which had been discovered over the past year, but even restricting the age range and specifying multiple injuries threw up too many to investigate. The world was an unsafe place, especially for women. And he had no idea when the woman had died, of course. The file could be years old. Sound files did not degrade with the passing of time.

No, Lapslie was at a loss. He didn't know what his next move should be. If there even was a next move.

Perhaps he should have a chat with Jane Catherall. The pathologist might be able to spot something in the sound file that nobody else had noticed. That was the kind of thing she was good at.

On a sudden impulse, he pushed himself up from the desk and left the office. The corridor outside ran past an open-plan office of the kind he had always hated, this one set aside for civilian support staff who were doing all the administrative work for Essex Police, but the small offices were set aside for meetings, video-conferences and confidential work. Through the plate glass windows on the far side of the open-plan office he could see the uninspiring grey architecture of Chelmsford, where the Essex Force was headquartered. Not the most appealing town in the world, even in the bright winter sunlight.

He felt several pairs of eyes tracking him as he walked towards the stairs. Obviously the sound of the screams had drifted further than he had thought.

He sprinted up the stairs, two at a time, until he reached the fifth floor. Previously he would have used the lift and thought nothing of it, but two things had changed. First, being with Charlotte had made him aware of his weight in a way that he hadn't thought about for years, and he was determined to shed a stone or two. And secondly, his synaesthesia combined with the echoing stairwell had previously caused him to taste something unpleasantly like india rubber and vinegar whenever he used the stairs, but now, with the drugs and the therapy, he could happily run up and down them all day with nothing more than a tingle in his mouth.

Chief Superintendent Alan Rouse's office was based at the end of a long, wide corridor lined with photographs of previous chief superintendents and assistant chief constables in various artificial poses, either standing out in the open and shaking hands with someone, fixed smiles on their faces, or carefully posed against a wooden panel and lit to make them look ten years younger. Rouse appeared in the background of most of the open-air ones. He had been a fixture of the Force for more years than Lapslie could happily count.

For a while they had been assigned together to Brixton, but Rouse's career trajectory had climbed up and up while Lapslie's had flattened out, due to his medical problems and his general attitude.

'Is he in?' Lapslie asked Rouse's personal assistant, a large lady named Gill.

She looked up at him from her desk, which was adjacent to the frosted-glass frontage of Rouse's office. Behind her Lapslie could see Rouse's silhouette at the desk.

Her mouth twisted sceptically. 'You know there's an electronic diary on the system? You know you can book appointments with a few clicks of a mouse?'

'Yeah,' he said, 'and I also know that Rouse rations his open diary slots to a couple a day and most of them are booked three months in advance.'

'I'll see if he's in,' she said.

'I can see he's in – he's sitting just the other side of the glass. And he's alone.'

'Yes, but he might not be in to *you*,' she said, raising an eyebrow.

She levered herself from her ergonomically designed chair and moved towards Rouse's door. She knocked gently, opened it just enough to poke her head through and said something Lapslie couldn't hear. Rouse replied in his guttural growl. She pulled her head back and turned to Lapslie, smiling sweetly.

'Chief Superintendent Rouse will see you now,' she said.

'You're very kind,' Lapslie murmured as he squeezed past her. 'No coffee, thanks, although it's nearly time for his post-lunch whisky.'

'I wouldn't know about that.' She sat heavily in her chair.

'Everyone knows about that,' Lapslie said, entering the office.

Rouse looked up. His face looked even more swollen than usual: his jowls heavy and his eyelids dipping low over his eyes. He was in uniform, but his jacket was slung across the back of his chair.

'You look like shit,' Lapslie said undiplomatically.

'You're no oil painting yourself,' Rouse rumbled. 'Pull up a chair, Mark. Tell me why you wasted a couple of thousand pounds of Her Majesty's money flying to Pakistan and then flying back again.'

'Ah. Dain Morritt has been in touch.'

'Detective Inspector Morritt has indeed been in touch. And he's not happy.'

'Did the presentation not go very well?'

Rouse tried not to smile. 'Apparently the presentation went very well. Your script and your viewfoils were immaculate. It was the question session that went badly.'

'Ah.'

'Yes, he'd concentrated so much on getting the presentation right that he forgot he didn't have any background. The first couple of questions were so technical they floored him completely. After that the audience scented blood, and they were coming at him thick and fast. He eventually had to call the whole thing short and retreat to lick his wounds.' He glanced at Lapslie over the top of his spectacles. 'What happened – that health issue of yours suddenly get worse? I thought you had it under control.'

'I do,' Lapslie replied. 'I'm on a drug regime to control the synaesthesia, with therapy to help me deal with the residual effects. It seems to be working.'

'Good.' Rouse nodded approvingly. 'You're a good officer. Too good to lose.'

'That's not what you said when we were investigating the murder of Catherine Charnaud.'

Rouse's fleshy lips twitched in the nearest his face ever got to a smile. 'No, you were a liability then. Fortunately you've pulled yourself together since.'

'Still got a result, though.'

'And not through standard police work. You sniffed the killer out, as I recall. Literally in that case, although it's something of an old copper's metaphor.' Rouse leaned back in his chair. 'I remember what you were like when we were on the beat together. You had an instinct for police work that officers today seem to have lost. It's something that can't be trained or taught.' He tilted his head to one side. 'I suppose it's occurred to you that your instincts back then might have been the synaesthesia, just starting up in your head and giving you that competitive edge. I do wonder if you'll still be as good with it suppressed.'

Lapslie shook his head. 'Don't go there. I never relied on the synaesthesia. I tried to ignore it for years. I never really came to terms with it.'

'Do you know yet how it started?'

Lapslie sighed. Thinking about the synaesthesia inevitably threw him back to the days when he and Sonia were together and things were different. Not necessarily better; just different. 'I think it started when Jamie was born. He was one of those babies who would cry all the time. Not because he was hungry, or because he was cold, or in pain, but just because. And after a while, when he used to cry, I could taste something coppery in my mouth. I thought it was just the sleeplessness of having a baby, but it kept on going, and bit by bit I started tasting different things. It took a while before I connected the tastes up to noises I was hearing, which was when I started researching the condition.'

'It was a difficult birth, as I remember,' Rouse said

softly. Lapslie nodded. The memory caused a shiver to run through his shoulders.

'But synaesthesia isn't caused by stress, is it? Otherwise everyone would get it. There must be another component.'

'I guess.' Lapslie shrugged, and looked past Rouse, out of the window at the deep-blue sky. 'Perhaps it's genetic, although I don't recall my parents or my sister ever mentioning it. Perhaps it's just a malformation of the brain, the neurological equivalent of a club foot or a hair lip. All I know is that it was more or less quiescent in me until Jamie's birth, and then it just revved up.'

'And it's got worse, hasn't it? I don't mean gradually – I mean suddenly, every now and then.'

Lapslie nodded. 'The first time was when my mother and father died. Car crash. It got worse then. And later – you know I had a relationship with another police officer a few years after Robbie was born?'

Rouse was inscrutable. 'I heard.'

'When that relationship ended, and it ended badly, the synaesthesia escalated. And then again, when Sonia and I first separated and I moved out, it escalated again. So yes, it's obviously related to things that are going on in my life, but I don't think it's directly caused by them.' He blinked, taking a deep breath as if waking from a dream. 'How the hell did we end up talking about this?'

Rouse steepled his fingers in front of him. 'I think we needed to. I think we've been needing to for a while. And perhaps we couldn't until you were actually in treatment.'

'You know that's not why I popped in?'

Rouse shrugged. 'My door is always open to you, Mark. Doesn't matter what you want.' He paused. 'So – if it wasn't your state of health that made you fly back, what was it?'

'I got sent something. An email.'

'Bad news?'

'For someone. It was a recording of a woman being murdered.'

'Ah, that. Yes, I seem to remember seeing something about it from Forensics. I would rather have expected to hear about it from you first.'

'And here I am. I wanted to make sure it *was* a crime before bothering you.'

Rouse pursed his lips and hesitated for a moment before saying: 'Did it happen on our patch? In Essex?'

Lapslie stared at him. 'Does that matter? A woman is dead.'

'If one of my officers is investigating a murder using my budget, I'd at least like to know that the murder occurred on my patch.'

'The email was sent to me from a hospital in Essex. Is that enough?'

'For now.' Rouse frowned. 'Sent to you directly?'

'Yes.'

'By somebody that knows you?'

'Presumably.'

'So this is personal.'

'At first blush, yes. I've sent the file to Forensics, as you know, and they've analysed it for me. They can confirm that it's a genuine killing, but that's about all at the moment. I've checked recent discoveries of dead bodies of women but there are too many to narrow down without further evidence. And that's where I am at the moment.' He paused and grimaced. 'I'll need to set up an incident room. Would Emma Bradbury be available to help?'

'Actually,' Rouse said, 'she's been assigned to another case. You weren't around, and besides, it's apparently a straight murder, although there are some odd details. You'll have to run with it by yourself for a while. Make sure you keep me informed. This has the hallmarks of something that could come back and bite us on the arse if we don't get a grip of it.'

'Do you ever think about anything apart from budgets and publicity?' Lapslie asked, standing.

'*Is* there anything else?' Rouse asked, apparently without irony.

Rather than head back to the office and spend the

rest of the afternoon listening to the sound file, over and over, Lapslie headed down to the canteen on the first floor and grabbed a sandwich and a cup of coffee. The sandwich was actually a muffuletta with a marinated olive salad and layers of capicola, salami, mortadella, emmental and provolone, while the coffee was a medio Americano with an extra shot, but to him it was still a sandwich and a cup of coffee. He had almost finished it when a figure loomed up beside his table. He looked up to find the diminutive Sean Burrows staring at him. 'DCI Lapslie,' Burrows said. 'They said I could find you down here.'

'Mr Burrows. Please, join me.' Burrows sat down, and Lapslie added, 'Can I get you a coffee?'

'Thanks, but no. I was up for another meeting, and I wanted to tell you that my people have been able to extract some more information from that sound file.' He smiled. 'They're like terriers, that lot. They just don't give up.'

'Good thing too,' Lapslie said, feeling a little flutter of anticipation in his stomach. 'I haven't got any further in identifying the victim.' He stared expectantly at Burrows. 'What have you found?'

'Best I show you,' Burrows replied. 'Or, at least, let you listen. I've brought a copy with me. Have you access to a computer around here, by any chance?'

'Funnily enough, I believe there are a couple in the building.'

Lapslie led Burrows up to his office. The forensic expert took a memory stick from his pocket and plugged it into an empty USB socket on the computer.

'I hope you've virus-checked that,' Lapslie murmured. 'Apparently, it's regulations.'

Burrows glanced up at him with a raised eyebrow. 'Believe me,' he said, 'our software checks against viruses that haven't even been invented yet. My technicians have a game where they try to build computer viruses that can get past the software. None of them has succeeded yet.'

'Have they ever considered going out and getting a life?'

Burrows grimaced. 'Given what they know about murder and computer viruses, I'd rather they stayed in their offices for as long as possible. If I were allowed to make them sleep there, I would.' He paused. 'Sadly, they'd probably prefer sleeping there to going home.'

Turning back to the computer, he pulled up the Windows Player and located a file on the memory stick. Double-clicking it, he stood back.

Lapslie braced himself, waiting for the first scream, but it never came. Or, rather, it came but it was pushed so far into the background that it was hardly audible.

In the foreground was static, a continuous hiss like a waterfall, and a sound like someone shifting around.

'What's this?' Lapslie asked.

'We've used a graphic equaliser to push the foreground sounds to the back and amplify the background sounds. It helps that the recording was in stereo, because that meant we could work out where the victim was standing at any moment and filter out sounds from that area as much as possible. You can hear that she's still there, but faintly. What you're hearing now is the killer.'

And as Lapslie listened, that's exactly what he heard. Footsteps. Breathing. The sound of clothes rustling. And then, chillingly, a voice whispering, 'No, that's gash. That's just gash.'

And there was something about that voice he thought he recognised, although without the crutch of his synaesthesia he wasn't sure. Just something about the tone, the timbre.

'Can you amplify that voice?' he asked urgently.

'That's as good as it gets,' Burrows said. 'We've run every technique we know, but anything more than that ends up distorting so badly that it's unrecognisable.'

'But it's a man's voice?'

'Difficult to tell, with the whispering, but it sounds like a man, yes.'

Lapslie took a deep breath. It wasn't exactly a case-breaking moment, but it was something. 'Thanks, Sean.'

'Not a problem, Mr Lapslie. We'll keep on working, of course. Sara has some hopes that she can isolate the acoustic signature of the building. We might be able to tell you something about where it was recorded.'

'Anything would be helpful at the moment,' Lapslie said, shaking Burrows' hand.

After the Head of Forensics had left, Lapslie played the file again, setting it on 'loop' so that it repeated over and over. That voice – 'No, that's gash. That's just gash.' Where did he know it from? Did he, in fact, know it at all? Was he just projecting the fact that the killer obviously knew Lapslie, or knew of him, onto a vague whisper and trying to reconstruct something that just wasn't there?

The more he replayed the file, the more he found himself listening for the screams of the victim, now suppressed into near-silence in the background. He had listened to the original sound file so many times that he knew where the screams would come.

Listening to the killer and his victim in their dance of death, Lapslie found himself thinking about the hospital internet café where the sound file had been sent from. According to Burrows' people there was no way of finding out from the file who had sent it, but as his mind drifted Lapslie found himself staring at the webcam that sat upon the top of the LCD monitor. It was switched off now, but Lapslie had used similar devices to conduct video-conferences with investigating officers from the silence of his cottage when his synaesthesia was particularly bad.

And he suddenly remembered that the computers in the internet café in the hospital had all had a little blue light glowing in the top-centre of their screens. Webcams? It was possible. And that meant an image of the killer might have been accidentally captured as they were sending the email – especially if the default setting of the computers was to have their cameras 'on'. It was a long shot, but he'd taken longer shots before and hit the target.

He pulled Burrows' memory stick from the computer, turned it off with a brutal press of the power switch and headed for the car park. Within five minutes he was in his Saab 9-3 and heading again for the hospital that, for various reasons, was playing a more and more important role in his life.

As was becoming more and more common these days, it was eye-wateringly expensive to use the car park at the hospital. Lapslie assumed that the intention was to dissuade hundreds of people from parking there for hours on end while visiting relatives, but the problem was that people often turned up at Accident and Emergency, or Obstetrics, or some other part of the hospital for treatment or with a partner and not knowing how long they were likely to be there. And the shock of paying for parking while you spent twelve hours in A&E would be enough to trigger another heart attack, if that's what they were in for in the first place.

He put two hours on the car and strode into the hospital. He knew the place well enough now to head straight through the wide white corridors, past the abstract paintings and sculptures that were meant to soothe the patients and their visitors, to where the internet café was located. Part of him missed the choking smell of antiseptic cleaner that he associated with hospitals from his childhood. Science had obviously moved on since then, and come up with something that probably smelled faintly of pine or lemon. Or, God help the world, lavender.

Three computers were occupied – two by patients in dressing gowns and one by a bored kid who had probably been forced to accompany his mother on a visit to her bed-ridden aunt – and Lapslie walked across to the counter where a girl with pink foam swirls in her hair was chatting on a mobile phone. Her nametag said 'Kari'. She raised her eyebrows at him and smiled. He just stared at her until she whispered into her mobile, 'Got to go – call you later,' and cut short her call.

'Detective Chief Inspector Lapslie,' he said quietly, holding his warrant card out towards her. 'I'm investigating a murder. I need to know about the webcams on your terminals.'

'Wow – a real policeman. Okay, yeah, what do you need to know?'

'Are they switched on all the time?'

She shook her head. 'No way. That would be an invasion of privacy. We have strict rules.' She leaned forward confidentially. 'It's to do with, you know, perverts. We don't want people thinking they can hack into the computers, turn the cameras on and watch the kids. We have to activate the webcams from the desk here.'

'Okay.' He thought for a moment. The chances of the killer having switched the webcam on while they were sending Lapslie the email was, while superficially attractive, almost laughably improbable, but he had to try. 'If I give you a date, a time and an IP address, can you see whether a particular terminal had its webcam switched on?'

'Sure.'

He handed across the information that Sean Burrows' team had given him and watched as she typed it into her terminal and frowned at the screen. 'Yeah,' she said, pointing. 'It's that one over there. Looks like we had one camera switched on at that time, but it wasn't that one.'

'Thanks.' He turned away, disappointed, then turned back as a sudden thought occurred to him.

'Do you log the images from the webcams?'

'Yeah. We have to. As proof in case, you know, people are doing something inappropriate.' She looked around at the ranks of terminals. 'Although you'd have to be pretty weird to want to touch yourself up or whatever in the middle of a hospital.'

'Oh, I don't know,' Lapslie found himself saying. 'Nurses' uniforms – you know?'

She gazed at him blankly.

'Okay. Anyway, any chance you still have the images from the webcam that *was* on at the time?'

'Yeah. I guess.' She turned back to the terminal, typed and clicked away, then swivelled the screen around to face him. 'Hey, look,' she said. 'It's me!'

Lapslie stared at the boxed image on the screen. The person using the terminal was a middle-aged lady, and she was talking away nineteen to the dozen. A time-stamp and date-stamp had been inserted at the bottom of the image. There was no sound, but Lapslie felt fairly sure that she was updating some family member in Australia or South Africa on the medical condition of some relative in the hospital. The image was updating several times a second; not quite movie quality, but enough to be able to see what she was doing. Better than a still image, certainly. Behind her was a reverse angle back to the counter. Kari was, indeed, sitting behind the counter. The swirls in her hair had been purple that time. Lapslie spent a couple of seconds orienting himself, trying to work out which terminal the images had been sent from.

And the terminal that Lapslie was interested in – the one from which the scream sound file had been sent – was located directly between the middle-aged woman and the desk with Kari behind it.

Lapslie's breath caught in his throat. Someone was sitting at that terminal. The image quality wasn't perfect, but he could make out enough to tell sex, age and colour of hair.

Lapslie checked the time-stamp and the date-stamp again in disbelief. There was no doubt. The images had been captured at the exact time that the sound file had been sent. And the person at the terminal was the person who had sent the file.

It was a girl. A teenage girl with red hair pulled back into a ponytail.

CHAPTER SIX

Emma Bradbury slept fitfully, bothered by the constant traffic outside her window and what sounded like a wedding reception being held in a room below her. Seventies and eighties dance hits – the one thing musically that she and Dom McGinley could agree that they both hated.

She'd eaten at the hotel, after leaving Sergeant Murrell at the police station. The restaurant had been decorated in *faux*-baronial style, with shields and crossed swords hung on walls painted a deep-red which, reflected in the windows looking out into the darkness, made it appear that the sunset outside had been forever frozen in time. A bit like Canvey Island itself, she thought. The menu, like the music that she would spend the next few hours lying awake and listening to, was also frozen in more ways than one: trapped in the 1970s: prawns in Marie Rose sauce, pâté on toast triangles, beef tournedos, mushroom stroganoff . . . She ordered a pint of gassy keg beer from the bar: she had a feeling that if she'd looked at the wine list it would have been filled with Blue Nuns and Black Towers and rosé wines in bulbous bottles nestled within wicker baskets. Naff. The whole place was naff, as if civilisation lapped out in slow waves from London, and Canvey Island was the point where the tide washed up the old, faded flotsam and jetsam of history.

Having said that, the food was actually nicely cooked, and the beer relaxed her enough that she started enjoying herself despite her surroundings. Listening to the conversations of the diners around her – mainly middle-aged or elderly couples, with a smattering of youngsters on what was probably their first date – she kept dropping in and out of parallel conversations along the lines of: 'You remember 'er, she used to live on Arnely Avenue. Had 'er, you know, 'er tubes tied at the 'ospital two years ago, but it all went wrong and she got an infection. She went to live wiv 'er mum and 'er mum's boyfriend in the end . . .' Not so much a conversation as a stream of consciousness interrupted by the occasional 'Yeah' and 'Uh?' from the other person.

Eventually the wedding reception degenerated into what sounded like a fight, and from there into silence. Emma drifted off to sleep, and woke hours later to find weak sunlight washing in through the double-glazed window.

She showered, dressed and went downstairs to find that the restaurant had been rearranged as a breakfast buffet. She loaded her plate up with scrambled egg, hash browns and bacon, and washed the lot down with a pot of strong coffee, then went out for a walk in the cold and damp morning air.

The Cocklecatcher had its own car park which opened out onto a small shopping centre of the Euronics and Iceland variety. A mist had drifted in from the estuary, muffling sounds and making people appear like ghosts as they walked. She located a cashpoint and got out some money, just to keep herself going.

She returned to the hotel and got into her car. Checking her watch she found that it was heading towards nine o'clock, but she was in no rush to get to the police station. The main event of the morning was getting the body formally identified by the Dooley family, and she wasn't particularly looking forward to that. It was the part of the job she hated most. So instead she started her car and drove out along one of the main roads, keeping going past more Dutch-sounding road names, like Ziderbeck, Wilrich, Baardwyk and Vanderwilt, past the strangely inappropriate and deserted Canvey Island Transport Museum, until the road stopped dead at a scrappy grass bank topped with a grey concrete sea wall. She parked her car and got out, feeling the chill wind run its fingers through her hair. Climbing the bank, she found herself gazing out across the Thames Estuary. Away in the distance a bird was calling, a repeated 'tueep, tueep, tueep', and somewhere else she could hear the whine of power saws and the 'beep, beep, beep' of a reversing forklift truck. The breeze pushed the otherwise waveless water this way and that, causing small ripples that criss-crossed each other like the grey, reticulated hide of an elephant. The grey, damp mist hung low, obscuring the horizon and giving the impression that reality just faded out into grey nothingness a few hundred yards away. What with that and the sea wall that ran all the way around the island, Canvey felt more and more to her like a fortified castle desperately clinging on to civilisation while surrounded by the besieging forces of chaos.

On the other side of the sea wall was an algae-covered concrete lip, some four feet wide. It was accessible via gaps in the wall every hundred yards or so that could be closed off with thick metal gates if there was a particularly high tide. Sloped down into the water beyond was the sea wall, built from massive blocks of stone that had been coated in thick black bitumen. Decades of hot summers had caused the bitumen to soften and run like ancient wrinkled skin.

Looking down onto the concrete lip, Emma could see three men in parkas and woollen hats clustered around a telescope mounted on a tripod. The other two had binoculars slung around their necks. The telescope was pointed sideways, along the wall, and following its line Emma could see in the distance a marshy area where banks of mud emerged from the rippling water like the backs of wallowing animals. Small wading birds scurried across the mud with splayed feet, probing for worms. The men ignored them, spending their time instead chatting and sipping tea from thermos flasks held in gloved fingers. They were obviously waiting for rarer prey.

'Morning!'

Emma turned, surprised, to find a woman in a green Barbour jacket and a headscarf wandering past. She had a chocolate Labrador at heel.

'Good morning,' Emma replied.

The woman smiled and walked on. The dog sniffed at Emma's trousers, waited for a moment to see whether it might be stroked, then wandered off.

Turning back to the estuary, Emma noticed that the birdwatchers' attention had been gripped by something out on the mudbanks. The man with the telescope was bending over with his face pressed up against the eyepiece, while his two friends had their binoculars clamped to their eyes with an eagerness that Emma would have considered suspicious if she had seen it displayed in a park near a children's playground. Following their rapt gaze she couldn't see anything different about the mud banks. The birds looked exactly the same to her. People were strange.

She looked back out across the water. The mist was beginning to clear now, pushed off by the stiffening breeze. A weak sun was now visible as a white circle the size of a penny held at arm's length in the sky. Beneath the rippling, wind-blown water Emma could see the dark shadows of sunken mud banks. The ripples seemed to change shape as they crossed the shadows. Further out, where the angle of the light on the water meant that the mud banks were invisible beneath its surface, Emma found that she could still tell where they were from the patterns of ripples. The estuary had a geography all its own, if you knew what you were looking for.

She was avoiding having to get the body identified. She knew that, but her willpower appeared to have evaporated. All she wanted to do, for the moment, was stand there and look out across the water, like the bird-watchers, waiting for something meaningful to happen. She didn't know what it might be, but she would recognise it if she saw it.

Emma wandered along the wall towards where the mud banks lay, heading in the same direction as the lady with the Labrador. She tried to work out which of the birds had got the birdwatchers all of a twitter, but they still all looked the same to her: dun-coloured little bundles with thin beaks and wide feet. Surely, if you were going to go to all the trouble of spending hours standing in the cold and the rain you would do it for something bright and tropical, or at the very least something bigger than the average, but to Emma it seemed that all the men were getting excited about was a bird the same size and shape as the rest of them but with a black edge to its wing feathers, or an extra toe, or something.

Past the mud banks, Emma saw a forest of slender wooden poles pointed towards the sky. For a few moments she couldn't work out what they were, then she realised. Masts. As she got closer she saw that they were all attached to boats that were drawn up on a concrete causeway that sloped down towards the water. And not just any boats. These were all small one- or two-person catamarans – two narrow hulls like canoes linked by narrow struts with a mast projecting right from the centre. A sign on a building nearby said: 'Canvey Island Boat Club'. Obviously there was more going on here than just birdwatching.

Her way forward was blocked by a fence that marked the boundary of the Boat Club. The Labrador woman had headed down the slope to where she had parked her car. Emma turned around and headed back along the wall.

The mist had rolled back now, revealing more of the water. Faintly, in the far distance, Emma thought she could make out a mass of land: sketchy suggestions of hills and dips across on the Kent side of the estuary. Gravesend, perhaps? Years ago, centuries before the Dartford Tunnel had been dug, and before the Queen Elizabeth Bridge had been built, both of them ten miles or so upstream, the only way from one bank to the other would be by boat. To make the trip by cart or by foot would require you to go all the way up to – where? Walton-on-Thames, perhaps? Or further?

This was stupid. She couldn't keep putting it off. The body would have been transferred from Jane Catherall's care to the mortuary nearest to the parents by now. It, and they, were waiting for her.

Reluctantly, she headed down the grassy bank towards her car.

She arrived at the police station just before nine o'clock. Murrell was in his office sifting through a pile of papers. He glanced up as she walked in.

'Morning. Sleep well?'

'Not so's you'd notice.'

He nodded. 'Wedding party?'

'You guessed. You weren't there, were you?'

'No, but there's a wedding party on there most nights. Which is odd, considering there aren't that many weddings occurring on the island. Someone ought to look into that.'

'You ready to go?'

His eyes narrowed for a second, as if he'd just been told he was being taken to the vet to be neutered. 'I suppose so.'

'Problem?' Emma asked.

'No.' He stood up, but hesitated before coming out from behind his desk. 'Well, yes. In a way.'

'Go on.'

'It's . . .' He paused, and swallowed. 'Look, this is going to sound pathetic.'

'What?'

'We're going off-island, aren't we?'

Emma sighed. 'You say that like it's a bad thing.'

Murrell raised his hands defensively. 'Not as such, but a lot of us are kind of *tied* to Canvey Island. It's more than our home; it's like it's separate from the rest of Essex and the rest of England. We feel comfortable here, and we've got everything we need – shops, pubs, night-clubs, cinemas. And apart from a few weeks in the summer we get the beaches as well.' He made a vague gesture with his hands. 'Most of the men who live on

Canvey marry women from Canvey. What does that tell you?'

'That the incidence of people with six fingers is higher than the national average?'

He had the grace to laugh. 'Well, yeah, in-breeding is certainly possible, judging by some of the people that I see out on the streets – but no, what I mean is, it's a community in the true sense of the word, with the kind of ties that bind a community together. Off-island, in Essex, over the course of centuries, little villages joined together to form larger villages, and then towns. Here, on Canvey, we didn't. We're still separate from the rest. In our minds we're still that little village, bounded by the sea.'

'Look,' she said patiently, 'I didn't need a passport to get here. There's no customs at the border and you're not going to be cavity-searched when you leave. The people in Essex still talk the same language, and they don't have nits. Just take a deep breath and force yourself.'

'Okay.' He nodded. 'Right. Yes. Let's go.'

They took his car, giving Emma a chance to do some more sightseeing as they drove out past the caravan park and the tall metal chimneys of the refinery, past the large supermarket and the several small round-abouts, along the long, curving causeway that carried cars over the marshes and which, Emma noticed, was called Memorial Way, presumably in remembrance of the people who had died in the floods of the 1950s. Murrell was quiet as they drove, and Emma couldn't help wondering about his reluctance to leave the island. It was almost medieval; but then, she reflected, so much of what she had seen on the island made it feel like a village walled off against the barbarian hordes that roamed the marshes. Some kind of race memory? Who could tell?

Once across the causeway it was about a forty-minute drive to Maldon. The first twenty minutes took them along wide A-roads built up above the Essex country-side as if by architects who were frightened of letting their roads touch the soil; the second half of the journey was along minor B-roads through small villages and past farms and industrial parks. Eventually they got to the outskirts of the town. The mortuary was on the other side, and Murrell had to drive right through the centre of town to get there. Maldon's town centre seemed to consist of one very long High Street that was a mix of nondescript buildings, old churches and new flat-fronted shops. They passed a particularly impressive hotel named the Blue Boar, and Emma made a mental note to look it up with a view to staying there if work or play ever brought her back to the Maldon area.

The mortuary was part of the new local hospital. Murrell parked in the hospital's car park, and together they walked through the large sliding doors at the entrance and on through the central spine corridor following the cryptic signage and the equally cryptic instructions given to them by the woman on the reception desk.

A tastefully furnished waiting room was set to one side of the doorway that led into the main mortuary area. Three people were waiting there: a small man whose tanned skin was almost as leathery as his coat, but not quite as scuffed, a woman who probably massed twice his body weight but who was leaning on him for comfort, and a large man in a tight police uniform whose hair was sandy turning white. He walked over to them. 'George Rossmore,' he said, hand outstretched.

'Keith Murrell,' said Emma's companion, shaking hands.

Emma did likewise, murmuring 'Emma Bradbury.' She looked across to the man and the woman. 'Mr and Mrs Dooley, I presume?'

'Indeed,' Rossmore said.

'Boyfriend not here?'

'Apparently not.'

'Shame,' Emma said. 'I wanted to talk to him.' Something about the voices of the parents caught her attention. After a few moments she realised that the tearful wailing and the muttered reassurances were being said in another language. 'They're not British?' she asked.

'They're Travellers,' Rossmore answered; 'a people without a land, if you believe them. Even the ones who have settled down, or who have been settled down against their will, and don't actually move around any more. They have their own traditions, their own ways of doing things and their own language.'

'Just like the people of Canvey Island,' Emma murmured, 'apart from the language bit.' She thought for a moment. 'What language do they speak? Romany?'

'No, you're thinking of true Gypsies: the Roma. They have a bit of a downer on the Travellers. They called them "Didicoy", which is the same word they use for the half-breed children of Roma and ordinary people. That language they're speaking is Shelti. It comes in two dialects – Gamin and Cant. These two are speaking Gamin, unless I miss my guess.'

'Wow.' Emma was impressed. 'A whole culture that I wasn't even aware of.'

'They don't integrate,' Rossmore agreed, 'but they don't set up an obvious counter-culture of Traveller shops, Traveller churches and Traveller community centres either. They're the perfect neighbours, as long as you ignore the petty crime and the caravan sites.'

Emma walked across to the two grieving parents. 'Mr and Mrs Dooley? I'm Detective Sergeant Emma Bradbury. Thank you for being here.'

'Can we get this over with?' the husband said gruffly. He wouldn't look Emma in the eyes.

'Of course.' She paused, trying to work out how to phrase the necessary qualification. 'We don't know for sure that this is your daughter, but we strongly suspect it is. We need you to confirm it for us. Is that okay?' She tried to meet their gaze, to gauge whether they understood what she was trying to tell them, but they were both looking away: Mr Dooley towards the window and his wife at the floor. Emma looked towards the door. A hospital worker was standing there. He nodded to her solemnly. 'Please – come this way.'

He led them through the door into the mortuary itself. The air was chillier there, and it smelled of pine and lavender. Vases of flowers were placed on tables and shelves; anything to disguise the fact that this was a place of death within a place of illness and disease: the final destination for some of the patients who passed through its large sliding doors. He stopped at a doorway. The room inside was darkened. He gestured inside. 'Please – whenever you are ready.'

Inside, on a table, a body lay. It couldn't be anything else. The smell of pine and lavender was almost overpowering. Mr and Mrs Dooley, Emma and Murrell all shuffled in, like actors walking on stage but unsure of their lines or their stage directions. The hospital worker walked over to the body, took hold of a corner of the sheet nearest the head, and folded it back, exposing the face.

It was the woman whose body Emma had seen in Doctor Catherall's mortuary, but someone had done a lot of good work on her. Emma remembered with a shudder how the woman's scalp had been peeled forward by the pathologist, exposing her skull and covering her face, but none of that was evident now. Her face was composed, her eyes peacefully closed, her forehead unwrinkled, her hair carefully brushed, A dressing had been applied at the place where Emma remembered that the flesh had been sliced away. It would have been possible to believe that she was just asleep, pale and cold and asleep, if Emma hadn't seen her with her chest and skull opened up and her organs being removed and weighed with no more ceremony than a load of groceries.

Mrs Dooley let out a shocked wail, then clapped her hand over her mouth. Her eyes were wide and disbelieving. Her husband's face seemed to age ten years in as many seconds.

'Yes,' he said, as flat and as hard as concrete. 'That's me daughter.'

Emma led the parents out of the room where their daughter lay and back to the waiting room. It seemed like a different room now. The flowers that had previously been vibrant looked artificial, and the soothing paint scheme pointed up the scuffs and cracks in the walls. Even the neon light strips were buzzing more than they had before.

''Ow did it 'appen?' Mr Dooley asked, still with his arm around his wife's shoulders.

Emma knew the police code: never answer a question except with another question if you're interviewing witnesses or suspects, in case you give something away that could later prove critical to the investigation, and this was still a murder investigation. She shook her head. 'We're still in the process of establishing exactly what happened,' she said. 'But please accept my condolences.' She paused for a heartbeat. 'When did you realise that your daughter was missing?'

'She didn't come 'ome,' Mrs Dooley said; the first words Emma had heard her utter in English. Her voice was raspy, roughened by too many years of smoking, Emma assumed. 'Normally we wouldn't bovver about that, but we knew 'er boyfriend weren't around.'

Mr Dooley's hand tightened on his wife's shoulder. Emma noticed the flesh beneath the blouse bulge beneath his thin fingers.

''E were out wiv 'is mates,' Mrs Dooley amplified. 'Cat hadn't said she was goin' to be out, so we phoned a few of 'er mates. They 'adn't seen 'er. Nobody 'ad seen 'er.'

'So you called the police,' Emma said, not so much a question as an anticipation of the next statement.

'No,' Mr Dooley said. 'We went out lookin'. Me an' some others. We checked all the usual bars an' clubs, but she weren't there. We phoned 'er bloke, just in case, but she weren't wiv 'im either. We drove around lookin', but she weren't nowhere.'

'And *then* you notified the police?' Emma asked.

Mr Dooley looked away. His expression suggested that he wanted to spit on the floor, but was restraining himself. 'After some . . . discussion, yeah.'

'The Parve usually try to sort things out themselves,' Sergeant Rossmore said from the other side of the room. 'They don't like bothering the police with trivialities like missing people.'

'We keep ourselves to ourselves,' Mrs Dooley offered when her husband said nothing. She looked up at him. 'And look where it got us.'

He remained silent, but his fingers clamped hard enough on her shoulder that she winced.

'Are you sure her boyfriend couldn't have seen her?' Emma asked.

'I'm sure,' Mr Dooley said. 'I know the blokes who was with 'im.'

'What's his name?' Emma asked.

Mr Dooley glanced at her, briefly, suspicion in his eyes. 'I told you, it ain't 'im.'

'None the less, we need to talk to him.'

'Why?' Blunt, flat.

Emma thought quickly. She wanted to talk to the boyfriend because he was probably her chief suspect, but the Dooleys were convinced he was innocent. 'Because he might have talked to her on the phone, and he might be able to narrow down the time when she was ... when she died.'

'Donal,' Mrs Dooley said, after glancing at her husband. 'Donal O'Riordan. 'E's a decent enough lad.'

'And where does he live?'

Mrs Dooley glanced at her husband again, but this time he shook his head briefly. 'I dunno,' she said lamely.

'If she was attacked,' Mr Dooley said before Emma could follow up the question, 'if my baby girl was assaulted, I want to know about it. I got a right to know about it.'

'And then what?' Rossmore asked. 'You round up a lynch mob? You hunt down someone you think might be guilty and you cut their bollocks off?'

'We keep ourselves to ourselves,' Mr Dooley said as if

reciting a mantra. 'We sort out our own problems in our own ways.'

'Which would be all fine and dandy,' Rossmore said, 'if you always get the right bloke. But you don't. You just choose someone you don't like the look of, usually an outsider, and you set on them like you set those lurchers you keep on hares. And, of course, if one of *you* has raped or assaulted an outsider then you close ranks. You let them get away with it.'

Mr Dooley shrugged, as if he wasn't interested.

'Mrs Dooley,' Emma said, calming her, 'can you think of anyone who might have held a grudge against Catriona? Did she mention anyone bothering her, or following her around? Had she been in any fights?'

'Nothing.' Mrs Dooley shook her head violently. 'She were a good girl. Everone loved 'er.'

'Did she work?'

'She was on the tills at Sainsbury's. Just to get by 'til the summer, when she could get a job at the amusements.'

'Lovely,' Sergeant Rossmore muttered from the other side of the room.

'Have either of *you* seen anyone round the area, anyone you didn't recognise, or who looked out of place?'

'Not a soul.'

Mr Dooley made a little gesture with his head. 'We

know what goes on in our manor. If there was a stranger around, we'd know about it. People would call other people, and pretty soon we'd 'ave someone checkin' 'em out.'

Emma shook her head. 'I won't keep you any longer. Thank you for your help, and once again – I'm sorry for your loss. Sergeant Rossmore will assign a police officer to act as family liaison, keeping you abreast of developments and making sure you know what's going on.'

'We don't need no family liaison,' Mr Dooley snarled. 'All we need is a name. Just a name.'

'And we need our daughter back,' Mrs Dooley said, almost apologetically. 'For the funeral.'

'It may be a few days,' Emma said, 'depending on the state of the investigation, but I'll get your daughter's body released as soon as possible. Can we give you a lift back to your home?'

'We'll make our own way.' Mr Dooley took his wife's elbow and guided her away, towards the door.

She watched them go, thinking about how little she'd actually got from them, and how tight-knit the Traveller community appeared to be. She'd never really had any dealings with them before. From the outside they looked just like anyone else, but scratch the surface and there was a whole set of beliefs, habits, traditions and customs there that marked them out from the rest of the society whose boundaries they lived so quietly within.

'This Donal O'Riordan,' she said, looking at Rossmore. 'Is he known to you?'

'Local Jack-the-Lad,' Rossmore replied. 'We've had him up for joyriding on too many occasions to mention, plus we've suspected him of some minor burglaries, a bit of breaking and entering. He likes his beer and he likes to get into a fight on a Saturday night. We know where he lives. Council house on the same estate as the Dooleys.'

'Then let's go there,' Emma said. 'Before the Dooleys warn him off.'

'We'll need backup,' Rossmore declared, scrawling the address on a scrap of paper. 'The old boy was right – if we turn up there'll be a flashmob surrounding us within ten minutes, and they'll be bringing bricks and base-ball bats to the party.'

As Emma walked with Murrell back to his car, Rossmore was talking on his mobile behind them. The drive from the hospital took less than twenty minutes, heading out of the centre of Maldon and into an estate that grew out of it like a cancer, its cells being hundreds of houses made out of grey breeze-blocks and discoloured PVC cladding, the only thing distinguishing one from another being the various different kinds of weather damage and the remains of old Christmas decorations clinging like dead vines to the gaps between the masonry blocks. By the time they got to O'Riordan's house they were part of a convoy of five police cars. It wasn't quite a raid, but the speed with which the police got out of their cars and formed a protective barrier against the rapidly developing crowd of locals made it feel like one.

Emma strode up the cracked path towards the front door, past the rusted carcass of an old Ford Mondeo that sat in the front garden. She could sense Murrell sprinting to keep up. She banged hard on the door, trying to ignore the mutterings from the growing mob behind her. 'Donal O'Riordan? This is the police. Please answer the door – we need to talk to you.' She paused, then added, 'It's about your girlfriend – Catriona Dooley,' just in case he had more than one girlfriend.

Two constables headed around the back to intercept O'Riordan if he tried to make a run for it. Either Rossmore had sent them or they'd been on enough encroachments into Traveller territory that they knew how it worked.

No sound from within. Emma turned to Murrell. 'What do you reckon?' she asked. 'We've got no grounds to go in, even if we suspect he's inside, and the locals aren't going to be much help. We'll never find a local gossip who can tell us where he's gone around here.'

'Actually,' Murrell said, 'I think we have got grounds to go in.' He pointed to the white PVC door. 'Look.'

Emma looked closer at the area Murrell was indicating, beside the Yale lock. What she had at first taken to be a grease mark looked more like a smear of blood, as if someone with bloody fingers had pulled the door too and left a thumbprint.

'Right,' she said, beckoning two constables. 'I want this door open, pronto.'

The constables looked at each other uncertainly, then back at the car.

'I don't think we've got the door-breaking equipment with us,' one of them, a lad with ginger hair and freckles, said.

Emma tried not to imagine what Mark Lapslie would say at that point. 'Policemen have been breaking doors down for hundreds of years,' she said patiently. 'Use your initiative.'

'Are we allowed to do that?' the other one asked. He was shorter, with spiky dark hair. 'Health and safety, like.'

'Just do it,' Murrell said before Emma could explode at them. 'I'll make sure you're covered. And whatever you do, don't try and kick it in like they do on TV. You'll just injure yourself. Brace yourself and use your shoulders.'

'That was my point,' the ginger-haired constable murmured, but he took a step back and threw himself against the door. It shuddered under his weight, and bowed at the top, but the lock stayed intact. He stood back further and took two steps this time before hitting the door. This time the wood holding the lock splintered and the door flew open.

'Get in and look for O'Riordan,' Emma instructed. The constables piled inside; one heading left and up a set of stairs that were all but invisible in the shadows of the hall, the other heading right. She and Murrell followed on.

The living room, directly off the hall, was dark; curtains drawn against the afternoon sunshine. It smelled of unwashed clothes and takeaway Chinese food. Emma looked around the living room: leather sofa, massive LCD TV, Xbox 360. No sign of O'Riordan.

One of the constables thudded down the stairs and into the living room. 'Nobody,' he said. 'Place is a mess, though. Don't reckon he's got a cleaner.'

'I think you need to see this,' the other constable called from the hall. He appeared in the doorway, face white and adam's apple bobbing as he swallowed. 'I *really* think you both need to see this.'

Emma glanced over at Murrell. He was frowning. Together, they headed towards the kitchen. Emma got through the door first.

The cooker was covered in half-empty plastic take-out

containers with snap tops, and the dried remains of spilled meals, but it was the kitchen table that her gaze was drawn to. It was covered in dark red blood. Smears and tracks on the centre of the table indicated that something had been dragged across it. Trickles of blood had made their way to the edge and hung like glutinous stalactites down towards the floor.

'Dear God,' Murrell said from behind Emma.

On a hunch, she crossed to the fridge and opened the door.

Revealed in the actinic white glow, the fridge was stacked up with plastic take-out containers. Unlike the ones on the cooker, these were washed and clean. And unlike the ones on the cooker, they were all full.

Emma felt her stomach lurch. Each plastic container was filled with gobbets of dark red flesh.

'Find him,' she snarled. 'And arrest him for murder.'

CHAPTER SEVEN

It was only when Lapslie got back to his Saab that he remembered he hadn't paid the hospital's extortionate parking toll. He looked around the car park, but there were no ticket machines – only a few well-disguised signs telling him that he had to pay in the hospital reception area. Grumpily, he walked back to the reception and found the only machine that seemed to have been fitted. There was a queue of people waiting in front of it, muttering to themselves in what was either irritation or the first indication of mental illness. The woman at the front of the line was rooting in her handbag for the right change. Judging by the look on her face she already knew that she hadn't got it but was hoping either to locate a previously unknown hoard of 10p pieces underneath her knitting or that a kindly soul waiting in the queue would donate the money to her. Looking at the people in the line Lapslie thought they were more likely to mug her for the coins she already had than give her more.

After a minute or so of fruitless waiting he turned and strode off to the reception desk. A middle-aged woman in a blazer was sitting behind it, scanning her computer screen and making notes on a sheet of paper with a ballpoint pen. She glanced up as he approached.

'Can I help you?'

'Police,' Lapslie said, holding his warrant card up where she could see it. 'I need my parking ticket validated.'

Her face creased into what was obviously a well-used expression that encompassed regret, sadness and a slight hint of reproach. 'I'm afraid I can't do that,' she said. 'It's not hospital policy. Everyone using the car park needs to pay for a ticket. Our facilities cost money, you know.'

'You must be joking.'

'You could have come by public transport,' she retorted. 'It's hospital policy to reduce our carbon footprint, and that means encouraging our visitors to leave their cars at home wherever possible.'

'In that case,' Lapslie replied, 'I have reason to believe that a crime was committed at this hospital. I need to collect the evidence, and I'm afraid I'm going to have to charge you for my time.'

'You can't do that,' she protested.

'Police time costs money, you know,' he said, and shrugged. 'Our policy is to reduce crime by charging people if they let crimes happen on their premises. What can I do?'

She just looked at him, obviously waiting for him to change his mind or tell her that he was only joking. Instead, he maintained a level gaze.

'Would you like me to write you out an invoice?' he asked eventually.

She half-opened her mouth, realised that she didn't know what she was going to say, and closed it again. She clicked her ballpoint a couple of times.

'The longer I stand here, the higher the bill gets,' he added when it became clear that she was still waiting for something to happen – a coincidental interruption, or divine intervention, or something. Anything.

Her lips pursed tightly and she snatched the parking ticket from his hand. She fed it into a machine below the counter. 'There,' she said, poking it back at him in a way that would have led to a paper cut if he'd had his hand extended too far.

'Do you know,' he said, smiling, 'that when you purse your lips like that it makes your mouth look like a cat's arse: all pink and scrunched up.'

The sound of her pen snapping was something that

Lapslie would remember for some time to come, and the memory would always bring a smile to his face.

He walked back to his car, passing the queue of people still waiting behind the woman at the ticket machine. She seemed to have given up trying to find the last few coins, but didn't know how to get the ones she had already deposited back from the machine, so she was pressing every button she could see in the hope that one of them would return her money.

'Excuse me,' Lapslie said, pausing at the queue. He pointed back at the reception desk. 'The lady over there told me that the machine is faulty. She's offering free parking tickets. All you have to do is to go and ask her.'

The queue broke up into a rugby scrum of people all jostling to get to the reception desk first. Lapslie walked off, feeling a lot better than he had for a while.

He pulled out of the car park, feeding his validated ticket into the machine and accelerating before the barrier was fully up. He had no clear idea of where he was going, but he knew he didn't want to go back to his office at Chelmsford Police HQ. He wanted time to think about the sound file, and the girl who had sent it.

Remembering the noodle bar he had seen at the junction of the A13 and the M25, he swung the car around and pointed it towards London. The thought of food unexpectedly made him feel hungry. It wasn't a feeling he had got used to yet. The synaesthesia that usually flooded his mouth with inappropriate tastes at inappropriate moments had pretty much burned out his hunger over the years. Usually he just ate because he knew he had to in order to function. He was surprised to find that it was still there.

The noodle bar was a single-storey building with a wide frontage, more like a tyre dealership than a restaurant, but when Lapslie pushed through the swing door that led inside he was confronted with an almost tangible wall of smells: garlic, ginger, hot oil and a hundred other things that he couldn't immediately identify. For a moment – just a moment – his suppressed synaesthesia kick-started and went into reverse, turning the smells into a choir of angelic voices singing to him, some impossibly higher and some far, far deeper than ever a human voice could manage. He wasn't sure whether they were singing in some unknown, ancient language, the first language that ever graced the Earth perhaps, or whether the sound they were making was bereft of meaning, like birdsong. The terrible, glorious sound made him catch his breath. It was what he imagined Heaven might sound like.

And then it was gone, leaving a void in his chest that made him catch his breath in shock. His synaesthesia settled into quiescence once again.

'You wan' a table?' said a young waiter in a red T-shirt and black trousers as he walked up to Lapslie.

'Yes,' Lapslie said, looking around. For somewhere that wasn't in the middle of a town or located at a convenient point on a major road, it was surprisingly busy. Long wooden tables stretched from one side of the restaurant to the other, with bench-like, backless seating arranged along them. The waiter led him to an empty space at one end of a table, opposite a bearded man in a dark suit who was just finishing a bowl of thick, fleshy rice noodles and vegetables drenched in a red sauce.

Lapslie sat, nodding to the man opposite, and took the menu that the kid handed him. His gaze scanned the list.

'You wan' something to drink?' the kid asked.

'Green tea,' Lapslie replied. 'And I'll have the fried noodles with pork, chicken and prawn in oyster sauce.'

'You got it.' The kid left. He must have waved an invisible signal at one of his colleagues, because a few moments later a small, handleless cup and a teapot with a wicker handle appeared at his elbow.

Lapslie looked around at the mass of humanity represented in the restaurant: everyone from schoolkids in blazers and wide ties that barely made it past the third button on their white shirts to businessmen in suits, students in hoodies and mothers meeting up with friends for a chat. A true democratic melting pot of noodle-lovers.

His plate arrived just as the man opposite him was paying for his finished meal. Lapslie looked down into the curved bowl. The smell rising from it was enough to make him salivate. The food had been ladled out over a base of thin noodles that had been fried to a crisp. Since the synaesthesia had infiltrated itself into the nooks and crannies of his consciousness he'd got out of the habit of going to restaurants, of even enjoying food. For years now he had been deliberately eating things that didn't have any taste, on the basis that he tasted too many things anyway, and now he wasn't sure where to start.

Eventually he slipped his chopsticks out from their paper wrapper, snapped them apart at the base and manipulated a chunk of chicken into his mouth.

The taste was exquisite: a salty, dark and slightly burnt flavour that seeped over his tongue, seeming to change and deepen as it went. He bit softly into the chicken, feeling it break into fibres beneath the pressure of his teeth. Is this what he had been missing all these years, with his monotonous diet of mozzarella, white rice, boiled chicken, swede and potatoes? This was perfection, boiled down to a morsel of food.

There were mushrooms mixed in with the meat and

the noodles – some wide and flat, some smaller and more rounded. He took one of the small ones and bit experimentally into it. The taste was indescribable, so rounded and complicated that it was as if this mushroom was the Platonic precursor of which all other mushrooms were pale shadows, but the taste was complimented by the way the flesh of the mushroom squished between his molars, leaking hot liquid into his mouth. He quickly took one of the flatter, larger mushrooms between the prongs of his chopsticks and popped it into his mouth. The flavour was almost the same, but the texture was different: the flesh of the mushroom was almost slimy, slippery, like a mollusc. And then there were the bamboo shoots: fibrous in texture, like the chicken and the pork, but woody and dry to the taste.

Unexpectedly, Lapslie's mobile rang. He retrieved it from his jacket pocket. 'Mark Lapslie,' he said, mouth still full.

'DCI Lapslie? Sean Burrows here.'

'Mr Burrows.' Lapslie could hear a faint echo of his voice a half-second behind the real one. It threw him, making him forget what he was saying.

'Am I interrupting?' Burrows said, his voice tinny.

'Not at all. What can I do for you?'

There was silence for a few seconds, apart from the

ever-present static from whatever ether mobile phone messages pass through. 'I just wanted to tell you that we've been carrying out some further analysis on that sound file. The one of the girl screaming.'

Lapslie looked around at the other diners enjoying their noodles, oblivious to the horror that he was talking about. And yet, did he know what *they* were talking about, to each other or on their own phones? Each person was an island, separated from the others by a gulf of ignorance. 'Go on.'

'We've isolated some more background noise.'

Lapslie's attention suddenly snapped into sharp focus. 'More stuff from the killer?'

'No.' Burrows' voice sounded regretful. 'No words. Just some noises.'

'What kind of noises?'

'That's the thing; we're not sure. Could be a musical instrument, like a glockenspiel, or a kid's chime bar, if you remember them from school. Or a tubular bell. Like in the Mike Oldfield album.'

'Okay.' Lapslie paused for a moment, in case Sean Burrows was going to say something else. 'Thanks. Can you send the new sounds through to me via email?'

'Will do. Have a nice day, now.'

Burrows rang off, leaving Lapslie wondering whether this new fact actually added to his store of knowledge in any useful way or whether it was just another distracting fact.

Putting the phone away, he tried the pork next. The little cubes were coated on one side with a marinade of some kind: sharp and tangy. Like the chicken, they broke up in his mouth into fibres of meat, but the pork fibres were smaller and drier than the chicken ones. The prawns, by contrast, burst between his teeth, exploding into salty, fishy liquid.

And then there were the noodles. By the time he'd got down to them they had absorbed the tastes of all the food above them and were beginning to lose their crispness. The ends, projecting out of the sauce, were still breakable, but the middles were soft. The contrast was incredible.

By the time he was chasing the last bits of chicken and prawn around the bowl his stomach was full and satisfied and his mind was quietly content. He couldn't remember having felt like this since he had been young. It was as if he had never tasted anything properly before. And as if he had never realised how much of the simple enjoyment of a meal was due to factors other than the flavours: the way the food felt in the mouth, whether it broke apart or stayed intact, whether it was dry or moist or coated in sauce, whether it was hot or cold. Looking around he couldn't help but wonder whether the other people in the restaurant appreciated the true variety of experiences that were held in their bowls. Or were they, like him when the synaesthesia had his mind in its tight grip, just concentrated on one thing in particular – in his case, texture over taste, in theirs taste over texture?

'Mind if I join you?'

The voice was familiar. For some reason Lapslie thought of vinegar and mustard seeds, although he couldn't actually taste them. He looked up to find Dom McGinley towering over him like a cliff that might give way to an avalanche at any moment.

'It's a free country,' he growled.

'If it's free, why does everything costs so much?' McGinley asked rhetorically, slipping his bulk between the bench and the table opposite Lapslie. His stomach pushed against the wood, forming a horizontal crease in his shirt from one side to the other.

'I'm surprised you even *know* how much things cost,' Lapslie found himself saying, 'given the amount of stolen cash you've squirrelled away over the years.'

'Now, now,' McGinley chided. His voice had tasted of piccalilli for many of the years that Lapslie had known him, but now Lapslie found that there was no taste to it at all, and it seemed to rob McGinley of a dimension, reducing him to something less substantial than he should have been. 'What with bribes and depreciation I'm not worth anywhere near as much as you'd think. And I've offered to give you some chunks of it over the years, but you've always turned me down. Don't get sniffy about it now.'

'How did you find me?' Lapslie asked. 'It's not like this place is one of my regular haunts. Or is it true that you pay people in each of the mobile phone providers to tell you where any person is based on the regular update signals their mobiles send, just so long as you know their number?'

'Don't even need to know their number,' McGinley rumbled. 'As long as I know their name my people can track down their mobile number, then find out which phone mast their mobile is currently registered with. Depending on the size of the cell around the mast, it's child's play to work out their actual location. Once your phone had stopped moving from cell to cell I had you pegged down to about two hundred metres. You probably weren't browsing porn magazines in the petrol station shop, not for that long. They would have thrown you out after ten minutes. This place was the next best bet.'

'With all that drive and energy,' Lapslie said, 'you could have been a world-class politician or something big in the City of London.'

'What,' McGinley said, sounding genuinely affronted, 'and work for a living?'

'McGinley,' Lapslie chided gently, 'if you'd dedicated the same amount of time to honest work as you had on planning bank robberies, insurance scams, blackmail plots and confidence tricks then you'd have just as much money as you do now without running the constant risk of arrest or being killed at the hands of some underworld rival.'

'Yeah, but where would the fun be in that?'

Lapslie shrugged. 'You have a point there.'

'After all, *you* could have gone into teaching, but instead you went into a job that paid the same but with a higher chance of being bottled breaking up a nightclub fight or hit in the face by a flying chunk of concrete at a riot.'

'What are you saying?'

'I'm saying that you and me, we're not so different. We're both thrill seekers. We both hate the nine-to-five routine. We both like getting up in the morning and not knowing what problems the day has in store for us.'

'You've never liked getting up in the morning.'

'I was speaking metaphorically.'

Before Lapslie could laugh, the young waiter turned up by the side of the table.

'You want a menu?' he asked.

'Get me something with beef and rice,' McGinley said without looking away from Lapslie.

'We don' do beef,' the kid said.

'You do,' McGinley corrected gently, 'for me.'

The kid drew a breath, ready to argue, but McGinley just reached across with his left hand and pushed his right cuff up. On the skin of his wrist Lapslie could see a tiny tattoo of a fish; pink and blue scales and an uplifted tail, barely the size of a 1p piece.

The waiter seemed to stiffen. 'I go get something with beef,' he said, and backed away.

'You'll be lucky if it's not a cup of Bovril,' Lapslie said to break the silence after the kid had left.

'I like Bovril,' McGinley replied as if nothing untoward had happened.

'Don't mind me asking, but what *is* that tattoo?'

McGinley shrugged. 'Never found out. I got it in Kowloon, in a backstreet parlour some years ago in an alley that smelled of rotting cabbage and fish. I was blind drunk and I asked the bloke for something scary. I was expecting him to do a dragon, or a snake, or a tiger, or something. Instead, when I woke up, I found this pansy fish on my wrist. I was ready to take exception to it, but someone came into his parlour, saw my tattoo, and left in a hurry. I assume it's some Tong or

Yakuza symbol.' He smiled. 'Maybe it marks me out as a ninja assassin or something.'

'Yakuza are Japanese, Dom. Tongs are Chinese. It's like mixing up the Mafia and the Ku Klux Klan.'

'They're both slant-eyes, aren't they?' McGinley asked calmly.

Lapslie stared at McGinley. McGinley stared back. There was a slight quirk to the corner of his mouth that told Lapslie he knew exactly what the tattoo was and what it signified, and that he'd either earned it or been awarded it for some action that was best not exposed to the light of day, but that he would never admit it and he would laugh if Lapslie ever raised the question.

'So what can I do for you, Dom?' Lapslie asked. 'You've gone to all the trouble of tracking me down here when you could just have phoned my mobile and arranged to meet. You're sending me several messages, but I'm too jet-lagged and too tired to decipher them. Just tell me. What do you want?'

A bowl of rice covered in strips of cooked beef was slid in front of McGinley by a waiter who quickly backed away. Another waiter dashed in with a teapot of green tea and another small cup without a handle. The smell of ginger and pineapple rose up with the steam from the food. McGinley gazed at it for a long moment.

'It's your sergeant,' he said eventually. 'Emma.'

Lapslie felt a wave of weariness wash over him. He'd known this conversation was coming, but he would rather have had it with Emma and on his own terms, than at a time and place of someone else's choosing.

'She's shacked up with a villain, Dom. I can't let that go unremarked.'

Dom glanced up at Lapslie. 'Definitions are funny things,' he said softly. 'I've never been convicted for anything, and if you linked my name to any serious crime in public then I would sue your arse from Land's End to John O'Groats. As far as justice is concerned, I'm as much a villain as Mother Teresa was a high-class call-girl.'

'We both know what you've been responsible for. The beatings. The tortures. The deaths. Remember, you once told me that you cut Dave Finnistaire's tongue out, back in the 1980s, and left him tied to a wooden pile holding up one of the piers on the Thames and bleeding down his shirt.'

'Bluster, Mr Lapslie. Pure bluster. I was taking credit for someone else's crime, as I have done on many occasions before.' McGinley sighed, and poured himself a cup of green tea. 'It's a cliché, I know, but there's less difference between the criminals and the police than there is between the police and the teaching profession. You go on about what I've done, but what about you?

If I commit a robbery – which I never have – then I know which side of the dividing line between law and disorder I sit. But you and I both know that your hands are far from clean, Mr Lapslie. You've planted evidence from time to time to secure a conviction. Yes—' He held his hand up to forestall Lapslie's protest – 'to secure a conviction against a criminal when you couldn't find any real evidence. I know the verbals, but how did you know he was a villain in the first place? Because you did. Because you had a feeling about it. Because God told you. It doesn't matter. You ignored the law in order to enforce the law. And what about the times you've beaten a confession out of a suspect, just because it's late at night and you know you'll have to release him if you don't get something out of him? I may be a villain, in your eyes, but I'm not a hypocrite. I know what I am.'

'We all know what you are, McGinley,' Lapslie said, nettled by what the man had said. 'You're a ponce and a thief and a killer.'

'I could ask you where your evidence is,' McGinley replied, 'but we both know there's two different kinds of evidence: the detailed facts and statements that you fellas collect in your little notebooks and your files, and the kind of rigorous scientific stuff that impresses juries and stands up in court. And when you say you know I'm a villain, you're basing that on the first kind of evidence, not the second. But they're like apples and apricots: they're both kinds of fruit but you can't turn the one into the other. You may *know* I'm a villain, you may have a thousand little facts that all add up to it, you may even feel it in your bones and the way your knee twinges in the rain, but it'll never stand up in court. There's no exchange rate between the two. So it doesn't matter that Emma and I are an item; you can't use that as leverage against her. You can't discipline her or demote her or fire her. She'll take it to appeal and she will win, because as far as justice is concerned I'm just an innocent member of the public without a blemish on my character.' He sighed heavily. 'And if you even try to take action against her then I will have you tied to a tree and I will personally pick up a large branch, stick it up your arse and hammer it upwards until you can taste it at the back of your throat.'

'She means that much to you?' Lapslie asked, mouth dry.

'I love her. Strange as it sounds from a man of my age and character, I love her. And believe me, I'm as surprised as you are. I can't remember loving anyone before; not even my mother, God bless her alcohol-rotted soul.'

'And she loves you?'

'So she says. So she says.'

Lapslie sighed. McGinley had a point. Several of them.

'Okay then, McGinley. I say this as her boss and her friend, and also as the man who probably knows the black depths of your character better than anyone else apart from your alcohol-rotted mother: you're right, I can't do anything apart from try to persuade her that you are bad for her. I can't, and I won't. I don't care about any threats that you make: I've been threatened by people who make you look like a lollypop lady. The trouble is that any action I take is doomed to failure; the system just won't pick it up and run with it with any enthusiasm and the Police Federation will back her to the hilt. But I swear this: if you hurt her in any way, mental or physical, then one dark night I will cut your prick and your balls off and feed them to the foxes outside my cottage.'

McGinley smiled. 'Then we understand each other.'

'Like an old married couple.'

McGinley gazed at Lapslie curiously. 'I don't suppose you're in love with her as well, are you?'

Lapslie raised his eyebrows. The thought had never occurred to him. 'I'm divorced, but I'm still trying to fall out of love with my ex-wife,' he said, 'and I think I'm falling in love with the woman I'm currently seeing.'

'The pretty blonde doctor,' McGinley murmured. 'Charlotte, isn't it?'

'Don't push it,' Lapslie snapped. He took a deep breath.

'But no – I respect Emma's tenacity, and her intuition, but I'm not in love with her.'

McGinley picked up his green tea and clinked it against Lapslie's. 'And long may that continue,' he said.

There was a silence for a few moments as Lapslie and, presumably McGinley, tried to work out how to have a normal conversation after the mixture of threats and bluster that had gone before.

'Emma didn't say you were back from Pakistan,' McGinley said finally.

'Do I often crop up in your bedroom talk?' Lapslie asked sourly.

'She has a lot of respect for you,' McGinley replied. 'So she talks about you. And, sad to say, old son, I like listening to stories about you. Even the ones that don't involve you castrating some petty criminal somewhere.'

'He was a paedophile,' Lapslie corrected, 'and I didn't castrate him. Not technically.'

'He spent the rest of his life peeing out of a hole that the surgeons had to cut for him. I think that counts.'

'I got sent something.' Lapslie found himself explaining what had happened to McGinley without quite knowing why. 'It was a sound file of a woman screaming while she was being murdered.'

'Nasty,' McGinley agreed. 'Why was it sent to you?'

'No idea. I thought at first it might be someone I

knew – Sonia, Charlotte, maybe even Emma – but I checked and they were all still alive. I thought maybe it was sent to me by accident, but the forensics people found out it was sent from the hospital where I'm being treated.'

'Ah, the one where your girlfriend works.'

'I told you, McGinley – don't push it. Anyway, I'm at a loss. I know who sent the file – it was a teenage girl, and I've got a photo of her – but given the nature of the murder itself I can't believe the girl was responsible. Or even involved.'

'How was the woman killed?' McGinley asked.

'Morbid curiosity?'

'More like professional expertise. I might be able to help.'

Lapslie gazed at McGinley for a long moment, trying to work out whether he could trust the man or not. Eventually he said, 'We're not sure what happened, exactly. There's no body. But she screams twenty-seven times, so I'm guessing that maybe she was cut, perhaps, or stabbed or burned, twenty-seven times before she died. There aren't that many options. Strangling, for instance, wouldn't have enabled her to scream properly, and poisoning would have been a one-off event.'

'Odd,' McGinley mused.

'What's odd?'

'The way you say that whatever made her scream happened twenty-seven times.'

Lapslie frowned. 'What makes you say that?'

'Emma's currently in charge of a case on Canvey Island. The cops there discovered the body of a woman.'

'I know that.'

'What you don't know is that according to Emma she'd been cut twenty-seven times, all over her body.'

CHAPTER EIGHT

Emma Bradbury was glancing through Donal O'Riordan's criminal record on the police database when the warning came through. Crumbs from her sandwich lunch were scattered across the table.

The phone on her desk rang. 'DS Bradbury – this is Lucy on reception. I've got a DCI Lapslie here—' She broke off. 'Sir – you can't just . . .' and then she was talking to Emma again: 'I'm sorry, Ma'am, but he just barged right past me.'

'It's okay, Lucy – he does that. A lot.'

While she waited for Lapslie to locate her incident room, she browsed through O'Riordan's record on the screen. As DS Rossmore had indicated, he was what judges liked to call 'an habitual criminal', albeit dealing in small things like breaking and entering, theft, assault and battery, possession of stolen goods, joy-riding and a whole litany of other minor crimes. They were what Emma tended to think of as survival crimes – the kinds of things a man without a conscience and without a job did to get money and to pass the time. No drug dealing, no fencing, nothing that indicated any connections to organised crime. Two incidents of possession of a small amount of a Class C drug. No incidents of violence towards women, interestingly, although DS Rossmore had re-emphasised to her the tendency of the Traveller community to assume that violence was a standard part of a long-term sexual relationship.

'You're on a case,' Mark Lapslie's voice barked from the door.

Emma looked around the incident room – the newly fitted whiteboards and computers, the phones and the staff – as if she'd never seen it before. 'Good God – you're right. Where did all this stuff come from?'

'You need to tell me all about it.'

'No, Sir,' she said patiently, 'I need to get on with solving the case.'

'It's *my* case,' he said.

'I don't think so. I'm pretty sure I got the original call. I distinctly remember being at the location where the body was discovered. I also have a pretty good recollection of arresting a man for murder this morning in a local public house. I may have a low attention span, but I don't remember you being there at all. In fact, I'm pretty sure you're meant to be in Pakistan on a law enforcement conference.'

'I came back early,' he said defensively.

'Obviously. I was surprised you ever agreed to go in the first place.'

'That's not important.'

'Then what is? Don't tell me ACC Rouse has parachuted you in on top of my murder investigation? It's not as if it's particularly high-profile or sensational. The dead girl isn't a TV reporter, and the killer didn't use some obscure poison. Apart from what looks like marks of torture on the girl's body, there isn't anything that would warrant the presence of a detective chief inspector. I don't *need* top cover on this one, Sir.'

'That's what you think,' he said grimly. 'Your dead girl was cut, what, twenty-seven times?'

'Yes,' she answered cautiously, 'although we're keeping the exact number from the press at the moment, just in case we can use it against a suspect. We're just saying that she was cut repeatedly.'

'The reason I came back from Pakistan is that I was sent an email containing a sound file of a woman screaming. She screams twenty-seven times before dying.'

Emma leaned back in her chair, trying to fit this new

information in to the context of what she already knew. 'She screams twenty-seven times, exactly?'

'Over the course of three minutes and twenty-seven seconds.'

'Was the time between the screams constant, or did it vary?'

Lapslie nodded. 'Good question. It was variable.'

'And this file was sent to you personally?'

'Yes.'

'By who?'

'You mean, "by *whom*?"'

Emma suppressed a twinge of irritation. Lapslie could be infuriatingly pedantic at times. She had occasionally wondered if his synaesthesia came with additional baggage – such as a touch of obsessive-compulsive disorder. 'By *whom*?' she asked.

'I'm not sure. I know the email was sent from Chelmsford Hospital, and I have video images of a girl sitting at the computer terminal it was sent from at the same time it was sent, but I haven't been able to track her down yet.'

'What about the file itself?' Emma asked. 'Anything strange about it?'

'I've let Sean Burrows and his team look over it. There's an unidentified voice in the background at one point saying, "No, that's gash. That's just gash," and what might be some musical instrument, but that's it. No other identifying characteristics.'

'"Gash". Odd word to use.'

Lapslie shrugged. 'I assume it's a reference to the woman who died. "Gash" is a fairly common slang term for the female genitalia.'

Emma took a deep breath. 'You realise this just confuses my case? I've already arrested the boyfriend of the murdered girl.'

'Means?'

'The cuts on the girl's body were odd, according to Doctor Catherall. They weren't like normal knife wounds. The boyfriend had lots of fishing line at his house. I'm wondering if he tied her up with the fishing line, or whether he somehow tortured her with it.'

Lapslie nodded. 'Okay – a cautious "yes" for means. Motive?'

Emma shrugged. 'Domestic row?'

'Good enough to explain a beating, not quite so good at explaining a torture session. Any evidence that he is a sexual sadist or a psychopath, or that their sex life involved S&M sessions?'

'Not so far.'

'So motive is unclear, as yet. What about opportunity?'

'The girl's family have said that they've already established that he has an alibi—'

'God preserve us from the general public helping us to solve our cases.'

'Indeed. We're checking his alibi out at the moment.'

'If the alibi holds up, then we don't have opportunity. That just leaves us with one-third of what we need. And it still doesn't explain who sent me the sound file – or why.'

'If the sound file is connected in the first place.' Emma felt a sinking feeling, deep within her chest. 'Is it possible that the girl who you saw on the hospital video imagery was a friend of the dead girl?'

'How old is the dead girl?'

'Twenty-three.'

'The girl in the video is barely fifteen.'

'Probably no school connection, then.'

'Could it be a sister?'

'The dead girl doesn't have any brothers or sisters.'

'Okay.' He thought for a moment. 'Let's put the sound file to one side for a moment. We'll interrogate the boyfriend, see if he coughs to anything. Come on.' He walked off down the corridor.

'Sir!' Emma scrambled after him. He was not going to take her case away from her. Not if she had anything to do with it.

DS Murrell was standing in his doorway, talking to one of the Police Community Support Officers as they passed. He gazed at Lapslie with the uncertainty of a man who doesn't know whether to defer or pull rank. His gaze switched to Emma. 'DS Bradbury: anything going on that I ought to know about?'

'DCI Lapslie and I are going to question the suspect, Donal O'Riordan,' she shouted over her shoulder as Lapslie barrelled on down the corridor.

'Let me know how it goes!' Murrell called after her.

'If any forensics come back on the contents of his house, interrupt us,' she shouted as Lapslie went round a corner with her in his wake.

Down in the interview room, Donal O'Riordan was talking to the duty solicitor. O'Riordan was a lean six-footer with tattoos of snakes writhing up his forearms and diving into the sleeves of his black T-shirt, then emerging from the collar and wrapping around his neck. She hated to think where else they were going. He was in his early twenties, and the tightness of his T-shirt emphasized the muscle tone on his chest and the flatness of his stomach. The duty solicitor, in complete contrast, was a balding man in a suit that needed dry cleaning and a good going over with a lint roller.

'What you want to go and arrest me for?' O'Riordan said before anyone else could speak. 'I suffered a bereavement, di'n I?'

'My condolences,' Lapslie said, sitting down and

switching on the tape recorder that sat on the table. 'This is Detective Chief Inspector Lapslie, commencing the interviewing of Mr Donal O'Riordan. Also present are Detective Sergeant Emma Bradbury and ...' He glanced at the man in the suit.

'John Knightsbridge: duty solicitor.'

'Thank you. The date is the twenty-seventh of November 2010 and the time is nineteen fifteen precisely.'

'If I may ask,' the duty solicitor said, 'why is a detective chief inspector conducting this interview? Isn't that a little like having the Archbishop conduct mass at the local church?'

'He's not conducting the interview,' Emma replied before Lapslie could answer. 'I am. DCI Lapslie is here as an observer.' She looked at O'Riordan, weighing him up. 'Mr O'Riordan, let's come straight to the point. When was the last time you saw your girlfriend, Catriona Dooley?'

'Three weeks ago, weren't it?' O'Riordan said. 'Wednesday the fifth.'

'How do you know what day it was, exactly?'

''Cos we—' He glanced at the duty solicitor, who nodded. ''Cos we was at the greyhound races. I won a shed-load of cash.'

'Good for you. I hope you bought her a present.'

O'Riordan frowned. 'Why should I? It was my money.'

'My client still has the receipt for the winnings,' the duty solicitor said in a tone of voice that indicated he'd said variants on those words so often that they had become a rote phrase, like an actor who had spent too long playing a minor role in *Hamlet* but kept going on, night after night.

Emma could feel Lapslie burning to ask a question, but she kept on going. 'Was the greyhound track the last place you saw her?'

'Nah.'

'So where did you last see her?' Emma continued patiently.

'At 'er mum and dad's place, wun'it?'

'And what time was that?'

'We was at the pub, then we went back to 'er folks' place. She didn't want to come back wiv me. 'Er mum was a bit funny about us spendin' the nights together. 'Er dad didn't care one way or the other. I stayed for a drink wiv' her dad, then I went back to my gaff. I left about one o'clock.'

'Mr and Mrs Dooley will be able to substantiate that,' Mr Knightsbridge added in his trademark dull grey monotone.

'No doubt.' Emma didn't take her eyes from O'Riordan, He didn't seem particularly grief-stricken at the death of his girlfriend; more like indignant over the fact that he had been arrested. 'And you maintain that you didn't see her at all from that night until now?'

''S right.'

'You didn't come to help identify the body.'

'Her folks didn't need no help,' he said darkly.

'Even so, I thought you might want to be present. As a mark of respect.'

'Either it was her an' she was dead, in which case I didn't want to see 'er, or it weren't 'er, in which case there was no point.' He paused. 'Anyway, I don't like seeing no dead bodies.'

'How squeamish.'

'Mr O'Riordan,' Mark Lapslie suddenly asked, 'where were you three days ago?'

Emma silently cursed. He just couldn't stay out of it, could he?

The suspect glanced sullenly at the table. 'I ain't sayin'.'

'Oh yes you are,' Lapslie growled. 'We can stay here until you get sick of the sight of me and the smell of Mr Knightsbridge's aftershave, but you are going to tell me where you were between those times.'

O'Riordan pursed his lips, but remained silent.

'Mr O'Riordan,' Emma said, trying to regain control of the interview, 'we found traces of blood and flesh in the kitchen of your house, along with quantities of fishing line. If you can't explain how they got there then we can only assume that they are connected to the torture and murder of Miss Dooley.'

'Have the forensics results confirmed that the traces of blood and flesh are human?' Mr Knightsbridge interrupted.

'Not yet.'

'So they are merely circumstantial.'

'But highly indicative, unless your client cares to provide us with a more innocent explanation of their presence.'

Knightsbridge leaned over and whispered something in O'Riordan's ear. The suspect nodded reluctantly.

'If, in theory, Mr O'Riordan's alibi involved admitting to a different and minor criminal act, what would be the position of the police?'

Emma leaned back in her chair. 'The position of the police would be that it's for the Crown Prosecution Service to decide on whether Mr O'Riordan would be prosecuted for any other crime, but I would remind him, and you, that murder trumps most other crimes. He needs to ask himself what he would prefer to be arrested for.'

O'Riordan glanced at Knightsbridge with a question in his eyes. The duty solicitor nodded wearily, with the expression of someone who has been through this routine so many times it had all begun to blur together.

'It were crows, weren' it?' O'Riordan said reluctantly.

'What?'

'The blood and the meat in my gaff. I'd been trappin' crows, 'adn't I?'

Emma felt as if the conversation had suddenly veered left when she was expecting it to go right. '*Crows?*'

'Yeah.'

'Why would you trap crows?'

'For food. The Albanians love 'em.'

'Albanians?'

'The Eastern Europeans. Albanians, Serbs, Poles, Croats, whatever. There's a lot of 'em work in Essex as labourers and farmhands an' cleaners. They can't afford to eat stuff from the supermarkets, and they've got a different taste in meat 'cos of what they were used to back 'ome. So what if I've set up a business satisfying their tastes? Bit of crow breast goes down a treat wiv' them, in a stew or a pie. Thing is, crow meat is dark and bloody, more like human flesh than chicken or lamb.'

'And does it taste like human flesh?'

He shrugged. 'How would I know? I don't eat the stuff. I just supply it.'

'And how do you catch the crows?'

'Scatter some bait on the ground then use a shotgun on them. Load the shotgun wiv salt crystals, not pellets, an' it kills 'em wivout leavin' pellets in the body.' He grinned. 'Seasons the meat as well.'

Emma shook her head in disbelief. 'What else do you supply them with?'

'I do carp. They love a bit of carp, 'specially the Poles. Can't get enough of it. You don't find it on the fish and chip shop menus here, but over there it's like a national dish.'

'And where do you get the carp from?'

He shrugged. 'Rivers, lakes . . .'

'Ornamental fishponds in people's back gardens?' Emma added.

O'Riordan frowned, and looked away.

'Tell me, Donal,' Lapslie asked, 'does a Koi carp taste different from an ordinary one?'

'They all taste of mud to me,' he said. 'Can't see what all the fuss is about.'

'And that,' the duty solicitor said, 'would be the explanation for the fishing line. Mr O'Riordan is a fisherman.'

'This is all very well,' Emma said, 'and even if I accept that the blood and the flesh in your house was from crows and not from Catriona Dooley, then it still doesn't provide an alibi for her time of death. Killing crows and carp and selling them on for human consumption may go against cultural prejudice in the UK, and probably contravenes the Wildlife and Countryside Act of 1981, which is punishable by a six-month prison term and/or a fine up to £5,000, as well as probably breaking all kinds of health and safety regulations, but I still don't know what you were doing when Catriona Dooley was murdered.'

O'Riordan glared at her. His eyes were dark beneath thick brows. 'We was trappin' and killin' swans, aw right?'

'Were you?'

'We'd driven in to Wanstead Flats. There's a whole load of ponds there where swans make their nests. A big 'un 'll fetch a few quid, in the right hands. Feeds a family for a week, they say. Never tried it myself. Tastes fishy, people say, although ducks swim in ponds an' they don't taste fishy.'

'So what's so different about killing swans?' Emma asked. 'Why is it different from killing crows?'

'Magistrates take it a lot more seriously,' he replied. 'Wiv crows they just treat it as a bit of a lark, a bit juvenile, like. Wiv swans, it's like you're attackin' the Queen.'

'So your alibi is that you were in Wanstead, on a fun trip killing swans.'

''S right. We was staying at a mate's flat. Kinda like a party.'

'How many of you.'

'Five.'

'We'll need names and addresses so we can take statements.'

He nodded sullenly.

'Anybody else apart from your mates who can verify your story?'

'The people downstairs complained about the noise. An' the people upstairs. An' we had some takeaways delivered. The bloke who delivered them saw me a couple of times. We had a bit of a barney about what we owed him.'

Emma had a sinking feeling in the pit of her stomach that told her this arrest was going to fall apart in her hands. It had looked so good when she'd seen the bloody thumbprint and the mess in the kitchen, but perhaps, looking back, it had all been too convenient. 'Do you know anybody else with a reason to want Catriona Dooley hurt or killed?' she asked.

'On behalf of my client,' Knightsbridge said, 'I object to your use of the word "else", as it implies that my client himself had reason to want Catriona Dooley hurt or dead.'

'Very well,' Emma said tiredly, 'I withdraw the word "else". Mr O'Riordan, do you know of anybody at all who might want Catriona Dooley hurt or dead?'

He shook his head. 'Nobody.'

'What about her parents? Did she get on with them?'

'She loved 'em to bits, an' they adored 'er.'

'Very touching.' She glanced across at Lapslie. He shook

his head. 'I'm halting this interview at – ' she looked at her watch – 'eight o-five p.m.' She pressed the 'Stop' button on the tape recorder. 'Mr Knightsbridge,' she said wearily, looking at the duty solicitor, 'we reserve the right to question your client further at some later time. He will be taken up before the magistrate tomorrow morning, at which time bail can be discussed.'

'You know perfectly well that he didn't commit the murder,' Knightsbridge said mildly. 'Why not let him go now?'

'Call me old-fashioned, but I want to wait for the forensics report on the blood and flesh found at his house before releasing him.'

Knightsbridge nodded. 'I'll see you tomorrow morning in court,' he said to O'Riordan.

Leaving a police constable to take O'Riordan back to his cell, Emma leaned against the wall outside the inter-view room. She checked her watch. 18.08. 'I hate inter-views,' she said. 'People either lie to you or they don't give you the answer you want. Either way, your nice, neat little case gets increasingly messy.' She opened her eyes and glanced up at Lapslie. 'That treatment of yours must be working. A year ago you'd never have managed to be in the same room as a suspect being questioned.'

Lapslie smiled. 'I tell you what – let's go and do some

real investigating,' he offered. 'Let's go to Chelmsford Hospital and see if we can identify that girl.'

'What makes you think that someone at the hospital can identify her?'

'I'm guessing she was there for a reason. Maybe she was an outpatient; maybe she was visiting a friend or a relative. Either way, someone in that hospital will recognise her photograph.'

Emma nodded. 'Okay, I'm up for it. Let's go "off-island".'

He raised an eyebrow. 'Off-island?'

'Don't ask.'

'I'll drive, and I'll drop you back here when we've finished. And on the way I'll tell you about the conversation that Dom McGinley and I had earlier on today.'

Her heart sank. They'd been talking. She needed to score some points quickly, otherwise he'd be overbearing for the whole journey. 'Okay. Will I get to meet your new girlfriend, if she's on duty?'

'Not a chance.' He scowled at her. 'How did you know about her?'

'Dom told me,' she said, feeling like she'd evened the score in advance.

The drive to Chelmsford Hospital took about forty minutes, and despite Lapslie's threat he actually said almost nothing about meeting Dom, apart from the fact that Dom had tracked him down in a noodle bar. That in itself surprised Emma more than anything else – the fact that Lapslie had willingly spent time by himself in a restaurant. Things really were changing.

Lapslie swung his car into the hospital car park and prowled the lanes until he found a particular slot, passing several other vacant slots on the way. Emma got the impression that he was a regular there, and had fallen into habits. She followed him in through the main entrance. He looked around for a moment, then went up to the woman on the reception desk. She flinched when she saw him. They obviously had a history together, and it wasn't a good one.

'I'm trying to identify this girl,' he said, fishing an A4 sheet of printed paper from his jacket pocket and unfolding it. 'Have you seen her around this hospital?'

The woman took the photo from Lapslie as if it, or he, might bite. She scanned it and then handed it back. 'We get all sorts of girls like that coming in here,' she said dismissively. 'On Friday and Saturday nights it's because they've drunk so much they're suffering from alcohol poisoning. On Saturday and Sunday mornings it's because they ended up in the wrong bed and need to get hold of a morning-after pill. The rest of the week they're just visiting some pregnant schoolfriend in the maternity unit.'

'You have even more of a twisted and cynical view of life than I do,' Lapslie said admiringly. 'I might even pay for my own parking this time.'

Emma followed him towards the lifts, feeling the woman's heated gaze on the back of her neck. 'Where are we going?' she asked as the lift travelled upwards. It was large enough to hold twenty people, or perhaps just five people and a large hospital bed being wheeled from ward to X-ray or back again.

'Paediatrics. Assuming she's a patient and not a visitor, the girl is probably too young to be on an adult ward. Someone in the paediatric ward might know who she is. She might even still be there herself.'

Emma checked her watch. 'Do you know what time it is?'

'Yes, but patients don't generally go home at night, and they'll all be in the ward getting ready for bed. We can check them all out while they're vulnerable.'

'They're patients in hospital,' she protested. 'They live in their pyjamas and dressing gowns.'

'While they're *more* vulnerable,' he corrected himself. 'And besides, the nurses on at the moment will be the same ones who were on during the last set of visiting hours. They might well remember the girl in the photo.'

In point of fact, they didn't. Emma spent half an hour with Lapslie in the paediatrics ward, twenty-five minutes of which were spent persuading the sister in charge that they weren't suspicious characters trying to get close to vulnerable children. The place made her edgy. The sound of several children sobbing themselves to sleep drifted through the ward, and the oversized cut-outs of cartoon characters stuck to the walls and the room dividers that presumably looked cute and friendly in daylight were ominous black shadows at night. The nurses in their white uniforms moved silently, like ghosts, between the beds. It could almost have been deliberately designed to give kids nightmares. The sister eventually told Lapslie pointedly that the girl in the photo wasn't a patient now, had never been a patient for as long as the sister had been working at the hospital, and was not a recent visitor either.

Lapslie managed to get them a good look at most of the beds as they left by deliberately wandering down the ward pretending that he couldn't remember the way out, but there was no sign of the girl. Or, at least, if she were there, and if the sister were either mistaken or lying, then she was hidden beneath the covers.

'So, what now?' Emma asked as they left.

Lapslie rubbed his chin. 'Short of stopping people at random and asking them whether they've seen this girl, or copying the photo and plastering it on every notice-board in sight with a message asking people to phone us if they've seen her, I'm at something of a loss.'

'Anyone you know here you could ask? Your girlfriend, for instance?'

Lapslie smiled. 'Nice try, but you're still not going to meet her.' He frowned. 'Actually, I'm still under the care of a psychiatrist here – Doctor Garland. I could ask his advice.' Catching her raised eyebrow, he added, 'It's nothing suspicious. I'm not having a nervous breakdown. It's just that synaesthesia, being a neurological condition, shades across into the area of psychology. Doctor Garland is running the support group that I attend.'

'Will he still be working this late?'

'As I've found out,' Lapslie said ruefully, 'doctors are like policemen – they don't stick to a regular nine-to-five working day. They stay until the job's done – or later, if they're committed to finding an answer.'

Lapslie led Emma back to the lifts, and up to a different floor, then across a bridge between buildings and along a wide spine corridor until they came to a side corridor marked 'Neurology'. He pushed the swing doors open and entered the darkened corridor. Light spilled from the open door of an office at the far end.

'I think he's in,' Lapslie said, sounding pleased.

He led the way down the corridor and stopped in the open doorway. 'Doctor Garland,' he said, 'may I interrupt?'

Emma joined him just as a burly, middle-aged man with a handlebar moustache rose from his chair. 'Mr

Lapslie,' he said. 'Surprised to see you. Didn't know we had an appointment.' He glanced at Emma, and smiled. 'Alan Garland,' he said, holding out his hand.

'Emma Bradbury,' she replied, shaking it. 'I'm the sergeant to his detective chief inspector.'

'Not a standard police relationship, surely,' Garland said. His grip was warm and firm. 'There's at least one level in between those two. Shouldn't you have an inspector hanging around somewhere?'

'He's never followed the normal rules,' Emma said, nodding her head towards Lapslie.

'Actually,' Garland said, 'it's not so unusual. I used to be in the Army. Lieutenant-Colonel. My Staff Officer was a captain – two ranks down.'

'You used to be in the Army?' Lapslie said, apparently amazed.

'Left ten years ago. Royal Army Medical Corps. Qualified psychiatrist, even then. Specialised in combat stress reaction, acute stress disorder and post-traumatic stress disorder.'

'How reassuring,' Lapslie said, obviously taken aback.

'Strange, isn't it?' Garland said, obviously enjoying the reaction. 'I know everything about your history, but you know hardly anything about mine.'

Emma decided that she liked Doctor Garland. He had a friendly bonhomie about him, an old-fashioned, old-world approach to life. If anyone was going to help Lapslie, it would be him.

'I need your help,' Lapslie said, chiming strangely with Emma's thought processes.

'Medical or criminal?'

'Criminal.'

'I'm not well up on forensic pathology.'

'That's okay,' Lapslie said, glancing at Emma and wincing. 'We've had bad experiences with forensic pathologists. No, it's more a case of you recognising a photograph of a suspect who we know has been present at this hospital.'

'Lot of people pass through reception every day,' Garland pointed out. 'I don't see more than a handful of them.'

'But you know me,' Lapslie pointed out, 'and that may make a difference.'

'Delusions of grandeur?' Garland asked, a twinkle in his eye. 'Fascinating.'

Lapslie shook his head. 'Don't get so excited. I actually have reasons to believe that I am being singled out by the murderer for special attention.'

'And a former patient of mine who swore blind that he was the secret ruler of the Earth, sent here from Jupiter to save us from destruction, had reasons to believe that as well. Spurious, of course, but he believed them.'

Lapslie glanced at Emma. 'You tell him,' he said wearily. 'I'm getting nowhere.'

'You're a patient,' Emma said calmly. 'I'm not.' She smiled at Garland. 'Detective Chief Inspector Lapslie here was sent a sound file attached to an email. The sound file was—' She hesitated, glancing at Lapslie, and when he nodded she continued – 'a recording of a murder. The email was sent from the internet café attached to this hospital. We have a recorded image of the person we believe sent the email. It's a young female suspect, and we're trying to identify her.'

Garland raised an eyebrow and glanced from Emma to Lapslie and back. 'The email was sent to you personally? So you're a target. Murderer wants you to know that they know you. Or the email wasn't sent by the murderer, but someone who knows about the crime and wants you to investigate it.'

Lapslie nodded. 'That about covers it. I'm not delusional. This person, whoever it is, really has me in their sights.'

'Can I see the photo?'

Lapslie handed the folded A4 sheet across to Garland. He unfolded it, and although his expression didn't change from professional detachment crossed with aloof amusement, the atmosphere in the neurology department suddenly changed. A chill wind blew across Emma's neck, and she wasn't sure whether it was a premonition or a product of the air conditioning.

'This is her?' Garland said carefully.

'Yes,' Lapslie replied. 'Have you seen her around the hospital?'

'I have,' Garland replied levelly. 'I don't think I'm breaking any confidentiality agreements by telling you that she's the daughter of that new chap in your workshop – Stephen Stottart.'

CHAPTER NINE

The family interview room in Chelmsford Police HQ was decorated in the same pastel colours as the paediatrics unit at the nearby hospital, with the same table in the corner with a wireframe toy where children could run beads along coloured wires which wound and spiralled around each other. The paint on the walls had dulled over the years and there were scuff marks at exactly the height where a five-year-old would run a toy car around the room. The ghost of a smell of spoiled milk and full nappies hung in the air. Like all the similar units Lapslie had seen over the years, it was depressing rather than relaxing. Or perhaps that was just because of the pain and misery that had been absorbed by the furnishings and the plaster and the paint; the tales of abuse by family, by babysitters, by teachers, by priests and vicars; by anyone, in fact, in a position of authority. The media often fulminated about sexual abuse being rife in some institution or another; in fact, it had nothing to do with institutions. It occurred everywhere that grown men had power over youngsters. There was something fundamentally wrong about the male brain, about the way sexual satisfaction and power were so often squashed together; something that had presumably grown as an unwanted by-product of human tribal evolution and now hung around like an appendix, ready to become sick and inflamed at the slightest notice. Most men had a mental cut-out that stopped them thinking and therefore acting inappropriately. Most men. But Lapslie, by nature of his job, tended to meet more than his fair share of men who didn't possess that cut-out.

Like most policemen, Lapslie firmly believed that paedophilic tendencies couldn't be treated with drugs or counselling. Cognitive behavioural therapy wouldn't work, and neither would neuro-linguistic programming. No fashionable psychological intervention was going to make a difference. Paedophiles were built that way because humans were built that way; it's just that the little mental fuse box that most people had that stopped them from finding small kids and relatives sexually attractive had blown, and there was no replacing it short of going in through the skull and doing some radical brain surgery. With a screwdriver.

The door to the family interview room opened, and

a female police constable walked in: 'They're here,' she announced. 'Shall I send them in?'

'Please,' Lapslie said. 'And send DS Bradbury in as well.'

She left, and the door swung to behind her.

Lapslie was sitting in a comfortable chair, his paperwork and notes balanced precariously on his knees. He felt like a fool. He would far rather be sitting behind a desk, separated from the person he was questioning by a solid barrier.

But wasn't that just emphasising his position of authority? Wasn't that just a step along the road that led to domination, and then abuse?

Best not to think about it too much.

A video camera had been set up on a tripod in a corner of the room. Lapslie had the remote control balanced on his knee along with his paperwork, and he carefully pressed the 'Start' button to initiate the recording. His notes nearly slipped off his knees, but he caught them before they could hit the floor.

The door opened again, and Stephen Stottart entered, his daughter behind him. He was holding her hand. She was shorter than she looked in the video image from the internet café in the hospital. She was wearing some kind of woollen hat, and corkscrew curls of red hair were tumbling out from beneath it. They were both looking wide-eyed and confused.

Mr Stottart glanced at Lapslie, looked away at the video camera, then looked back at Lapslie.

'You were at the synaesthesia workshop,' he said. 'Mark, wasn't it?'

'Detective Chief Inspector Mark Lapslie,' he said, standing up to shake hands while trying to clutch his notes and paperwork to his stomach.

Stottart shook Lapslie's hand. His grip was firm and dry. His mouth was a tight line and his eyebrows were furrowed together. 'I didn't realise you were with the Dibble. So, what is this? You've been following us? Checking us out?'

The Dibble. Lapslie hadn't heard that term in a while; not since he'd spent a year up with the Greater Manchester Police working with the Drugs Squad.

'Nothing of the sort.' Lapslie gestured to the sofa across from his chair. 'Please, sit down, both of you.' As they sat, father and daughter side by side, and as he slid back into the comfortable upholstery of his own armchair, he continued: 'This is something of an unusual situation. I am under the care of a consultant at the hospital, as you are, but I am also investigating a murder. The two are entirely unrelated – at least, that's what I thought until your daughter came to our attention.'

'You think she's involved in a *murder*?' Stottart snapped. His arm went protectively around his daughter's shoulders. 'She's *fourteen*, for God's sake!'

'I know,' Lapslie continued, 'and it's only a possibility at the moment, based on where she was at a particular time. She's not under arrest, and this interview is not being conducted under caution. We just need to know what she knows – if anything.'

The door opened again and Emma Bradbury slipped in. She nodded an apology at Lapslie, then took up an inconspicuous position against a wall.

'She doesn't know anything,' Stottart said, and glanced down at his daughter's head. 'Do you?'

She shook her head, avoiding eye contact with anyone in the room.

'Okay,' Lapslie said, 'then let's start off with you. Can you tell me what you do for a living, Mr Stottart?'

'I'm a biologist with an agricultural company.'

'And where do you live?'

'Basildon. Moved here from Manchester.'

Lapslie looked across at the daughter. 'And you, Tamara? That's your name, isn't it? Tamara Stottart?'

'Yeah. I live with my dad,' she said.

'Anyone else in the house?'

'My mum.' She paused. 'My brother. And Eddie.'

'Eddie?'

'The dog,' Stottart replied for her. 'I presume he's not a suspect?'

'Mr Stottart,' Lapslie warned mildly, 'this is a serious matter. A woman has died. Horribly. We need to find out why she was killed, and who it was who killed her.'

'Sorry. It's just that – this is all new to us. I've never even been in a police station before.' Stottart paused. 'How did she die?'

'Dad!' Tamara protested, appalled.

'That's not information we can reveal at the moment,' Lapslie replied. He switched his gaze to the girl. 'Tamara, we have no reason to believe that you committed any crime, or were present at the commission of a crime, but we do believe that you have – or had – evidence that a crime had taken place—'

'Who was it?' Stottart interrupted. 'Who was killed?'

'A young woman named Catriona Dooley,' Lapslie replied. 'Do you know her, Tamara?'

The girl shook her head, still avoiding Lapslie's gaze.

'Are you sure? I've got a photograph of her here.' He pulled an eight-by-five-inch print of Catriona Dooley from the pile of papers on his knees and held it out. 'Please – look at this.'

Stottart held out a warning palm. 'It's not – it's not

a photograph of this woman's body is it? Dead, like? I wouldn't want Tamara to see something like that. That would be rank.'

There it was again – another northern expression. Lapslie suddenly felt strangely nostalgic for Manchester.

Lapslie shook his head. 'No, nothing like that. It was provided by her family.'

'Okay.' Mollified, Stottart took the photograph and glanced at it, then held it in front of his daughter's face. 'Do you know her, Tamara?'

The girl shook her head without looking at the photograph.

'Please,' Lapslie urged, 'look at it.' He tried to gauge whether she actually did recognise the photo from the way she held herself, but the way she held her shoulders so tightly and had her arms folded severely across her chest could have been guilt or could equally just have been typical teenage passive aggressive behaviour.

She glanced quickly at the photograph, then glanced away. 'No,' she said in a quiet but firm voice. 'I've never seen her before.'

'She lived in Maldon,' Lapslie pressed. 'Does that help place her?'

'I told you,' Tamara said, 'I've never seen her before.'

'What about you, Mr Stottart?'

Stottart shook his head. 'Don't recognise her.' His

eyes scanned the photograph again. Lapslie sought for recognition in his eyes, but he just looked blank.

'Tamara, have you ever been to Canvey Island?' He watched the girl carefully as he asked the question, looking for a flinch, or a wince, or some kind of gesture to indicate that she recognised the place and identified it with something unpleasant in her life, but her expression was neutral. Carefully so.

'No,' she said.

Lapslie looked at her father for confirmation. He shook his head.

'She's never been, and I haven't been for at least fifteen years. Why – is that where the body was discovered?'

He was asking all the usual questions that people being interviewed came out with – How was she killed? Where was she killed? – not so much trying to build up some kind of picture of the crime in his mind as trying to level out the inequality of knowledge between himself and Lapslie. It indicated that he, at least, might not know anything about the crime. Lapslie still wasn't sure about the daughter, though.

'Tamara,' he continued, using the same relaxed tone of voice but conscious now that he was approaching the core set of questions, 'when was the last time you were in Chelmsford General Hospital?'

'You were asking about Canvey Island,' Stottart said, jumping in before his daughter could speak.

'Please – Mr Stottart.' Back to the girl. 'Tamara?'

The pale, smooth line of her brow furrowed momentarily. 'Dunno. A few days ago, I guess.'

'Why?'

'I was waiting for my dad. He had an appointment.'

Lapslie glanced at Stottart. 'Is this true?'

'Yeah. One of my regular sessions with Doctor Garland, like you. You can ask him, if you like.'

'I will.' Lapslie turned back to the girl. 'Was that two days ago, at about eight p.m.?'

She shrugged. It was amazing how much negative emotion a teenager could put into a simple shrug. 'I guess.'

'And did you use the internet café in the hospital while you were waiting?'

'Yeah. So? It's not a crime, is it?'

'Tamara,' her father warned, 'just answer the man's questions. Don't try to be cheeky.'

'Why did you use the internet café?'

'I was on BeBo, wasn't I?'

'BeBo?' Lapslie was suddenly thrown by the unfamiliar term.

'It's a social networking site,' Emma Bradbury murmured from her position against the wall. 'Like Facebook, but aimed at a younger market.'

'Ah.' Lapslie had a vague feeling that he knew what Facebook was: an internet site where you could put up details about yourself and engage in trivial email conversations with other people. 'Can you confirm that?'

'What do you mean?'

'I mean is there any evidence apart from your word that you were using this ... BeBo site?'

'She said she was,' Stottart said. 'Isn't that enough?'

'Much as I would like to believe the word of everyone I interview, I've found through long and bitter experience that people often lie to me,' Lapslie sighed. He turned back to Tamara. 'So – is there any proof? Were you talking to anyone else on-line?'

'I was just checking my messages,' she said, and paused. 'But you have to log on to the site, with a password. I guess there's a record of when I logged on and logged off. You could check that with ...' she hesitated. 'With the BeBo people,' she finished lamely.

Lapslie nodded fractionally at Emma. She could check that out later.

'Did you,' he asked, 'while you were using the computer at the internet café, send any emails?'

'No,' she said.

'Specifically, did you send an email to me?'

'No.'

'How would she know your email address?' Stottart asked.

A reasonable question, and one that Lapslie hadn't considered. It had seemed obvious to him that a murderer who wanted to involve Lapslie in their crime would be able to find it out, but a fourteen-year-old girl?

'Did you,' Lapslie continued, not responding to Stottart's question, 'send me an email with an attached sound file?'

'What kind of sound file?' Stottart seemed increasingly hostile as the interview continued and as Lapslie failed to volunteer any information.

'Well,' Lapslie went on after a few seconds. 'Did you?'

'No,' she said.

Lapslie pulled another photograph out of the pile on his lap, this time the one of the girl sitting at the internet terminal. 'Is this you?' he asked, passing the photograph to her. Again, her father took it and held it so that they could both see it.

'Yes,' she said, after a few seconds of looking at the picture. 'That's me. But I already told you I was there.'

'You did, but the email that was sent to me, the email that is connected to the murder we are investigating, was sent from that terminal at the same time you were sitting at it.'

'Maybe they put a timer on it,' she said with devastating simplicity.

'A what?' Lapslie asked.

'A timer.' She glanced up at him with the derision that only the young can manage for their technologically illiterate elders. 'You can delay emails so they get sent at a particular time. Everyone knows that.'

Lapslie felt like someone had kicked the legs out from beneath him. 'So you *didn't* send the email?'

'No,' she said, smiling now that she had realised she had him on the defensive. 'But it could have been delayed until the person who sent it had gone and I was sitting there.'

'Did you see anyone else sitting at the terminal before you arrived?'

'No. It was empty when I got there.'

'Okay.' He paused, and glanced over at Emma. She shook her head slightly. They'd closed off all the avenues of enquiry. 'Tamara, Mr Stottart, thank you for coming in today.'

'That's it?' Stottart suddenly switched from defensiveness to belligerence. It was a transition that Lapslie was familiar with. He saw it at every interview and every time a suspect was released without charge. It was as if, when the pressure that kept their mood defensive was released, internal mental pressure suddenly snapped them to the other end of the psychological scale. He'd seen fear suddenly snap to anger as well, and anger to fear. The mind was a funny thing.

'Yes, Mr Stottart,' he said heavily, 'that's it. We can now return to our murder investigation, and you can return home secure in the knowledge that you have done your civic duty by cooperating with a police investigation. If your daughter remembers anything else about that internet terminal, and people that might have used it before her, then please let us know. I'll have a constable escort you out. Do you have your own transport, or do you need us to arrange something?'

'Oh,' he said, deflating. 'Er, no. I've got my car outside.'

'Come on, Dad,' his daughter said. 'Let's go. I've got swimming tonight.'

Emma opened the door for them and watched them go. 'So, he knows you and his daughter was sitting at the computer terminal at the same time the email was sent. That strikes me as more than a coincidence.'

'Coincidences happen,' Lapslie said. 'As most barristers know, and are quick to point out to juries. Young Tamara had a convincing explanation as to how the email could have been sent when she was sitting at the terminal, but not by her.'

'Which doesn't mean that she didn't do it.'

'I know, but it does mean we can't prove it. And why

would she send it in the first place? Because she wanted to, or because her father told her to? As far as I know, I've done nothing to make him angry. I don't think we've ever met before the workshop the other night.'

'Even so, it's worth checking out where he was, and where his daughter was, for the period when we think that Catriona Dooley's body was dumped. Just to be sure. After all, we don't know when she was killed, exactly, but we can pin down when she was left at the play area.'

Lapsie nodded. 'And it's also worth checking for unexplained absences in the period of time between Catriona Dooley vanishing and her body being discovered. She was tortured, and that would probably take a while. Let's see whether Steve Stottart was absent on a business trip for any length of time.'

'Will do,' said Emma. 'So where do we go from here?'

Lapslie shook his head. 'I'm not entirely sure. I'm not sure that the autopsy has anything more to tell us. Are all the toxicology tests back?'

'Yes. Nothing that we didn't already know.'

'And I've not seen any new information from Sean Burrows on the sound file. Have you?'

'Nothing.'

'And now that we've had to let the boyfriend go we haven't got any suspects apart from Steve Stottart and his daughter, and I don't fancy them much for torture and murder, either separately or together.' He sighed. 'What about the crime scene where she was discovered? Any new evidence there?'

'Nothing. There's evidence that she was dragged across the floor at the kids' play area, dead of course, but there aren't any bloody footprints or fingerprints that we can separate out from the general flow of customers. The car park is a mess of tyre marks – no way of separating out those belonging to whoever dumped the body. And we've got all the CCTV footage from the area, but there's nothing that shows us the kids' play area specifically.'

Lapslie frowned. 'What, not even the security footage from the play area itself?'

'Ah,' Emma said, 'they only turn the CCTV cameras on when the play area is open, in order to save on storage costs for the data. The manager explained to me that they're only worried about kids being abducted by strangers or by relatives after a family split, or about paedophiles watching kids from the bushes and trying to take photographs through the windows. Once the customers leave and the doors are locked they just don't care any more.'

Lapslie's phone rang: the usual sweeping motif of the Bruch Violin Concerto. He answered it. 'Lapslie.'

'DCI Lapslie? This is Sean Burrows again. From the

forensics lab. You remember the sound file you gave us to analyse?'

Lapslie smiled. 'How could I forget, Mr Burrows? In fact, Sergeant Bradbury and I were just talking about it.'

'We've been continuing the analysis here. You remember that I mentioned there was a sound that we'd identified in the background? A distinctive sound, like a musical instrument?'

'Yes.'

'Well, we've tracked it down. It turns out that it's a bell. A church bell.'

Lapslie grimaced. 'That doesn't sound like it's going to help much. There must be thousands of church bells in Essex.'

'Yes, but not like this one. Church bells are usually tuned to fall in a diatonic scale without chromatic notes; this bell falls between the usual notes. I've managed to track it down: it was a special bell made for one particular church.'

Lapslie felt a thrill run through him. The hunt was back on. 'Which church?'

'All Hallows Church in Bishop's Stortford.'

'Thanks. I owe you one.'

Lapslie rang off and turned to Emma. 'We know where the sound file was recorded. Let's go.'

The drive took less than an hour, and Lapslie spent the time wondering how a church was connected to a murder. Emma Bradbury spent the time sitting in the passenger seat of Lapslie's Saab making phone calls and alternately cajoling and shouting at people to get what she wanted. Whatever that was. Lapslie didn't bother listening in.

The Church of All Hallows was a square, red-brick edifice set back from the main street by a low wall and a tarmac car park. Lapslie swung his car off the road and parked across several of the unoccupied bays. There were no fences, no chains across the entrance to the car park, no signs of any security at all. Perhaps the owners were trusting to God to look after it. Or, given that it had been deconsecrated, perhaps they were hoping Satan would arrange for it to be burned down by local arsonists, leaving them to collect the insurance.

Leaving the car, he gazed up at the building. It looked more Russian Orthodox than Church of England; more ornate and decorated than was actually necessary. Each corner of the building bore its own tower, topped with a grey lead spire that looked four-sided at first glance but on closer inspection revealed itself to be octagonal. The front elevation was enormous, rising higher even than the four towers, and framed a huge stained glass window. From the size of that window Lapslie assumed that the inside of the church must be one large space, but the outside seemed to be divided into two storeys by a band of cream-coloured stone. The windows that lined the first floor were arched and bordered in the same cream-coloured stone, while the windows on the ground floor were rectangular and narrow – too narrow for a burglar to get in. They reminded Lapslie of the kind of arrow slots one saw in castle walls. A few circular windows were scattered around the church's exterior, and a single narrow octagonal bell-tower rose from one side of the front elevation to tower over the rest of the building. Somewhere behind the towers and spires, Lapslie assumed there was a standard pitched roof covered in lead tiles.

'What a fantastic place,' Emma said, joining him.

'Isn't it. What have you learned?'

'It used to be a popular church, back in the thirties. The acoustics inside are apparently phenomenal. So good, in fact, that record companies used to come here in the fifties and sixties to record classical music albums – not just organ recitals – the organ used to be incredible, by the way – but also violin recitals, guitar recitals, choral pieces, all kinds of things. Trouble is that congregations in the area dropped away all through the seventies and eighties, and the church decided they couldn't afford to keep this one going. The first step was not replacing the vicar when he retired in 1995, but shipping in other local vicars on a roster basis to hold the fort. Inevitably the remaining members of the congregation drifted towards the vicar of their preference at their own church, and this building ended up a hollow shell. The organ was ripped out in 1999. The rumour is that the church wanted to sell the building to a development company to be split up into executive flats, so they had it deconsecrated, but there was some kind of covenant in the building's terms of ownership that stopped them, and it's been stuck in a legal limbo ever since.'

'Surprising that it's stayed intact,' Lapslie mused. 'I would have expected squatters and drug addicts to be using the inside, and local enterprising youths to have been peeling the lead off the roof. So what's the significance of the bells?'

Emma pointed to the slender tower that rose above the bulk of the church. 'There's only one, and it's up there. Most churches will have a set of bells, but for some reason lost in the mists of time this church had only one. It's called a Sanctus bell, and it's traditionally rung at the singing of the Sanctus and again at the elevation of the elements, to indicate to the locals that the moment of consecration has been reached.'

'Okay, so why's this one still making noise?'

'Apparently it was left in a fixed state, where it

wouldn't ring, but the support it was hanging from rotted when rainwater got into the tower. The thing swung loose, and now if the wind blows in through the louvres in a particular direction then the clapper gets blown against the bell. Which really annoys the locals, by the way. They're raised petitions to get it sorted out, but it's all tied up with that covenant thing.'

'Okay.' The sound of a car engine behind him made Lapslie turn. A car was pulling into the car park. It parked next to a metal pole that had been stuck in the ground outside the church. A yellow plastic box with vents in the side sat on top of the pole. It didn't look like something belonging to a church.

'Who's that?' Lapslie asked.

'That's the man with the keys to the building.'

'The caretaker?'

'Not quite. Again, it's all tied up with the covenant. The keys are lodged with a firm of solicitors. This is Mr Tulliver. He's the solicitor's clerk.'

The man who emerged from the car was young, small and birdlike, with a pointed nose and deep-set eyes under a thatch of blond hair. His suit was too large; his wrists emerged from his cuffs like twigs. 'Good morning,' he said, looking from Emma to Lapslie and back. 'Which one of you is DCI Lapslie?'

'I am,' Lapslie said. 'Can we get this place opened up?'

'Firstly, can I establish that you have no actual warrant?'

'We have,' Lapslie said heavily, 'no actual warrant. We actually have due cause for a warrant, and we actually have reason to believe that a crime has been committed inside the building, which means that we don't actually *need* a warrant, but do we actually *have* a warrant? No.'

'That's fine,' Tulliver said chirpily. 'I just wanted to check.' He delved in his pocket and brought out a set of keys on a ring, marked with a brown cardboard tag with a number written on it. 'Let's go, then.'

He scurried up the steps to the front doors of the building and hefted a large padlock attached to a chain that was strung between two large handles, one on each door. He glanced back over his shoulder. 'Lock doesn't appear to have been disturbed.'

'There are,' Lapslie pointed out, 'other ways into a building than through the front door.'

Within a few seconds the padlock and chain were on the stone steps and the doors were swinging open.

The smell that drifted out was a complex combination of wood polish, dry rot and something ammoniac, probably bird droppings. And overlaying all of that, a smell like rust. An old, familiar smell.

Blood.

The doors led into a small entrance hall lit only by the weak sunlight filtering in through the narrow ground-floor windows. A barrier straight ahead was set in front of what were probably the doors into the church itself, so that the parishioners had to file either left or right to get past it. Lapslie went left; Emma Bradbury went right. They came together in front of a set of swing doors. Lapslie pushed them open.

The church was, as Lapslie had surmised, a large, open space. Dusty buttresses of light braced the vaulted ceiling against the walls and the floor. The pews, altar and furnishings had been removed years before, leaving lighter patches on the stonework. Every movement sent echoes fluttering like birds.

For a moment, Lapslie thought that there was nothing in the building apart from dust and shadows, but then he saw a fine network of glints in the otherwise empty space. Glittering lines as fine as a spider's web caught in early morning sunlight. The more he looked the more he saw: they criss-crossed the space diagonally, horizontally, vertically; dividing it up into cells and sections.

'What's that?' Emma breathed.

'I don't know.'

Lapslie stepped closer, but the lines remained

maddeningly difficult to focus on. Tracing the lines to their ends, he could see that they were fastened to the walls with hooks and eyes that were either screwed into the masonry or stuck to it. He reached out with his fingers, brushing one that seemed to be closer than the rest.

A single, pure note rang out through the building.

'Wire,' he breathed. 'It's metal wire, under tension. Like a guitar string, but tens of metres long.'

'You mean this whole place has been strung like a musical instrument?' Emma asked.

'God knows why, but that's the effect.'

'This wasn't the way we left it,' Tulliver said from behind them. He sounded affronted, as if decorating the building with metal wire was equivalent to sticking upside-down crosses on the walls and sacrificing goats at the far end, where the altar had been.

And then he noticed the rust-like discoloration on some of the wires, and the strands of . . . something . . . that connected them to others and to the floor. And he saw the scraps of meat that lay on the ground beneath them, all dried up and leathery. And he imagined a woman, running through the building in the dark, panicked and blind, and blundering into the wires, feeling them cut into her flesh, slice it open, carve it off like turkey at a Christmas lunch. And out there, in the darkness, someone recording the whole thing. Watching and listening.

'"And through the cavernous slaughter-house,"' he murmured bleakly, '"I am the shadow that walks there."'

CHAPTER TEN

'I'm not even sure,' Sean Burrows said, 'how we're going to catalogue this place.'

Emma Bradbury, standing beside him, nodded in agreement. 'Rather you than me.'

'Thanks a bunch.'

Powerful spotlights had been set up in the corners of the deconsecrated Church of All Hallows, illuminating the inside with a bright wash of light, but the wires that had been strung across the inside of the nave were still nearly invisible, apart from the ones that were coated with the dried remnants of Catriona Dooley's blood.

'I can't send anyone in to look for evidence,' Burrows went on, 'because they might cut themselves to shreds. It's a health and safety issue.'

He was dressed in the usual CSI working gear of papery white coverall with hood, plus white gloves and white plastic bags covering his shoes. With his quiff of white hair emerging from the elasticated hood he looked like Frosty the Snowman. Or at least that's what Emma thought.

Behind him, his team of Crime Scene Investigators were standing around waiting for instructions.

'I don't want to tell you your job,' she said carefully, 'but I'd have thought that the first step would be to take the wires down, surely.'

'Not so,' Burrows replied. 'The position of the wires might be important. We need to be able to re-create the whole thing later, in the lab. Doctor Catherall might be able to make a better judgement about the injuries on the corpse if she can see how the wires are arranged. We also need to know what order the victim blundered into the wires – which one was first, which last. It's all grist to the mill. All stuff the Crown Prosecution Service will need later on, if you ever manage to nab the villain.'

'Thanks for the support,' Emma muttered, then louder: 'You'll need to catalogue the position of the fixtures in the walls, then work out which fixtures are connected together.'

Burrows sighed. 'So the first step is high definition pictures of each wall. I'll probably have to take several dozen photos and then mosaic them together. Once I've done that, I can get the resulting mosaics printed out onto A1 sheets of paper and number the fixtures.'

He was talking to himself by this stage, but Emma kept listening. She loved the way that Crime Scene Investigators thought: the rigorously logical, analytical way they broke everything down, no matter how difficult, into a series of very small things that could each be solved or accomplished. It was the ultimate reductionist approach to life, and that's what made them – Burrows especially – so good. It was the opposite to the way DCI Lapslie worked, which was largely gut instinct.

'We'll call the left wall "A", the wall ahead of us, where the altar used to be, "B", the right-hand wall "C" and the wall behind us "D",' Burrows mused. 'That way, we can locate every fixture.' He pointed to a loop of metal that projected from the wall over to their left. 'That one would be "A1", because it's the first fixture on wall "A". We'll number the fixtures on each wall from top left to bottom right. Then we'll have to work out a mapping, so that we know there's a wire from "A1" to –' he followed the nearly invisible wire that led across the nave from the fixture he'd identified as 'A1' – 'to, let's say, "C56".' He blew out his cheeks. 'Then we'll have to put labels on each wire, saying where it starts and where it finishes. *Then* we can start taking the wires down and storing them for later analysis, confident that we can re-create the room either practically or in a computer simulation later, knowing the dimensions of the room.'

'What about the fixtures on the ceiling?' Emma asked.

'Bugger,' he said. 'That'll have to be "E". And the floor will be "F" – there are some fixtures there as well.'

'This place,' Emma said, looking around, 'must have taken days, maybe weeks to put together.'

'Don't,' Burrows said soulfully. 'Just – don't.' He took a deep breath. 'We'd best make a start, then.'

'Okay,' Emma said. She glanced around. 'Just one thing . . .'

'Yes?'

'Where are you going to stand to take the photographs of each wall?'

Burrows's gaze flickered around the church, looking for some kind of access, some way he or his people could wend their way between the wires to a position opposite each wall so they could take pictures from the best vantage point.

'*Bugger*,' he said again. 'We might have to rig up a camera on a pole with a remote control, then somehow poke it in through the wires to the centre of the room.' He shook his head. 'There are days when I wish I'd taken my old grandmother's advice about careers.'

'Why?' Emma asked, 'what did she say?'

'I don't know,' Burrows replied dolefully. 'I didn't listen.'

Someone shouted Emma's name from the far side of the church. She looked to see who it was. DCI Lapslie was standing on the raised plinth where the altar would have gone.

'How the hell did you get over there?' Burrows yelled back before Emma could respond. 'I hope to God you didn't break any of the wires!'

'Don't panic,' Lapslie shouted back. 'There's another entrance round the back. Leads into a vestry and then out to the side of the altar area. Come round – I've found something.'

Emma walked out of the front entrance to the church and worked her way round to the back of the building, stumbling through clumps of weeds and unkempt bushes, across a patch of burned ground where someone had lit a fire, and past a couple of what had to be molehills. At the far end of the church she found a small door that led inside. It looked like it had been kicked in. DCI Lapslie, displaying his usual disregard for proper procedure.

'What is it?' she asked, entering the church at the west end. She found herself on the raised plinth, and glancing around, orientated herself to the different perspective.

Lapslie was kneeling down on one side of the altar

space. She joined him. He was gazing at scuff marks in the dust.

'I think this is where one of the microphones was placed,' he said. 'There's another similar mark on the other side. Burrows' people told me that the sound file was recorded in stereo.'

'Hmm. And there are some bigger marks over by the wall,' Emma pointed out, looking around. 'That might be where the recording apparatus was located.'

'Could well be.' Lapslie's gaze slid around the echoing interior of the church.

'It's like a bizarre version of that kids' playground we found the girl's body in,' Emma said, shivering.

Lapslie straightened up, brushing dust from his trousers. 'How so?'

'It's like a maze. The one on Canvey Island is all padded and safe and well lit, while this one was all razor-sharp and dangerous and dark, but the principle is the same. Catriona Dooley was set loose in it and had to blunder round looking for a way out. Except that for her, the way out involved a horrible death, rather than orange squash and cakes.'

'You're guessing,' Lapslie said gently.

'Yeah,' she sighed, 'but you know I'm right. This was some kind of sick game, and the bastard recorded the whole thing for entertainment.'

'And then what – dumped the body in a kids' play area because of some twisted, perverse sense of humour?'

'Why not?'

Lapslie considered. 'That means we're dealing with someone intelligent – too intelligent for their environment, so they seek kicks elsewhere. They're not desperate; they're enjoying themselves with whatever game they're playing and they want us to join in too.' He thought for a moment. 'And it goes against the words that were recorded on that sound file – "That's gash. That's just gash." Using a phrase like that to objectify a woman by referring in slang terms to her vagina doesn't accord with the idea of someone that intelligent.'

'Careful,' Emma warned. 'You're profiling.'

'Yeah,' Lapslie snorted, 'look how that worked out last time.' He grimaced. 'It's a tempting picture, but you know what it implies, don't you?'

Emma nodded. 'Nobody starts out with something this complicated, and they don't invite the police to join in first time around. They work up to it. They practise their sick art first. That means there are other victims out there. Other murders.'

'We need to trawl the records. Look for other unsolved crimes with similar characteristics.' He thought for a moment. 'Okay, I'll stay here and supervise the forensics. Doctor Catherall is on her way to look for traces of human flesh. We still need to tie this place in to Catriona Dooley's death by DNA or something, otherwise we're just pissing in the dark and hoping to hit something.'

'What a pretty picture you paint.'

'You head back to HQ and pull out the records of all unsolved murders with similar characteristics, going back, oh, five years.'

'Lovely.' She paused. 'What *are* the similar characteristics?'

'The obvious one is people who disappear and then their bodies are found after an unexpectedly long period, but it's clear that they've been alive for most of that time.'

'We don't know that that's a defining characteristic yet.'

'We've only got one body. Anything could be a defining characteristic, including hair colour and middle name, but we have to start somewhere. The two unusual things here are the length of time between disappearance and discovery, and the strange means of death. We would have heard if others had died this way, so that leaves the gap.'

'And the sound file,' Emma reminded him.

'But again, we would know if that had happened before. It would be a talking point. No, let's go with the disappearances.'

'Okay.' Emma turned to go. 'Have fun.'

She took the train back through the Essex country-side to the Police HQ at Chelmsford. She'd thought about going back to Canvey Island, which she was becoming strangely attached to, but it was quicker and easier to access the records in Chelmsford.

She found herself a quiet office with a terminal that wasn't being used, and settled down for a while. The database wasn't the easiest thing in the world to ma-nipulate, but she could access all unsolved cases and then gradually filter out the irrelevancies – the thefts, the muggings, the white collar crime, the accidental deaths and the manslaughters with obvious causes, the fights that led to one person or both people bleeding out in the street. That left her with a few hundred rather more suspicous deaths with no obvious suspects.

Her phone rang. She checked her watch as she answered. Bugger! It was past midnight! She'd been working longer than she expected.

The display said 'Dom.'

'Hi, babe.'

'Where are you?' he growled.

'I'm working.'

'Lapslie's pushing you too hard,' he said darkly. 'I'll have to have a word.'

'It's nothing to do with him.' She hesitated. 'Well, it is, but it's not. I'm looking for something.'

'It's his case and your case, isn't it? I shouldn't have pointed out the connection to him.'

'Oh, I've got you to thank for that, have I?'

He laughed. 'Someone's got to do your jobs for you. When are you going to be back?'

'Don't know. Might work through.'

'Okay. Let me know if you need a change of clothes or something. I'll run them over.'

'I've got two changes of clothes here, just in case.' A pause. 'Love you.'

'Yeah,' he growled. 'Same here.'

She disconnected the call, feeling a glow of happiness inside her.

Concentration broken, she wandered out and got a cup of coffee and a sausage and egg roll from an all-night café across the road. The only other people there were taxi drivers, insomniacs and various police and firemen on a break. Traffic flashed past in the darkness; tail lights glowing like the red eyes of some fantastical predator. A bus heaved itself past, belching diesel fumes. There were five or six people on it, each sitting in their own isolated world, and she wondered, as she always did in these situations, where they were going and why they were out so late. Were they going home, had they just left home, or didn't they even have a home? Did they just spend their time moving around the town, passing by as life went on without them?

She finished her food in silence, and returned to her desk.

Back at her terminal, she continued to whittle down the thicket of dates, times and injuries into a coherent pattern, trying her best to ignore names and stories and just regard them as parts of a puzzle. And, gradually, a pattern did begin to emerge.

Three disappearances. Three people who had gone missing under suspicious circumstances in Essex and the surrounding counties in the past five years and had been discovered, dead, several weeks later. Post-mortems had later revealed that they had been kept alive and fed, probably while bound, for at least ten days after their disappearance, and they had all died after sustained torture. No traces of rape – in fact, Emma noted with surprise, one of the three was male. All of the victims were aged between twenty and forty. The lead investigator on two of the cases was a former colleague of hers – DS Gary Ellender, based in Southend. They had worked together for three years and had always got on well.

Emma checked her watch – it was nearly seven o'clock, and she'd worked through the night. Her eyes felt hot and gritty, and the muscles around the back of her neck ached, but she didn't actually feel tired. The adrenalin was keeping her going. If she could face the drive down to Southend, she could catch Gary at his desk.

She logged off the police database, closed up the quiet room and headed for the car park, grabbing a coffee from the cafeteria on the ground floor on the way.

Her drive to Southend got caught up in the morning rush hour and school run, and she didn't hit the centre of town until nearly half past eight. She parked in an open-air car park between the Court and Southend Victoria railway station. According to the desk sergeant at Southend nick, Gary was giving evidence at a Coroner's Court that morning.

She booked into the court, flashing her warrant card but still having to pass through the obligatory metal detector before heading up the wide stairs to the first floor, where the courtrooms were located. She'd given evidence at several trials in Southend before, and she knew the ins and outs of the building; the side corridors, the ante-rooms, the impressive main courtroom with its wooden panelling and huge royal crest behind the bench, and the smaller, more down-at-heel courtrooms where minor cases were heard. She recognised the ever-present sense of desperation and seediness that hung over everything. A coffee-stand in the foyer was about the only trace of modernity in the entire place, and Emma felt it was a bit like putting lipstick on a corpse.

She found Gary in the waiting room outside court number three – not so much a room as a widened area in the corridor lined with chairs. He was sitting opposite a family group dressed in black and a separate group who looked like office workers. Gary was a big, bear-like man with a close-cropped beard and a twinkle in his eye. He was soberly dressed in a dark suit. Seeing her enter the room his eyebrows raised in surprise and pleasure. He got to his feet as she approached. She extended her hand awkwardly, but he grabbed her and gave her a hug.

'Emma, it's been ages. Where have you been?'

'Around and about.' She hugged back. 'It has been a long time. Sorry I drifted out of touch.'

'I hear you had your hands full with that mad DCI – Lapslie.'

'He's not that mad,' she said awkwardly. 'He gets results.'

'By witchcraft, I hear.'

'Hey – whatever works.' Changing the subject, she asked: 'So what's the inquest?'

'Actually a pre-inquest hearing,' he said quietly. 'The coroner wants to establish the ground rules before the inquest proper starts.' He nodded his head towards the group of office workers. 'They're from the Ministry of Defence. One of their scientists died during some secret experiment. There's some question about the Official Secrets Act, and the coroner needs to establish what can be revealed in open court and what needs to be held in camera. The family solicitor is pressing for everything to be out in the open; unsurprisingly, the Treasury Solicitors who are representing the MOD want it all hidden away in dark places. And the press are interested as well, which doesn't help. They can smell a cover-up a mile off, whether it's there or not.'

'So what are you doing?' she asked. 'It's not a suspicious death, is it?'

'First police officer on scene,' he said. 'I'm just a witness.'

'Have you got time to talk?'

He glanced around. 'The coroner's clerk popped his head around the door earlier to say that things were running late on the previous inquest. I think I've got time, but I have to stay here.'

'Okay.'

'So – what do you want to know? I presume this is business?'

'Do you remember two cases you worked on – Lorraine Gregory and Alison Traff?'

He nodded, face turning solemn. 'Yeah. I sometimes wake up sweating in the night, I remember so much.'

'Sorry to have to raise the ghosts.'

He shrugged. 'Comes with the territory, doesn't it. We're never allowed to forget.'

'What can you tell me about the cases?'

'Okay.' He exhaled heavily. 'Lorraine Gregory. Studying engineering at Essex University. Third year, lived in the halls of residence there. Attractive girl: brown hair, brown eyes, vivacious personality. She disappeared two months ago in the middle of the week after attending a rehearsal – she was lead singer in a band. No clues, no suspects. No boyfriend, for a start, and no stalkers that we could identify. We did all the usual things – canvassed the neighbourhood, did interviews for the local TV and radio stations, but nothing. No suspicious people hanging around, no strange cars seen motoring around the neighbourhood – nothing.' He stopped. Emma noticed him swallow. 'Her body was found four weeks after she disappeared, in the inspection pit of a car garage. Someone had broken in and left her there.'

'You checked out the mechanics and the owner, obviously.'

'First thing we did. They were clean. I mean, they had a nice sideline in taking write-offs from car accidents and welding the front end from one to the back end of another and flogging the resulting monstrosity on eBay as a functioning car, but they all had alibis for the time she was taken and the approximate time she was killed.'

'Okay. Sorry to interrupt.'

'She'd been . . . tortured,' he said starkly. 'Horribly, and over the course of several weeks. Her fingernails had been pulled out with pliers, for a start, and then the skin between her fingers had been cut and the fingers slowly pulled apart all the way down to the wrist. Her right hand looked like . . . like a bloody spider. Like something from a horror film.'

'What about her left hand?' Emma asked, feeling sick. 'What happened to that? Was it taken?'

Gary's normally pink face had gone pale now. 'No. No, it wasn't taken. It just wasn't there any more. Not in one bit, anyway. The wristbones of her left arm had been cut through with shears from front to back, from the hand towards the elbow, and then the same thing that had been done to the hand was done to the arm: the flesh was cut down for a distance, and then the two bones of the forearm – the radius and the ulna – were gradually pulled apart. And when I say 'gradually', I mean over the course of several hours. It must have been . . . unimaginably painful. When we found her, the two parts of her forearm were at right angles to each other.' He swallowed again. 'It's bad enough when things are done to people, and you find the bodies, but they usually still look like *bodies*, know what I mean? Lorraine – she looked like . . . I don't know. Like someone was trying to take her apart like you'd take a car engine apart to see how it worked, but stopped after a while when they got bored and left the bits scattered around.'

'And there was – ' Emma stopped to swallow the flood of saliva in her mouth; precursor to her throwing up if she wasn't careful – 'no clue as to the perpetrator?'

Gary shook his head. 'Nobody hated her enough to do that to her, and nobody who even disliked her had blank spots in their calendar long enough to cover what was done. Eventually we had it down to a predatory psychopath who'd just picked up a passing stranger, but then you would expect there to be an element of sexual crime. She was, as far as the pathologist could establish, still a virgin.'

Emma's forehead was hot, and she could feel sweat prickling it. The other people in the waiting area were looking at the two of them strangely; not hearing what was being said but aware from the body language that it was disturbing.

'And the other disappearance?' she asked. 'Alison Traff?'

'Some similarities, some differences.' Gary seemed glad to change the subject. 'She was thirty-five, married with two children. Disappeared one evening after filling her car up at a petrol station. She was on her way back from choir practice in the local church hall. The family lived out in the countryside, in a fairly remote farmhouse. The suspicion was that she'd either been run off the road or stopped to help someone in trouble, and been abducted.' He shook his head. 'The family were devastated. The husband had a rock solid alibi, and no reason to kill her. We did check. He's still seeing a therapist to try and come to terms with it. The council have put the children into care, because the husband is having such a hard time.'

'I hate to ask, but how was she found? I mean—'

'I know what you mean.' He seemed to brace himself. 'This time the body was dumped in the car park of a holistic therapy practice in Frinton. The body had been pierced repeatedly with what the pathologist estimated were meat skewers. Pierced in every place you could put a skewer and still keep someone alive. You know that kids' game when we were young where you had all these thin plastic rods going from one side of a Perspex tube to the other, going through all these small holes in the sides, and there were a whole load of marbles balanced on top of the rods, and you had to take turns pulling the plastic rods out and the loser was the one who caused the marbles to fall down the tube?'

'KerPlunk? Yeah, I got it for Christmas once. I was eight.'

'Imagine someone doing it in reverse, but to a human being. Imagine two people taking turns to stick skewers through another human being's body over the course of several days, maybe a week, and the loser is the one who kills her.' He paused, and Emma noticed that the corners of his mouth were turning downwards. 'They were stuck through her arms, her legs, her shoulders, her cheeks, her fingers, her ribs . . . anywhere you can imagine, and places you really don't want to imagine.'

'Any evidence of two people being present?'

'No. That was just an assumption on our part.'

'Did you recover the skewers? You say the pathologist had to estimate that's what did it.'

'No – they'd all been removed, very carefully. The pathologist did say two interesting things. The first was that the skewers had probably been sterilised with an antiseptic before being inserted, which indicates a desire to keep her alive for as long as possible, and a certain fastidiousness.'

'And the second?' Emma asked when it became clear that Gary wasn't going to continue under his own volition.

'The second interesting thing was that, judging from the scar tissue in the wounds, the skewers had been pulled in and out several times over the course of the days or weeks she was tortured.'

'Oh.' Emma tried to imagine it, and then quickly tried not to. 'What killed her?'

'In the end? Believe it or not, it was a simple infection. Although her captor had taken care with his sterilising procedures, some opportunistic bacterium got in.'

'Okay.' Emma was about to ask another question when the door to the courtroom opened and a small man in a suit poked his head through. He nodded at Gary, the family and the group of assorted civil servants, then withdrew.

'Got to go,' Gary said. 'You know how it is.'

'Yeah. Thanks.' Impulsively she hugged him again, and kissed his cheek.

'Stay in touch.'

'I will.' She turned to go, then turned back. 'I suppose the black humour of the situations occurred to you? The woman whose arm was dismantled was left in a car garage, and the woman who was stuck through with skewers was left in a holistic therapy centre where, I presume, they practised acupuncture.'

He nodded. 'It didn't escape us. We could never prove that the murders were carried out by the same person, but we always assumed they were. We called him "The Comedian". It would have been "The Joker", but the press would have connected that up to *Batman* if they'd got hold of it, and made us look stupid and unfeeling. Which we certainly weren't.'

Emma turned to go again, and this time it was Gary who stopped her. 'Has something else happened?' he asked. 'Another body?'

Emma nodded.

'How was this one killed?' he asked.

'Do you want to sleep tonight?'

'Ah.' A pause. 'Get him, Emma. Whoever this "Comedian" is, get him.'

'I will. *We* will.'

'You'll need a lot of luck.'

'Or witchcraft,' she said, and left.

In the car, driving on the long and curving road out of Southend, Emma's mind ranged back and forth over everything Gary Ellender had said. There was a distinct pattern there – a murderer who abducted his victims, kept them alive for several days or weeks while torturing them, and then disposed of them in some blackly ironic way. With only two cases there wasn't enough to make more than a cursory connection; Catriona Dooley's case hadn't been around for long enough, and the post-mortem results were still on sufficiently close hold, that nobody apart from Emma had made the connection. No sexual assault, which was odd. Perhaps the killer masturbated while he was torturing his victims. Perhaps that was the only way he could get off.

But then there was the fourth case; the one she hadn't talked to anyone about yet. The one she had discovered in the files.

On an off-chance she took a diversion, heading not for Chelmsford but up past Brentwood and towards Harlow. She recalled from the files that the fourth case – chronologically, the second – had taken place there.

Harlow Police Station was a two-storey building of relatively modern construction, built in a square around a central staff car park. It looked something like a new comprehensive school, a similarity emphasised by its location next to a sports centre.

Parking, and showing her warrant card again, Emma was soon inside. She found Detective Inspector Bill Ponting on the phone in his office. He waved her to a seat.

'Sorry,' he said as he put the receiver down. He was a big man, barrel chested, with cheeks that were too red to be healthy and a mass of back-combed white hair. He wore a pin-stripe suit that his size couldn't really carry off properly. 'What can I do for you?'

'DS Bradbury,' Emma introduced herself. 'I'm working on a case where a woman was abducted, tortured and then dumped in a public area. I believe you had a similar case. I was hoping you could tell me about it.'

Ponting looked surprised. 'Woman? Ours was a man. Decided it was gang-related. Lot of that in Harlow.'

'I don't want to rule anything in or out at this stage,' Emma said, and then added a little white lie. 'Ours might be gang-related as well, of course, even though it's a woman.'

'Where was she found?' Ponting asked.

'Canvey Island.'

'Ah. There you are.'

Emma wasn't sure where 'there' was, or why exactly she was 'there', but she smiled sweetly. Ponting continued: 'David Cave. Small-time drug dealer, car thief and runner for one of the larger gangs. Word was that he'd got someone's daughter pregnant. He disappeared. Found his body six weeks later. He's been worked over with what the pathologist concluded was a potato peeler. Whole top layer of his skin had been removed, front and back. Looked like a freakshow exhibit.'

'Where was he found?' Emma asked.

'Bakery,' Ponting said. 'Left bundled up in one of the ovens. Break-in. Someone has a sick sense of humour.'

'And you put this down to gang activity?' Emma asked, trying to keep the critical tone out of her voice.

'He ran with the gangs, he got someone's daughter up the duff, he was tortured and dumped. What else could it be?'

'Good question.' Emma stood. 'Thanks. I don't think I need bother you any further.' She crossed to the door, then turned back as a thought struck her. 'This may be a silly question, but I don't suppose David Cave was a singer in any way?'

Ponting fixed her with an unnerving gaze. 'Funny you should ask. Did a lot of karaoke in local pubs. Got quite a lot of cash winning competitions. Is that important?'

'Oh, I shouldn't think so,' she said sweetly, and left.

In the car on the way back, she mulled over the information she'd collected. Information that wasn't all in the official police records. Three disappearances that had turned into tortures and murders, and in all three cases the victims had some connection with singing. One sang in a band, one in a choir and one in pubs for money.

What were the odds that Catriona Dooley had been a singer as well?

CHAPTER ELEVEN

'Interesting idea,' Lapslie said. The cold mid-morning wind whipping around the corners of All Hallows Church in Bishop's Stortford cut into him like a shoal of piranhas. He could hear the growl of Emma's car engine in the background of the mobile phone transmission. 'Why would someone kidnap singers?'

'I've often thought of doing the same with Lady Gaga,' Emma replied.

'Who?'

'She's a singer. Kind of falsetto soul. Never mind.'

'I hope you're on hands-free,' he growled.

'I am.'

'It's just that I've never seen a hands-free kit in your car.'

She sounded aggravated. 'I'm on hands-free, okay?'

'I only mention it,' he said mildly, 'because judging

by the sound of your car engine you're doing well in excess of the speed limit, and if you're caught doing that *and* using your mobile phone the consequences could be horrendous.'

There was a pause, during which the sound of Emma's engine noticeably changed. 'I'd better go,' she said eventually.

'Yes, you better had. Have you slept, by the way?'

'Have you?' she asked.

'I managed to get home, grab six hours' kip and get back here again as fresh as a daisy. I suspect you've worked through. It'll catch up with you, you know.'

'But I'm young,' she said. 'I can take it.' He couldn't see her expression, but he assumed she was grinning.

'I'll check into Catriona Dooley's background,' he said. 'You go back and check the files again for people who have disappeared and never been found, alive or dead.'

'There'll be thousands of them!' Emma protested. 'You know how many people go missing in England every year?'

'Just check for singers,' Lapslie said. 'That appears to be the common thread.'

'I still don't understand.' Emma sounded frustrated. 'I already spent twelve hours checking through the files. I found all the disappearances that looked similar to Catriona Dooley's case.'

'No,' Lapslie explained patiently, 'you found all the disappearances where the bodies were found some weeks later, and it then turned out that all the ones you discovered had good singing voices. What I want you to look for now is reverse the process: look for all the cases where people who have good singing voices have disappeared and never been found.'

'You think he's still got some kidnap victims alive!' Emma breathed.

'We know he discards some in an obvious and blackly ironic way. The question is: does he discard all of them, or just the ones that don't match his twisted criteria? Remember the voice on the sound file – "That's gash", he said. He's looking for something, and I'm guessing it's connected with their voices. According to what Doctor Catherall told you, Catriona Dooley was given food and water. If you've got somebody tied up, you can keep them alive for quite some time if you're prepared to feed them.'

'Jesus.' Emma's voice was bleak. 'I don't want to think what he's doing to these people.'

'If there are any,' Lapslie warned. 'Let's get the facts first.'

'Okay. I'll be in touch.'

Emma rang off. Lapslie was about to put the mobile back in his pocket when it rang again.

'Lapslie.'

'DCI Lapslie? This is Patricia – Chief Superintendent Rouse's PA. He wants to see you straight away.'

'Does he have a telescope?'

A pause while she processed the comment and then threw it away. 'He has a gap in his schedule at one o'clock this afternoon. Can I tell him you'll be here?'

Her voice was sweetness itself, but there was an implicit threat lying behind the words. Even without the synaesthesia, Lapslie could taste it. 'Yes,' he said. 'Please tell him I'll be there.' Before she could go, he added, 'And can you have a large coffee waiting for me, two sugars? Maybe some of those lovely bourbon biscuits as well.' He rang off before she could make some comment about reducing police running costs by not catering for meetings of less that ten people.

Re-entering the church, he found that Sean Burrows' team had started deconstructing the cats' cradle of wire that was strung from side to side and floor to ceiling.

'How's it going?' he called.

'It's a slow and laborious process,' Burrows replied, crossing an open space towards him. 'I'm already two men down. One of the wires snapped as we were taking it off the hook that's attached to the wall. It whipped back and slashed across the face of one CSI and the hands of another. I've sent them off for stitches and for tetanus shots and HIV tests.' At Lapslie's questioning glance, he added, 'We just don't know what's on these wires. I know Catriona Dooley was clear of HIV, but there might be other blood here that we don't know about.'

'Emma's found three more murders that tie in with the Dooley one,' Lapslie confirmed, 'although they don't have the same wounds as the girl's body did. But I take your point.' He looked at the remaining wires. 'Do we know what these things are made of?'

'Curiously enough,' Burrows said, 'I'm leaning towards the view that it's piano wire, based on the tension and the breaking strain. Musical instrument strings are one of the most demanding of applications for wires – far more demanding than big game fishing, for instance. They're placed under high tension, they're subject to repeated blows and repeated bending, they're stretched and slackened during tuning and, while being expected to be up to scratch for concert performances, they are still expected to last for decades. They're made from tempered high tensile steel. If I were making someone run through a funhouse strung up with lethally sharp wire, I'd want to make sure that it stayed in place and they came apart, rather than the other way around.'

'Musical instruments,' Lapslie mused. 'Singers. Music teachers. It's all connected somehow, but I can't quite see the connections.' He shook himself. 'It would be nice if there were only one manufacturer of this wire in the UK, and we could trace who bought this lot.'

Burrows shook his head. 'It comes in coils and gets sold by weight. No chance of tracking it down, in my opinion.'

'What if it's a high-quality make?'

Burrows pursed his lips. 'In that case I might be able to track it down for you. But why do you think this is high-quality stuff? This is a torture device, not a musical instrument.'

'Perhaps it's both,' Lapslie muttered, and moved away, leaving Burrows staring after him.

Over in the centre of the church, in a cleared area, he spotted a familiar figure crouched down awkwardly on the ground and scraping something into an evidence bag.

'Jane? What are you doing out of your shell?'

Doctor Jane Catherall looked up at him. 'Mark! I'd heard you were back, and then this happened. You do have a habit of presenting me with cases that are out of the ordinary. Thank you.'

'Glad to help,' he said, smiling. For some reason, he was very fond of the diminutive pathologist. Seeing her always cheered him up. 'What's the lowdown here?'

'Blood everywhere, and traces of flesh on the floor,' she replied. 'I'm collecting up as much as I can. No way of telling how many people we're talking about yet – I'll have to identify how many unique DNA traces I have before I can tell you that, but I'll certainly check the DNA against that of Catriona Dooley. Oh, and I've found a couple of dead pigeons as well. They must have blundered in and flown into the wires. That'll have to be disentangled from any traces of human remains.'

'I wonder what pigeon tastes like,' he mused, thinking back to the carp and the swans.

'Unpleasant,' Jane said, 'if you're talking about the common town pigeon. They eat carrion and garbage. Wood pigeon is a different matter. Why do you ask?'

'No reason,' he said. 'Looking around, could this place have caused the injuries that Emma told me were evident on Catriona Dooley's body?'

Instead of answering, she extended a hand to Lapslie. He supported her weight while she climbed painfully to her feet. The top of her head was on a level with his chin. 'Yes, the injuries are completely consistent with wires either cutting through flesh like a cheese wire or snapping under tension and lashing back. You see the same kind of thing with construction workers and, strangely, circus performers.' She looked around sombrely. 'I hate to imagine what it was like,' she said. 'Pitch black and cold. The poor girl, stark naked and terrified; probably starving, given that the stomach contents I found indicated that she'd been fed enough to keep her alive but not to satisfy her gnawing hunger pangs. Released into this death trap and allowed to blunder around, feeling the wires cut into her flesh, carving away whole slices which flapped against her body as she ran, feeling the hot blood splattering against her skin and gushing down her arms and legs; feeling herself growing weaker and weaker until she couldn't go on any more and she sank to the ground, and died, alone and afraid.'

'Not alone,' Lapslie said. 'Every noise she made was recorded. There was someone here, listening. Not watching, but listening.'

For a moment they both remained silent, each in their own world of imagination. Then Lapslie said, 'You mentioned stomach contents. Do we know what she was fed on?'

'Does it matter?' she asked.

'It might help us profile her captor and killer if we knew how he treated her. Was he kind or unkind? Did he recognise her as a human being or throw her scraps? It's all part of the bigger picture.'

Jane Catherall shrugged. 'Analysis of her bowels and her stomach indicate that she was fed on a largely liquid diet, but one that contained most of the nutrients necessary for life. I'd suggest that whoever was holding her captive either fed her on soup or food that was cooked and then liquidised. It wouldn't have been terribly satisfying, and in the longer term it would have had a detrimental effect on her digestive system and her dentition, but I suspect that was the last thing on her captor's mind.'

'Why go to all that trouble?'

'If her captor had just cooked meals for her, he would either have had to release her hands so she could feed herself, thus risking her attacking him, or he would have to feed her himself, which would take a lot of time. Liquidising the food and then letting her drink it is quicker and minimises time and risk.'

'So we can surmise,' Lapslie said, 'that her captor was concerned for her welfare, so he made sure she was eating properly – at least, as properly as she could, under the circumstances – and was worried about her attempting to escape and overpowering him, which means that he is likely to be physically weak.'

'Or not a him at all,' Jane murmured.

'Statistically, almost all abductors of women are men,' Lapslie pointed out.

'But there was no sign of sexual interference in this case.'

Reluctantly, Lapslie nodded. 'Point taken. I'm using the words "him" and "he" as shorthand, but we might be looking for a woman.'

'You've made another unwarranted assumption,' Jane Catherall pointed out.

'What's that?'

'You're assuming that the care taken in the feeding indicates a degree of empathy. Of concern.'

'Yes?'

'It might alternatively indicate that he – or she – wanted her alive and in relatively good health in order that she be able to do something.'

'Like run a lethal maze?' Lapslie asked, looking around the church.

'Oh, I think this was just a means to an end,' Jane said. 'Not an end in itself.' She shivered. 'I should get going. These DNA samples aren't going to analyse themselves.'

Jane Catherall left, clutching her evidence bags, and Lapslie made his way to his Saab. He checked his watch. If he started out now he could get to Chelmsford in time to grab a bite to eat before seeing Chief Superintendent Rouse.

His mobile rang as he was driving. He touched the side of the Bluetooth earpiece – a new innovation in his life that Charlotte had persuaded him to try, now that his synaesthesia was quiescent.

He expected it to be Emma Bradbury on the line, but it was Charlotte calling.

'Hi,' he said, surprised.

'Hi yourself. I thought I saw you in the corridor of the hospital last night. I waved, but you were talking to someone and you didn't see me. You weren't looking for me, were you?'

'Sorry,' he said, feeling vaguely embarrassed at being watched without knowing it. 'I needed to find a psychiatrist in a hurry.'

'You've got me worried now.'

He laughed. 'Not for myself. I've got a case on, and I needed some advice. And for someone to look at a photograph and see if they recognised it.'

'Never ask a psychiatrist what they see in a photograph,' Charlotte said mock-seriously. 'They spend so long asking patients to look at black and white patterns and tell them what they see that their perceptions are permanently biased.'

'If I'd known you were there I would have bought you a coffee.'

'That time of night the cafeteria is closed. It's machine coffee or nothing. And besides, you were with another woman.'

'Jealous, much?' he asked.

She laughed. 'Funnily enough, no. Do you want me to be?'

'Absolutely not. That was Emma. She works for me, and she's going out with an old East End villain of my acquaintance.'

'I'm sure there's a whole story there that you can tell me about tonight.'

'You're not working?'

'No. You want to come over to my place? I've got concert tickets for tonight, remember?.'

He felt the colour drain from his face. Good thing she wasn't there to see it. 'Yes, of course I remembered.'

'You've got a key. Just let yourself in.'

'I will.' He paused, wanting her to say 'I love you', wanting to say it himself, but the moment passed, and he said, 'I'll see you later. Take care.'

'You too.'

The rest of the drive to Chelmsford Police HQ went without incident. He coasted over the raised entry road into the centre of the town just before noon and parked in the HQ car park. He walked away from the building, into the town, following a route that his feet remembered better than his mind did. After a few minutes he found himself standing outside a Café Rouge. It was the last place he'd had anything more than a passing conversation with his wife. Ex-wife. On a whim he went in, found the same table was free, and ordered the same chicken salad that he'd had last time. While he ate, part of his mind wondered exactly what he was doing. Trying to recapture a memory? Exorcising ghosts? The chicken salad which had been as adventurous as he could push himself last time he'd been there was now bland and nearly tasteless. He remembered the rice noodles and prawns and chicken that he'd eaten at the noodle house by the M25. In comparison with what he was eating now, they were bursting with taste.

He was a different person now.

'"That is the land of lost content,"' he said softly, '"I see it shining plain; the happy highways where I went, and cannot come again."'

'Sorry, Sir?' The waiter had paused by his table.

'Nothing.'

He left the meal half-eaten and walked back to the Police HQ. He got to Rouse's office, and the redoubtable PA Patricia, just on the stroke of one o'clock.

'Mark!' Rouse's voice boomed from inside. 'Come in! Come in!'

Rouse wasn't alone in the office. A woman was sitting at his meeting table. She was wearing a maroon jacket with a rough hessian weave over a white silk blouse, and trousers matching her jacket. Rouse, of course, was in uniform, with his jacket off.

'Mark, this is Margarita Haringay. She's with our legal services department.'

'That's a bit premature, isn't it?' Lapslie rejoined. 'We've not even got a proper suspect yet.'

'I said "legal services", not "Crown Prosecution Service". Margarita is here to give me some advice.' He scowled at Lapslie. 'Oh, sit down, for Heaven's sake. You're making the place look untidy.' As Lapslie sat, he continued blithely: 'We've had a complaint about your conduct.'

'Do I need a Police Federation representative present?' Lapslie asked mildly, although he could feel a small worm of concern start to twist and turn within his gut.

'Do you *need* a rep?' Rouse asked.

'Don't be cute,' Lapslie snapped, getting to his feet again. The woman's head lifted and she glanced at him, surprised at the tone of voice he was taking with a senior officer. 'Given that I don't know why I'm here, only you know whether I need representation or not. That's the kind of cheap psychological trick you and I used to play on suspects who asked to see a solicitor the moment they were brought in for questioning.'

Rouse spread his hands wide on the desk. 'Calm yourself, Mark. Calm yourself. This is just a preliminary—'

'Hearing?'

'—meeting. Please, sit down.'

As Lapslie sat once more, Rouse levered himself up from behind his desk and joined them at the meeting table. Sitting, he said, 'You interrogated a girl named Tamara Stottart in the presence of her father, Stephen Stottart.'

'I interviewed a girl who I believed had evidence in a murder investigation, yes. The interview took place in a family room, in the presence of another police officer as well as the girl's father, and was videotaped as per standard procedure.'

'Yes, I've seen the video.' Rouse sniffed. 'You don't think you were a little . . . overbearing?'

'No.'

'The girl's father does. He's raised a complaint with the IPCC. We need to work out how to respond.'

'Firmly,' Lapslie said, 'and quickly. This is rubbish. An over-protective father and a clever daughter who knows more than she's letting on. If we let them get the upper hand we'll never get any traction on this case.'

'And if the IPCC agrees with the father that you were intimidating his daughter then I'll have to remove you from the case and get someone else to take over.' He paused, and pursed his lips. 'I hear that Dain Morritt is free at the moment.'

The worm in Lapslie's gut began to wriggle more strongly, as if it were trying to get itself off a hook the size and nature of which it could barely comprehend. 'Sir . . .' He took a breath, aware that he didn't even know what to say. What might get him off the hook.

'This drug you're on to control your mental problem ... could it be affecting your judgement?'

'Sir, as you are well aware, it's not a mental problem in the same way that depression or bipolar disorder is a mental problem, it's a condition. That's number one. And number two, no, the drug I'm on does not cause confusion, aggression, paranoia or any other issue that might have made me act strangely in the interview.'

'These are the kinds of questions that the IPCC will have to consider,' Rouse said as if Lapslie hadn't spoken. 'We'll need an independent medical statement, of course. You need to tell us your side of the story, Mark. We know what you said, but we need to know what you felt. What you were thinking. What you were trying to elicit from the girl. Margarita will take you through it.'

Lapslie spent the next hour going over the entire interview, once from memory, then again from a transcript of the videotape that the woman had with her. Rouse, bored, moved back to his desk after ten minutes and buried himself in paperwork. In her calm, repetitive, uninvolved way she made Lapslie feel like a suspect, like he was saying things that she didn't believe, and all she was doing was looking for holes in his story that she could use to break it apart. By the time she'd finished, and was packing the transcript and her notes away in her bag, he felt drained. Tired. Old.

'Thanks for coming in, Mark,' Rouse said without looking up from his paperwork. 'We'll be in touch.'

Feeling like he wanted to lash out at someone, but aware that he'd only be making things worse for himself, Lapslie headed out to the car park. He wasn't sure whether he wanted to go back to All Hallows Church, drive out to the incident room on Canvey Island to see where the other strands of the Catriona Dooley investigation had got to, head across to the hospital and prowl around the internet café or sit on Sean Burrows' desk until Forensics came up with something. A dark, primal part of his mind even wanted to go to Stephen Stottart's house and goad the man into taking a swing at him, just so he'd have the satisfaction of breaking his nose, but he managed to keep that desire in check by turning it into a daydream that he could console himself with if he got too tense. In the end he decided to go and bother the forensics lab staff, if only because it was on the way home, and he wanted to get changed out of his suit before he headed over to Charlotte's flat.

The drive to the isolated, fenced-off area of land that marked out Sean Burrows' fiefdom did nothing to relax him, and he found himself stomping up the path that led past the small hills of the old Napoleonic fort to where the single-storey buildings of the laboratories were set. He felt ready for a confrontation. A squirrel ran across his path, breaking his concentration for a moment. He stopped and looked around. The mid-afternoon sun was filtering through the trees, casting dappled patterns on the path. Moss was growing up the sides of the oak trees. There was no traffic around, and the hush was suddenly magical. An acorn dropped at his feet, startling him.

He took in a deep breath of the nature-scented air, feeling it penetrating deep into his lungs and driving out the diesel and petrol fumes that characterised Chelmsford town centre; driving out also the feelings of impotence that a meeting with Rouse always managed to engender in him. Fuck the man. Lapslie had a job to do.

He was smiling when he knocked on the door of Sean Burrows' office. Unexpectedly, Jane Catherall was there as well.

'Mark,' she said, 'we were just talking about you.'

'I came looking for a fight,' he admitted, 'but the walk up from the main gates calmed me down.'

'Then can I pour you a small Irish whiskey, to improve your mood even further?' Burrows suggested. 'I was just about to offer Jane one as well.'

'That would be ... most welcome. What's the occasion?'

'Let's just say it's my birthday and leave it there.'

As Burrows poured three tumblers of soft, golden liquid from a bottle that he kept in a filing cabinet, Lapslie took his coat off and sat down. 'I know it's early days,' he said, 'but are there any initial results from the All Hallows Church crime scene?'

'We pushed it through as a rush job,' Burrows said, 'knowing that you would probably be up here asking that very question. I'll let Jane go first.'

Doctor Catherall sipped at her whiskey first. 'Very smooth,' she said judiciously, 'but without much depth. The alcoholic equivalent of the music of Ludovico Einaudi.'

'If you don't like it,' Burrows said, 'I'll take it back.'

'Not at all. There are times when a lack of complexity is exactly what is needed.' Turning to Lapslie, she continued, 'DNA tests on the blood and the scraps of flesh indicate that they all came from the same person. It will be a while before I can actually compare the DNA to that of Catriona Dooley, but the blood is certainly of the same type. I am minded to say that she was the only person who was either injured there or died there.'

'Okay.' Lapslie took his tumbler and sipped cautiously

at the liquid inside. For years now he'd drunk mainly water for its simplicity of taste. Now that the thorazitol was apparently suppressing his synaesthesia, he was gradually introducing flavours back into his life. With alcohol he'd started off with fairly subtle white wines like Chenin Blancs, Pouilly-Fuissé and Pouilly-Fumé, then moving on to similar reds, but he hadn't risked spirits yet, let alone beer. The Irish whiskey that Sean Burrows had poured for him seeped into his mouth like a spreading warmth flavoured with orange, leather and linseed, with a peppery aftertaste. Odd, and yet the disparate flavours blended together to form something rich and vibrant that left a line of fire behind it as it slipped down his throat. 'I'll await the DNA comparison. Sean, what about you? Any forensic samples you could retrieve from the church?'

'Interestingly,' Burrows replied, 'although the perpetrator of the crime had done a good job of cleaning up after himself, we did manage to retrieve some soil samples from where he had set up his recording and mixing desk. The soil is inconsistent with the local soil in Bishop's Stortford, so our working assumption is that the perpetrator tracked the soil in himself, possibly from wherever he'd been keeping the girl captive, or from where he lives.'

'I don't suppose,' Lapslie asked, 'that you can identify

where the soil comes from, like Sherlock Holmes always could?'

'It would be nice,' Burrows said, 'but there's nothing particularly distinctive about it. Except – ' he paused, obviously enjoying their reaction – 'that the soil contains traces of pollen. We did a quick scan to identify the plants that produce that pollen, in case that could help narrow down the location, and it turns out that the plants aren't indigenous to the UK.'

'So, what?' Lapslie asked. 'The murderer works in a garden centre where they sell exotic plants?'

'Not quite. It's actually a wheat. Garden centres don't sell wheat.'

Lapslie shook his head, still puzzled. 'Okay, so he's a farmer or farmworker. That helps narrow it down, but there's still a lot of farmland in Essex to check.'

Burrows had an irritatingly superior smirk on his face. 'Actually, it's better than that. We checked in the reference books, and this particular variety is actually part of an experimental batch of genetically modified plants.'

'Genetically modified?'

'They've had a DNA sequence artificially spliced into them that's supposed to make them resistant to frost and snow. Good thing, given last winter. And that—'

In an attempt to actually get control of the conversation back from Burrows, Lapslie interrupted, saying:

'Okay, so what you're going to tell me is either that a British company based in Essex is marketing the wheat across the UK, or that a company based somewhere in the UK has sold this wheat to a farm, or a number of farms, in Essex, yes?'

'One or the other,' Burrows replied with a trace of sulkiness. 'We're still trying to find out.'

'Well, let me know when you do.' Lapslie got up and reached for his coat. 'Oh, and happy birthday.'

Back at Chelmsford Police HQ, Lapslie heard someone call his name in the car park. 'Yes?' he snapped.

'Boss?' It was Emma Bradbury.

'Emma. Sorry – I was expecting it to be someone else.'

'I'm guessing Chief Superintendent Rouse, judging by your tone of voice.'

'You're right, which means it wasn't a guess, it was a deduction. You'll never make inspector if you don't understand the difference a word can make. Did you manage to grab some sleep?'

'A couple of hours. I'm feeling better now.'

'So – what's up?'

'Well, firstly you asked me to check up on where Stephen Stottart and his daughter were at the time Catriona Dooley's body was dumped at the kids' play area.'

'Go on – amaze me,' he growled.

'Turns out the father was rehearsing. He's in a band – a load of middle-aged men getting together to relive their youth and pretend they're fifteen. "Weekend Warriors", I think you'd call them.'

He felt his heart sink like a stone. Yes another potential lead cut off.

'He's in a band?'

'Plays bass guitar, apparently.'

'What do they call themselves?'

There was a pause, as Emma consulted her notes. '"Blue Croak", apparently.'

Lapslie laughed.

'What?'

'It's a reference to the title of a book about synaesthesia,' he explained. 'The Frog Who Croaked Blue, by a guy called Jamie Ward. Must have been Stephen Stottart's idea.' He shook his head. 'The murder victims are singers, the church is strung up with piano wire and Stottart's a wannabe rock star. This must be making sense, but I can't see how.' He took a breath. 'What about the daughter?'

'She plays on the school netball team. They had a match that evening. She was definitely there.'

'Okay. This is all very depressing. What else can you say to ruin my day?'

'Well, just a couple of things. First, I've checked with

the firm who run that BeBo thing, and after a bit of prompting they confirmed that Tamara was using the site at round about the time she said she was.'

'Round about the time?'

'I got lost in the explanation. Something to do with "internet time" versus "real time", and the lag in messages going around the world.'

'Great. And secondly?'

'Secondly, I've been back over the files, like you asked me to.'

'Yeah?'

She paused before continuing. 'You're not going to believe this. I'm not sure *I* believe this, but I reckon there are another six missing people out there who connect to our case. Cas*es*.'

'*Six?*' Lapslie was stunned.

'Six people aged between sixteen and forty who have good singing voices and who have disappeared in Essex in the past six months with no obvious explanation or suspects. Each of them was either in a choir or a band or sang solo in a professional or semi-professional capacity. We've got a gospel singer, a cabaret artiste and a member of the chorus at the Royal Opera House, as well as two lead vocalists with jazz groups and a singing teacher. One soprano, two altos, a tenor, a counter-tenor and a bass. Not in the same order, obviously.'

'*Six?*' He still couldn't believe it. 'I asked you to check as a long shot, and I expected one or two, if any, but not this. My God, what's he *doing* with them?'

'Apart from preparing an entry for the Eurovision Song Contest, you mean?'

'Emma!'

'Sorry, boss.' She looked contrite. 'The surrealism of the situation is getting to me.'

'He's *auditioning*! That's why Catriona Dooley and the other two were discarded. For some reason, they failed the audition.'

'But the torture? The skewers and the ripping apart of the arm and the running through the wires? What's that got to do with an audition?'

Lapslie's brain was spinning. 'That's part of it, somehow. The torture is an integral part of the audition process.' He felt a chill running up his neck and across his scalp as his brain caught up with what was going on. 'There's potentially six kidnap victims still out there. Still *alive*! We need to pull all the information together into one incident team. I'll brief Rouse. You get us some real estate. Move!'

CHAPTER TWELVE

'I want you to follow up this genetically engineered wheat angle,' Lapslie snapped.

'What are you going to do?' Emma asked him. The Essex Police HQ building loomed above them both. Cars drove past, their drivers looking for non-existent parking spaces.

'I need to notify Rouse that we've got a multiple kidnap and multiple murder case on our hands. He's going to require some convincing that this is all connected. I know what he's like. Then I'm going to go and see Jane Catherall and get her to compare the autopsy reports on the three other dead bodies you picked up on. Now we know they're part of a larger case there might be some similarities, some connections she can make.'

He was looking tired. There were grainy shadows under his eyes, and he kept running his hand through his hair. Emma didn't think she'd ever seem him this distracted.

'What's the matter, boss?' she asked.

He glanced at her with irritation. 'We need to find out where the killer might have picked up genetically modified wheat and tracked it into the church where Catriona Dooley was killed.'

'Yeah, that bit I know. What I meant was: what's the matter with *you*? Is your medication causing side-effects?'

He shook his head. 'No. I'm just ... It's Rouse. He's told me there's an Independent Police Complaints Commission investigation started against me.'

'That's bollocks!' Emma said, amazed. 'What for?'

'For the questioning of Tamara Stottart. The father reckons I was too heavy-handed. He's raised a complaint.'

Emma cast her mind back to the interview, trying to remember what had happened. 'He's trying it on. Angling for some kind of compensation.'

'Yeah, but how many decent officers do you know whose careers have been ruined by a baseless accusation from a member of the public? It's too easy for them.'

'Agreed. Let me know if there's anything I can do to help.'

He grimaced. 'I'm sure they'll want to talk to you. You were there, weren't you?'

'Anything you'd like me to say, or not to say?'

He shook his head. 'Just tell them what happened. That's what I'm going to do.'

Emma resisted the urge to reach out and put a reassuring hand on his arm. 'Listening to some of the stories that Dom's told me about actual things you've done,' she said, 'it would be a tragedy if you were brought down by a spurious complaint from an irritated parent.'

He glanced warily at her. 'What kind of stories?' he asked.

'Well, to hear the way he talks, there wasn't a lot to choose between the police and the criminals back in the 1980s, apart from which side you were on. It was like a game.'

'We did what we had to do to get a result,' he admitted. 'As A. E. Housman said: "Let God and man decree / Laws for themselves and not for me."' He shrugged. 'Some of the guys took it too far. As far as most of us were concerned, getting a result meant arresting the guilty party, even if we had to do something . . . unorthodox to make it stick. There was always a minority for whom getting a result meant arresting anybody at all, as long as the evidence could be twisted to match. I could never be a part of that. As far as I'm aware, everyone I ever arrested needed to be arrested.'

Emma nodded. 'Dom once told me,' she said cautiously, 'that he'd heard you were after a paedophile, back when he first knew you. A really nasty one. Did some things to kids that left them . . . physically wrecked, not just psychologically injured. He said you were just about to arrest this guy when he skipped across the Channel to a cottage he had in France, knowing that it would take you months, if not years, to get the extradition paperwork done, and even then there was a strong chance it would get turned down. So he said you hired an actor who looked like this guy, and set him up in a flat in Barking, and told him to be as obvious as he could. Get seen in the pubs and the shops locally. And you waited for a couple of weeks, then went across on the ferry to France with a couple of friends. You took this guy from his cottage while he was asleep and drove him back to the ferry, and you told him that if he said a single word to the gendarmes or the customs people at Cherbourg you would cut his balls off. And he said, "You can't take me back – I'm living in France now! You need extradition papers!" And you said; "No you're not – you're living in a flat in Barking, and we can prove it. And the great thing about Barking is that I don't have to get extradition papers."'

Lapslie's face creased into an unintended smile, the kind you get when you're reminded of a happy memory. 'He kept telling anyone who'd listen that we'd taken him all the way from France back to England, but he couldn't prove it, and we had piles of surveillance photos of the actor we'd hired reading newspapers with obvious headlines in the park. Nobody believed him. Not the barristers, not the solicitors, not the journalists and certainly not the Crown Prosecution Service. He was sent down for twenty years, and I don't regret what I did for a moment. He needed to be put away before he hurt anyone else. Some of those kids … they couldn't even shit properly afterwards, because of what he'd done. They had to have surgery to repair the damage. I've always taken the position that it's easier to seek forgiveness afterwards than to seek permission beforehand, and if you can avoid having to seek forgiveness then that's best of all.' He glanced over at her. 'Probably best you don't repeat that story,' he said mildly.

'Worried he'll get out on appeal?'

'No – he died in prison a few years into his sentence,' Lapslie said levelly. 'He was anally raped with a length of scaffolding pole by an inmate who found out that he had a history of hurting kids. Died of blood loss and shock. No, it's just that times have changed. Some people just wouldn't understand that story.'

'Okay.' Emma started to turn away, then looked back at him. 'I don't suppose it was you that told the other inmates that he was a paedophile?'

'I didn't tell them anything,' Lapslie replied.

Emma walked away, leaving Lapslie behind her. As she went, he was already making a phone call. Sometimes she just didn't know what to make of him. There was a part of him that was so strict about enforcing the rules, and another part which refused to acknowledge that the rules applied to him at all. It was a dangerous combination. It made him one of the best police officers she'd ever worked with, but he was only a step away from being one of the worst. Perhaps it was just a matter of perspective.

For a while Emma wasn't even sure where she was going. Lapslie had asked her to check into genetically engineered wheat, but how? Where? After she'd spent a few minutes in the car debating whether to head for the nearest library and spend the rest of the day with her head buried in books, it occurred to her that Essex University was bound to have a biology department, and they were bound to have someone who would know about genetically engineered wheat.

She drove out to the university campus, parked in a car park that seemed full of cars too expensive for students to own, and followed the signs to the Biology Department. Once there she asked a passing student with a little patch of beard just below his lower lip and nowhere else, who was the best person to talk to about genetically modified food. He directed her to an office with a sign on the door saying 'Professor Peter Wilkinson'.

Professor Wilkinson was sitting behind a desk reading

a report. Despite her preconceptions, he wasn't wearing a corduroy jacket and he didn't have a beard. He was about Emma's age, and wore jeans and a T-shirt that showed off a muscled abdomen. She guessed, from the relative width of his shoulders and the narrowness of his hips, that he was a swimmer, and a very good one. She felt herself flushing slightly as she introduced herself. He probably drove the female students wild. And some of the male ones as well.

'Hi,' she said hurriedly, 'I'm Detective Sergeant Emma Bradbury, Essex Police. I need some professional advice about genetically engineered wheat for a case I'm working on. Are you the right person to speak to, and do you have a few minutes?'

'Yes and yes,' he said, smiling. 'I lecture here on genetic engineering. Sit down. Can I get you a coffee?'

She shook her head. 'Thanks, but no. Time's pressing.'

'Okay.' He frowned. 'Is this about the protests? Because if it is, you need to know that I'm providing consultancy services to Greenpeace.'

'Protests?'

'A camp has been set up next to a field where genetically modified wheat is being grown. There have been some alleged incidents of vandalism, as well as harassment of the protestors by security guards working for the company who provided the wheat.'

'Interesting that the vandalism is alleged while the harassment is apparently real,' Emma pointed out.

He had the grace to smile. 'Fair point. You can see where my sympathies lie.'

'Actually, we've found traces of GM wheat at a crime scene. I'm trying to determine how it might have got there.'

'Okay.' He paused, obviously trying to compress all his knowledge and experience down into a few well-chosen sentences. 'I won't ask you about the case, but what do you know about genetically modified food in general?'

She shrugged. 'I know what's been on the Channel 4 news and in the papers. Some people say that it's the solution to world hunger; other people say it's dangerous. More than that, I'm not sure.'

'Do you know how the modifications are done?'

'Altering the DNA . . .?' she ventured hopefully.

He smiled tolerantly. 'Okay. Let me give you the condensed lecture version. Genetically modified foods are foods which are created using genetically modified plants or animals as ingredients. Let's call them "organisms". Genetically modified organisms have had specific changes introduced into their DNA. You're familiar with DNA, obviously?'

'The genetic blueprint.'

'Yes. It's the complex molecule found in the nucleus of every cell that describes and defines what the animal is: what it looks like and how it is put together. It's the plan, the knitting pattern, the music score, whatever you like to call it. There's actually no direct equivalent, but calling it the blueprint of life is probably as good as anything. It's the thing that the organism uses to build itself.'

He stood up, and started to walk back and forth across the office. Emma smiled at the way he so quickly slipped into lecturing mode.

'There are various ways that DNA can get altered,' he continued. 'It can happen by mutation, for instance, where a bit of the molecule is changed by radiation, or by chemical action. This is pretty hit-and-miss, of course. Most of the changes made to DNA by radiation or by chemical action are just random damage which cause whatever creature is built from it to not work properly – like a building blueprint where the concrete stairs have been rubbed out and replaced with slides made of peanut butter – but every now and then the DNA is changed in a way that makes it work better.'

'Can you give me an example?'

'Okay. Some ten thousand years ago, for instance, one particular person in northern Europe had their DNA accidentally mutated by stray radiation from the sun in a way that meant their digestive systems produced new proteins that could digest lactose. Up until then, drinking cows' milk would cause people to have digestive problems. We just weren't built for it. The mutation spread rapidly, because it helped people to survive in the cold northern latitudes if they had something else to eat when the crops were frozen in the ground and game animals were scarce. Now it's spread over a large chunk of the world, with the exception of Asia, to the point where it's generally assumed that humans have always been able to tolerate lactose—'

'And that's evolution,' Emma interrupted. 'Happy with that.'

'That is indeed evolution. And it takes time. A lot of time. Lots of bad or meaningless mutations have to occur before a useful one does. But humans, in their infinite wisdom, have found ways of increasing the odds that a beneficial mutation will occur. The earliest, of course, was selective breeding, which is really just speeded-up evolution. If an animal or a plant shows signs of something useful, breed from it and prevent the others from breeding, and pretty soon it will spread. More recently, we've been able to actually get into the DNA itself using processes like cisgenesis or transgenesis. With me so far?'

'I was until the last few words,' she said.

'Stay with me. These are ways of introducing a new gene into a living organism so that the organism will exhibit a new property and transmit that property to its offspring.'

'Okay, stop. A gene?'

'A gene is a portion of DNA that contains both "coding" sequences and "non-coding" sequences. The "coding sequences" are the bits that determine when the gene is active. The "non-coding sequences" are the bits that determine what the gene actually does. A gene is like a self-contained little unit of DNA. A piece of the blueprint that can be built in isolation.'

'And introducing these genes into other living organisms: does that work?'

'Oh yes. Transgenic and cisgenic organisms are able to express, or use, the foreign genes that have been introduced into their DNA because the genetic code is similar for all organisms. Although they're all built using different plans, different DNA, the plans are all written in the same language. This means that a specific DNA sequence will do the same thing in all organisms.' Seeing her sceptical expression, he went on: 'For instance, there's a specific protein called the green fluorescent protein, or GFP. Unsurprisingly, it exhibits bright green fluorescence when exposed to blue light. It was first isolated from a particular type of jellyfish. The gene that

causes the jellyfish to produce the GFP has been introduced into other animals as a kind of proof-of-concept
that a gene can be expressed throughout a given
organism. There's a fluorescent rabbit that was created
partly as a work of art and partly as a talking point for
social commentary. A US company markets green fluorescent mice to the pet industry. And green fluorescent
pigs have been created in Taiwan.'

'And this doesn't hurt the animals?' Emma asked,
aghast.

'Apparently not. They go about their business uncon-
cerned.'

'I'm probably going to regret this, but how does this
transgenesis work? How do you move genes around and
splice them in wherever you want?'

'There's a number of ways. In ballistic DNA injection,
for instance, genes are fired at a sample of target tissue.'

'Fired? Like, from a gun?'

He laughed. 'Trust a policeman to think of that. No,
the genes are coated onto gold or tungsten particles
which are then accelerated by an electrical field until
they reach sufficient velocity to cross a gap and hit the
target tissue, where they embed themselves.'

It sounded less like science and more like a fairground
to Emma. 'All pretty hit and miss, isn't it? And what
about the others?'

'Pronuclear injection involves the injection of fragments of DNA into a fertilised embryo at the pro-nuclear stage. The fragments become incorporated into the genome of the embryo. Plasmid vectors are little circular loops of DNA that can become integrated into a larger DNA molecule . . . I could go on.'

'Please don't.' She took a breath. 'I'm with you on the mechanisms for genetic engineering. What about the genetically modified food itself?'

'GM foods were first put on the market in the early 1990s,' he said. 'Typically, genetically modified foods are the products of transgenic plants like soybean, corn, canola, and cotton seed oil – plants which have had genes added to give them resistance against weedkillers, or to make them less attractive to insects that might otherwise eat them. But animal products have also been developed. A few years ago a pig was genetically engineered to produce omega-3 fatty acids. The way it was done was to snip out a section of DNA from a roundworm that is known to produce omega-3 fatty acids and introduce that section into the pig's DNA. The pig goes on being a pig, because none of its original DNA has been removed – the plan to build a pig is still intact – but another page has been added to the plan. It's a pig-plus.'

'But is it still a pig?' Emma asked. 'It's all very well

to say that the pig plan hasn't changed, but if I have a plan for a garden shed, and I add on a bell-tower, the building is still there but the centre of gravity has shifted upwards. It's going to be more unstable in high winds and earthquakes.'

He nodded approvingly. 'Well done. It takes some of my students weeks to spot that flaw in the argument. Yes, adding genes onto an existing length of DNA might affect the way it operates. That's one of the main objections to the widespread use of genetically modi-fied foods.'

'But the GM organism can be tested, surely? There are ways of checking that the pig is still a pig?'

'Yes-ish.' He shrugged. 'Just by splicing a section of DNA into a larger DNA sequence, you're moving the bits that are already there further apart. This might mean that particular proteins that were previously made correctly might now be made wrongly. This might not affect the animal or plant directly, but might affect whoever eats it. Or, worse, only affects them if some-thing else happens – maybe if another protein is intro-duced from somewhere else and the two react with each other. You just can't easily test for that kind of thing.'

'Hence the protesters.'

'Hence the protesters. They're campaigning about fields of genetically modified wheat that have been planted in Essex as part of a research project. The company conducting the research – Tolla Limited – say they need to grow the genetically modified wheat in real-world conditions so they can harvest it, make it into food products, feed it to various animals and then check the health of the animals generation after generation against a control group that hasn't eaten the GM foodstuff. The protesters say that it's too dangerous to grow the GM wheat under real-world conditions, because pollen might get picked up by the wind and spread to unmodified wheat in neighbouring fields where it could reproduce and spread. The company says in response that the gene they've introduced isn't expressed in the pollen. The protesters say that this is irrelevant, because the gene they have introduced might have an indirect effect on the production of pollen, just because it's moved existing parts of the DNA further apart. And so it goes on.'

'I presume the company have records of where these fields are?'

'Yes, and they've got monitoring stations set up around the area to check the drift of the pollen. They've also made sure none of the fields is anywhere near existing wheat fields, so even if the pollen drifts it shouldn't contaminate anything, but this is an inexact science. The fields are surrounded by fallow fields or fields growing something that doesn't interact with wheat pollen – cabbages, potatoes, that kind of thing.'

Emma tried to pick the bones out of what Professor Wilkinson had said. 'There's no easy answer, is there?' she said eventually. 'The ways of getting genes into DNA seem pretty rough and ready, and even to me the research into the long-term effects of eating the food made from the GM organisms is not as comprehensive as it should be, but I can't really see how it can be improved. And going back isn't an option. We can't pretend that genetic modification hasn't been invented, and we obviously need it to improve food yields to feed starving nations.'

'And that, in a nutshell, is a ten-week course on GM foods,' the professor said. 'Congratulations – by realising that there is actually no way ahead you've passed the course.'

'Really?'

'Well, there is a whole lecture about the idea of owner-ship – if you snip a piece of DNA into an existing wheat genome, does that mean you've invented a new type of wheat and should get paid by anybody who uses it?'

'What kind of percentage of the DNA are we talking about?'

'Minuscule. Less than one per cent. Much less.'

'Then no. If you make that small a change, you

shouldn't own it. It's like putting new tyres on a Toyota Prius and claiming you've built a whole new type of car.'

'With the proviso,' he pointed out, 'that the change you've made has cost you a lot of money, and will arguably provide a huge benefit to the grower of the plant, or whatever it is. If you don't get some kind of reward or recompense, then why would you do it in the first place?'

'Ah,' she said.

'So, not a distinction, then. Let's call it a good pass and have done with it.'

'Professor Wilkinson, you've been very helpful.'

'Peter, please. And it's nothing.'

'I don't suppose you have a map showing the locations of the fields where Tolla Limited are growing this genetically modified wheat?'

'I do.' He smiled. 'I probably shouldn't, but I do. Would you like a copy?'

'Please.'

He moved his computer mouse and clicked a couple of times. A printer on the far side of the office whirred into life, spitting out several sheets of paper.

'The information you need is there, along with the address of the Essex branch of Tolla Limited.' She flashed him a bright smile. 'Thanks.'

'If you really want to thank me,' he said, 'you could let me buy you a coffee.'

'Best not to,' she said reluctantly.

The smile faded from his face. 'Jealous boyfriend? I'm not worried.'

'You should be,' she said. 'You really should be.'

Driving away from the Essex University campus, Emma found herself regretting the polite brush-off she'd given him. He was devastatingly good looking, after all. But she was with Dom, for better or for worse, and she had a dark feeling that she would not be the one who was allowed to call the relationship off.

Perhaps she should have listened to Lapslie's warnings.

But then, by the time he had found out about her and Dom McGinley, it was already too late. She was in too deep.

Her mobile rang while she was driving. She clicked the Bluetooth button on the dashboard.

'Hello?'

'Detective Sergeant Emma Bradbury?' a voice asked.

'Yes. Who is this?'

'This is James Grimshawe, from the Independent Police Complaints Commission.' The voice was cultured, polite and had a tone buried within it that suggested its owner was used to getting his own way. 'Are you free to talk?'

'I'm driving at the moment.'

'I won't take up more than a few seconds of your time. I just wanted to arrange a time and place where I can interview you.'

She felt her heart sink. 'Can I ask what this is about?' she asked, although she already knew.

'Of course,' the voice said. 'We're investigating a complaint that has been raised concerning Detective Chief Inspector Mark Lapslie. I believe you know him.'

'I do.'

'And you were present at an interview he held recently with a girl named Tamara Stottart.'

'Has the interview already started?'

He laughed. 'Not yet. I just need to know that I have the right person.'

'Yes, I was at the interview, and yes, I know Mark Lapslie.'

'Then shall we say ten o'clock tomorrow? I can come to you. I believe you're working out of Canvey Island at the moment.'

She was just about to tell him that she was on a case and couldn't tell whether she'd be free at the time he wanted, or at any time if it came to that, and that the focus of the investigation had moved away from Canvey Island, but she stopped herself. If she could drag this Grimshawe away from wherever Lapslie happened to be then she might be doing her boss a favour. 'Yes, Canvey Island Police Station at ten o'clock tomorrow.' She paused, then added innocently, 'Shall I get you booked in at the front desk?'

'No need,' Grimshawe said with a trace of amusement in his voice. 'I can get in to any police station I need to. I'll see you tomorrow, then.'

'Looking forward to it,' Emma replied, but he'd already broken the connection and she was talking to dead air.

She parked her car back at Chelmsford Police HQ and went in search of Lapslie. She found him in the centre of a large, empty, open-plan room.

'I like your new office,' she said. 'It's bigger than Rouse's, isn't it?'

'Much bigger. Sadly, it's only mine until we solve the case.'

'He accepted that the murders and the kidnappings were linked?'

Lapslie nodded. 'It took a bit of doing, but he's behind us on this one. He's given us an incident room here, plus all the staff we need. And he's made it clear that if the IPCC investigation finds that I was too heavy-handed on Tamara Stottart in any way then he will personally pull me off and replace me with Dain Morritt.'

'Then let's make sure the investigation clears you.'

She took a breath. 'They want to talk to me tomorrow. At Canvey Island.'

'Good,' Lapslie said. 'That'll give you a chance to close things down there and bring all the paperwork and maps and stuff here. Oh, and the computers as well.'

'I'll rent a van,' Emma murmured.

'And I'm having Sergeant Murrell reassigned temporarily to us. He seemed competent.'

'I agree,' Emma said, wondering why it always seemed that she was a step behind Lapslie, rather than by his side or even, God help her, a step ahead.

'Let's think about it as a whole, rather than as a load of individual parts,' he said suddenly. 'Is there some commonality in the way the people disappeared? Something that all the kidnappings share that might direct us to the perpetrator?'

Emma considered the question. 'I've had all the files sent through,' she said, trying to remember the details. 'Lorraine Gregory was taken while walking back to her digs after a band rehearsal. She fronted a jazz-fusion band, and her walk back took her along an unlit canal towpath. The suspicion was that someone came up to her from behind, knocked her out and then dragged her to a car, but there's no evidence.'

'Any bruising to suggest she'd been knocked out?'

'No, but there were no traces of chloroform or anything similar in the blood or the lungs.'

'Fair enough,' he said moodily. 'What about the next one?'

'Alison Traff. She disappeared after filling her car up at a petrol station after spending a couple of hours at choir practice. Her car was found abandoned by the side of the road in an area that barely sees two cars an hour.'

'So we know the abductor and murderer chooses his location carefully. He obvious reconnoitres beforehand, and finds locations where he won't be disturbed.'

'There were no signs that her car had been forced off the road – no swerving tyre tracks or skid marks. She'd just slowed to a stop and vanished.'

'The abductor lay in the road, looking like a jogger who'd collapsed, waiting for her to come along?' Lapslie guessed.

'How did he know it would be her?'

'Maybe he followed her in his car from the church hall, then accelerated past her and drove up the road, parked out of sight then quickly lay down. If it wasn't her who stopped then he could just stage a miraculous recovery and leave. But it was her.' Seeing her sceptical expression, he went on: 'Or he overtook her, pulled over a few miles down the road and raised the bonnet of his car as if he'd had a breakdown, then flagged her down as she drove up.'

Emma felt her face settle into even more sceptical lines. 'Hey. I do Tae Kwon Do but I wouldn't stop at night for a man with a broken-down car. Too risky.'

'Maybe it wasn't a man,' Lapslie pointed out.

'What, Tamara Stottart again? It wasn't her, boss. She's fourteen. She can't drive. How would she get to all of these locations by herself?'

He sighed. 'Fair enough.'

'You just want it to be her.'

'She's got something to do with it. Mark my words. She knows something.'

Emma considered for a moment. 'Then what about the third victim? David Cave? A bit of a hard man, by all accounts. I can't imagine a fourteen-year-old girl subduing him. Not even with chloroform.'

'What's the story there? How did he disappear?'

'He'd been playing snooker at a late-night club. Left at three o'clock in the morning. Twenty-minute walk, but he never made it home. Somewhere along the line, he vanished.'

'What was that stuff the Russian Special Forces used in the Moscow theatre siege?' Lapslie asked.

'Dunno. Some kind of veterinary thing, I think. I'll find out.'

'Could have been that,' Lapslie continued, 'or he could have been bashed over the head with a baseball bat and shoved into a car. Any signs of damage to the corpse?'

Emma shuddered. 'There were sufficient signs of damage to the corpse to obscure almost anything that might have knocked him out, according to the autopsy. He really was messed around with.'

'And that brings us to Catriona Dooley.'

'Returning from a night out with the girls. At some point between getting off the bus and her parents' house, she disappeared.'

'Again, the attack from behind with the chloroform pad seems the most likely means.'

Emma nodded. 'Which takes us to where? All the attacks took place at night—'

'—implying that the abductor either lives alone or has reason to be out of the house after dark without anyone being suspicious—'

'—and occurred as far as we can tell in badly lit locations—'

'—suggesting a degree of prior reconnaissance—'

'—with the probable use of an anaesthetic of some kind—'

'—indicating some chemical knowledge on the part of the kidnapper, along perhaps with some physical weakness which means he had to subdue them quickly—'

'—following which captor and victim vanished into the night—'

'—which tells us that he has a car.' Lapslie snorted explosively. 'We've got nothing!'

A uniformed constable entered the bare room and walked up to Lapslie. He handed over a sheet of paper. Lapslie scanned it quickly, then again more slowly. He rubbed his chin, considering, then nodded at the constable. 'Okay, tell them we'll be there right away. And tell them that I'm the senior investigating officer. Make sure they understand that although their investigation is already under way, they're reporting to *me* now.'

The constable nodded and left. Emma frowned up at Lapslie.

'What's happened?'

He was gazing straight ahead, out of the windows. 'It's happened again,' he whispered. 'A family, this time. An entire family. Father, mother and two sons, all abducted from their house in Loughton last night. The police were alerted by the cleaner this morning. She found the dog dead in the kitchen and the family missing.' He seemed to come to a decision. 'Right, let's get over there before the local plod tread dirt all the way through and wipe any fingerprints away with their fat arses as they rest themselves against all the work surfaces. Get Burrows and Catherall down there straight away.'

'Doctor Catherall? I thought you said the family were kidnapped, not killed?'

'They were. I want Jane to take a look at the dog.' At her questioning gaze, he explained: 'It's like that Sherlock Holmes thing – the strange case of the dog in the night time. The strange thing was that the dog didn't bark, suggesting that it knew the criminal. Well, here we have another strange case of a dog in the night time. The strange thing here is that the dog has died, and we don't know why. Not a mark on it.'

'One question, Sir?'

He glanced at her in irritation. 'What? Time's ticking away.'

'How do we even know that this case is connected to ours?'

'Didn't I say?' He swung back. 'They're a folk group evenings and weekends. They call themselves the Singing Baillies.'

CHAPTER THIRTEEN

The Baillie house was located at the end of a narrow and winding road in the area of Loughton known locally as Little Cornwall. The drive through the town took Lapslie and Emma up and down steep hills and past weatherboard houses, along narrow lanes and past high holly hedges, as well as occasional outthrusts of the nearby brooding mass of Epping Forest. It also took them past Loughton Underground station, which was over-ground at this point. The station was located four stops from the end of the Central Line and a reminder that despite the ever-present trees and the bushes they were less than fifteen miles from the centre of London. Every now and then, as they crested another hill, Lapslie could see past the houses and across the tops of the forest: a sea of bubbling green canopies.

The house was huge: two wings either side of a central block, the whole thing a relic of the Victorian era updated with a satellite dish on the roof and a garage off to one side. Creepers covered most of the sides. The house sat in its own small grounds, walled around and connected to the road by a short gravel drive. The gravel crunched under Lapslie's wheels as he brought the car to a halt in front of the main portico, next to a set of other police cars and a CSI van. People were moving back and forth between the vehicles and the house like bees foraging for pollen and then returning to the hive.

'Nice place,' Emma said as she got out of the passenger side. 'I might get Dom to buy me one like this for my birthday.'

Lapslie scowled at her. He knew she was winding him up, but he wasn't in the mood. 'Paid for by the blood money he's obtained as the unjust gains from a hundred armed robberies?'

'He told me he won the lottery,' she said, smiling. 'Numerous times in a row.'

Lapslie didn't reply.

'What's the background here?' she went on when it was clear that Lapslie wasn't going to rise to the bait. 'What does this bloke do for a living?'

'Mark Baillie is an investment banker,' Lapslie replied, remembering the scant facts on the sheet of paper that the constable had brought in to him. 'Works in Canary Wharf for one of the big Japanese clearing houses.

Probably brings home in excess of a million pounds a year, when you factor in bonuses.'

'So could this kidnapping have a financial motive?' Emma asked.

Lapslie shook his head. The thought had occurred to him already, but he'd dismissed it. 'If a ransom had been demanded they'd have taken the wife or the daughter and left the husband. Taking him means there's nobody to organise getting the money to pay the ransom.'

'There's his company,' Emma pointed out.

'But who do you phone if you've taken one of the employees captive and want a ransom? There's no hotline for that. You could try the managing director, but there's scant chance he'll take the call, and all the while you're wasting time telling more and more people what you've done. No, I maintain that a ransom attempt is based on leaving the person who has the money and taking the most precious thing in his world, not the other way around.'

The door opened as Lapslie ran up the front steps. A constable stepped back to let him and Emma in. 'DCI Lapslie?' he asked.

'Yes. Who's in charge here?'

'Er, you are, Sir.'

Lapslie glared at the man. This wasn't the time for

anybody to be funny. 'Who was in charge fifteen seconds ago?'

'Inspector Barnes, Sir.'

'Where is he?'

'Conservatory, last time I looked, Sir.'

Lapslie led the way through the house towards the back, where he guessed the conservatory would be. There was a smell hanging in the air: a sweetish, slightly medicinal odour. He filed that away for later consideration. The paintings on the walls were originals: mainly vibrant abstracts in reds and oranges that looked, from the corner of the eye, like landscapes but which, on closer inspection, were just collections of horizontal and vertical lines. The thick white carpet covering the floor would, Lapslie estimated, have to be vacuumed twice a day to keep it from going grey. The furniture was Swedish in its simplicity, but it certainly wasn't from Ikea.

'Inspector Barnes?'

There were five or six people in the conservatory, but the man who turned around was the smallest. His eyes were set deep on either side of a sharp nose, giving his face a rodent-like appearance. His blond hair was brushed straight back from his forehead.

'DCI Lapslie? Glad to have you here.'

'What have you got?' Lapslie asked.

Barnes indicated the conservatory window behind him. It had a large hole cut in the centre, about the right size for a man to put his arm through. 'All the windows and glass doors in the house are protected with metal foil around the frames. There's a current runs through the foil. If the glass is broken, the electrical current is disrupted and the alarm goes off. Problem is, if you cut a hole in the centre of the glass big enough to get a hand through, like chummy did here with what I reckon was a carborundum-tipped cutter, the electrical current remains undisturbed.'

'Surely that's not the only alarm system?' Lapslie questioned. 'The man was loaded.'

'Indeed,' Barnes said, nodding eagerly. 'There's also sensors on the frames.' He indicated two small boxes on the window: one attached to the window itself and the other, just above it, to the frame. The box attached to the frame had thin wires leading away from it, along the line of the wood. 'The magnet in one of those boxes pulls a contact away from a circuit in the other. If the boxes are separated the contact closes again and the resulting signal sets the alarm off. Except that in this case chummy reached in through the hole he'd cut with the aforementioned carborundum-tipped cutter and introduced a thin magnetic strip between the two boxes. When he then opened the window from the inside the strip stayed attached to the upper box and kept the contact from closing.'

Lapslie sighed. They were dealing with a professional, that much was for sure. Not your bog-standard breaking-and-entering merchant. 'And I'm guessing the locks I can see on the window catches were bypassed with equal ease?'

'There's only so many designs of window catch,' Barnes said, shrugging. 'If you have enough keys, you can usually find one that fits. Even more likely if you've cased the joint beforehand and sussed out the type of locks you're dealing with.'

'Any other invalid security precautions?' Lapslie growled.

Barnes pointed towards a corner of the conservatory, where Lapslie noticed a small white box had been attached to the wall. 'Each room is apparently protected by a passive infra-red sensor which detects body heat. I say "apparently" because a prospective burglar can see the sensors and should be scared off, but in this case the sensors were turned off because the dog had the run of the house. The family only turn the sensors on when they're all on holiday and the dog's either with them or in kennels.'

'Anything else?' Lapslie sighed.

'Just in case he'd set anything off without realising

it, the burglar went straight to the main alarm box and injected it full of liquid nitrogen, freezing all the circuits. He knew he'd have about thirty seconds before an alarm went off, if he *had* tripped one, because that's how long the alarm company usually allow householders to type in their key code, get it wrong and type it again when they get in the house at night.'

'So, what do we learn from that?' Lapslie asked, looking at Emma. She'd been cheeky enough earlier that he wanted to bring her back down to Earth for a while.

'That we're dealing with someone who is methodical and cautious, someone who conducts a detailed reconnaissance before making a move.'

'What leads you to that conclusion?'

'Whoever it was couldn't know about the metal foil in the window frames, because it's not visible after the frame's put together, so he assumed the worst and planned for it. He also came prepared with a glass cutter and a thin magnetic strip, and had worked out that the presence of the dog meant that the passive infra-red sensors would be switched off. Oh, and he must have known exactly where the main alarm box was, because he got to it and neutralised it within thirty seconds. That probably means he's been in the house before, or at least spent time prowling around the outside and looking through the windows. Does that cover it?'

'Pretty much,' he conceded. Turning to Barnes again, he asked; 'What about the family? How did he manage to subdue them?'

'It's looking like an anaesthetic gas,' Barnes replied. 'Like the stuff that thieves use on French caravan sites to rob tourists: they find a caravan parked up then pump gas in through the window to make sure the people are completely knocked out, then go in with face masks and rob them of their cash and jewellery. Here it looks like chummy pumped something similar through the hole in the window and waited for long enough that he could be sure they were all unconscious.'

'What gave away the fact that it was a gas?'

'You heard about the dog?'

Lapslie nodded. 'I heard the dog was found dead.'

'Respiratory failure, it looks like. It just lay down and died. That, and a slightly sweet smell in the air when we arrived, led us to that initial conclusion. We're awaiting forensic tests on the air in the house and the pathologist's view on the dog.' He paused, shaking his head. 'Had to send one of my constables home earlier. Whatever the stuff is, there was enough of it lingering around to make him feel woozy.'

'And the entire family were taken. How the hell did the kidnapper get them all out?'

'No,' Barnes said simply.

Lapslie wasn't sure he'd heard properly. 'No what?'

'No, the entire family weren't taken. One of them was left behind.'

Lapslie was aghast. 'Which one?'

'The daughter. Still asleep upstairs when we arrived.'

'Let me get this straight – the husband, wife and two sons were kidnapped, but the daughter was left behind?'

Barnes nodded. 'That's right.'

'But why?'

'Don't know. Maybe he didn't have time to carry her to the car after taking the other four. Maybe he just didn't like the look of her. Maybe ...' He trailed off. 'Actually, I don't know. I really don't know.'

'Where's the girl now?' Emma asked.

'She's been taken to hospital for a check-up, just to make sure there's no health problems from breathing in the anaesthetic. Social Services will look after her until we find her parents. *If* we find her parents.'

'We will,' Lapslie promised. And he meant it. 'You'll be questioning her? See whether she saw anything or heard anything?'

'I'll make sure she's interviewed when the doctors say we can. Unless you want to talk to her instead?'

Lapslie shook his head. Given what was happening with the IPCC, it probably wasn't a good move for him to question another vulnerable girl just yet. 'Thanks, but I'll let you cover that. Forensics here?'

'Yes. And we're moving the dog's body to the mortuary. I must admit, I don't know whether there's a special pet pathologist, or whether the normal pathologist can handle it.'

'Oh, I think she'll enjoy the challenge,' Lapslie murmured.

He glanced at his watch. Just shy of five o'clock. 'Can I leave you to liaise?' he asked Emma. 'I have somewhere I need to be. It looks like we're dependent on the CSIs for the time being to process the scene. Do all the usual things: set up a tap on the home phone and so on, but I really don't expect a ransom demand. Then go and get some sleep.'

She nodded. 'Leave it to me. You go and enjoy yourself.'

He raised an eyebrow at her. 'Sarcastic?'

'Not at all. It's nice to be able to do something for myself rather than stand behind you and watch you do it.'

Rather than reply, he just nodded and left.

It was dark when he got to Charlotte's flat.

'Don't take your jacket off,' she said as she opened the door. 'We're going out.'

'What do you mean?' he asked.

'It will all become clear.' She smiled quizzically at him. 'For a man who spends his life conducting interrogations, you're surprisingly slow on the uptake when it comes to assimilating information.'

'We don't call them "interrogations",' he said mildly. 'We call them "interviews". "Interrogations" usually implies thumbscrews and pliers, and that's an image we're keen not to encourage.'

'Well, tonight there's not going to be any interrogations *or* interviews. There's going to be some conversation and some listening.'

'Don't I even get a chance to wash my face and change my shirt?' he asked. 'I've been wearing this one all day, and it's getting a bit old.'

She raised an eyebrow. 'You've been sneaking flannels and spare shirts into my flat while I haven't been paying attention?'

'Given the amount of time you spend here compared with the time you spend on the ward, I could sublet the place and you'd hardly even notice.'

She hit him playfully on the chest. 'You're wasting time. Brush your teeth and change your shirt if you need to. You've got ten minutes.'

Ten minutes later they were in her car – a black Lexus that gave Lapslie a slight shiver whenever he saw it, remembering the men from the Home Office who had spent time shadowing him on the Madeleine Poel case – and heading towards London.

'How was your day?' she asked as she drove.

'Could have been worse,' he said non-committally

'In medical terms,' she said, eyes on the road, 'any medical result other than death could be described that way. Amputations, brain damage, disfigurement – "could have been worse".'

'In this case, I've got a kidnapped family of four and a daughter left abandoned in the house. But none of them is dead so, yes, it could have been worse.' He paused, thinking. 'And, if we don't get a break soon, it still might.'

The car drove onwards, into the night. As they crossed the M25, Lapslie assumed that they were heading towards Central London. A restaurant? A gala event? What?

'Can I ask a question?' he said as she drove.

'You just did.'

He took a deep breath. 'Funny girl.'

She smiled and squeezed his hand. 'You've got out of the habit of relationships, haven't you? I sometimes get the impression when we're talking that it's a series of questions and answers, rather than a conversation.'

Lapslie felt a sudden lurching sensation, like vertigo. 'Is that a problem?' he asked carefully.

'It's something we need to work on,' she said. 'Over time. So – what was the question?'

'You're an anaesthetist. What would you use if you were going to knock out an entire family in their home?'

She thought for a moment. 'Difficult. Calculating the dose is critical to ensuring that you minimise the risk of brain damage or death. I take it you're not asking me as an anaesthetist, but you want to know what an ordinary member of the public might use.'

He nodded. 'I was thinking along the lines of those reports of French criminals gassing people in parked-up motor homes.'

'The commonest narcotic gas available is diethyl ether. You can get it in cold-start sprays for cars – the kind of thing you spray into your engine to help it turn over when the weather's below freezing. You'd want to purify the ether, I guess. The best way I've heard is to take a piece of PVC pipe and a jar, then spray the can down the pipe and into the jar. The propellant gas is expelled and the diethyl ether condenses on the pipe and runs down into the jar. When the entire can is empty you end up with a very high-content diethyl ether solution. There's still some impurities in there, so you add an equal volume of water and shake it, then let it stand for a few minutes. It'll settle out into two layers: pure diethyl ether in the top layer and everything else in the bottom layer. You then take the diethyl ether and introduce it into the house. It vaporizes at around thirty-six degrees centigrade, so surrounding it with hot water would do the trick, and you can use a rubber pipe to direct it into the house.'

'You know your stuff,' Lapslie admitted. 'I didn't realise you had to know how to make your own anaesthetics. I thought you just bought them wholesale.'

She laughed. 'I had some odd friends at medical school. They used to try all kinds of tricks.' She thought for a moment, her face becoming more serious in the head-lights of the oncoming cars. 'The alternative is something like propane. That's not narcotic, but it does replace the oxygen in the air, and effectively suffocates people. The trick is to stop pumping it in before they die. Either way, I wouldn't want to try it myself. Too much risk.'

'Okay.' He let the thoughts coagulate in his brain. 'Thanks.'

The main flow of traffic was heading out of London, not in, and they got to the Thames Embankment within an hour. Charlotte parked in a slot in a car park next to St Thomas's Hospital. 'Medical perk,' she said as he raised an eyebrow.

He'd already guessed that they were heading for the South Bank Centre, and he was right. Charlotte took his hand and guided him through the concrete pathways towards the Festival Hall. She stopped in front of a row of restaurants and bars that ran alongside the Hall, between it and the trains coming off Hungerford Bridge. 'We've got half an hour,' she said, checking her watch. 'Time for a quick bite. You up for it?'

'OK.' He looked along the line. 'Not sure I can choose. I'm still trying to get used to the concept that tasting something can be pleasurable, rather than painful.'

'Then let's go for sushi,' she said. 'It's fast and it's not in-your-face. Or, in your case, in-your-mouth.'

The restaurant was small and basic, and the food was indeed fast, but with little explosions of flavour. On Charlotte's advice he avoided the wasabi sauce, but the slices of vividly fresh fish against the plain rice backdrop were amazing. When she told him it was time to pay up and go, he was disappointed.

She took his hand and led him into the massive bulk of the Festival Hall. He tried to see if there was a poster or a sign advertising what they were about to see, but there were too many posters advertising too many forthcoming events for him to make anything out. Not a theatrical event, not in the Festival Hall. An orchestra? A recital? What? The unexpected anticipation was making him feel tense.

She already had tickets, which she produced from her bag.

'What if I'd been late?' he asked. 'I'm on a case. Things can drag on.'

'Then we'd have missed tonight's event,' she said. 'Things happen. I'm a doctor in a hospital, remember? I work unusual hours too. That's no reason not to plan on going out. If the plan fails, it fails.'

Overcome by a sudden rush of emotion, he pulled her to him and kissed her. She responded, surprised. 'What was that for?'

'For reminding me that life should be lived, not endured.'

She stopped at a kiosk to buy a programme, and then they entered the hall itself, which was already nearly full. The sound of hushed conversations would previously have made Lapslie feel like he was drowning in his own blood, but now he could taste nothing apart from the lingering remains of the sushi. Even the nervousness with which he normally faced large crowds was nearly absent.

The tickets put them at the front of the main circle. The stage was bare apart from seven chairs and music stands, a piano, two electronic keyboards and what looked like a couple of xylophones or vibraphones, although Lapslie wasn't sure he'd seen a xylophone since school. Like a recorder, it had always seemed to him to be an instrument designed solely for schoolchildren to use.

'OK,' Charlotte said, leaning towards him so that their heads were touching. 'I'll put you out of your misery. It's a performance of a piece of music called *Music for Airports*, which was written by Brian Eno. It's an example of what's called "ambient music".' She opened her programme. 'It says here that he's described ambient music as being "music that's designed to modify one's perception of the surrounding environment".'

'Ah,' Lapslie said, disappointed. 'Elevator music.'

'Exactly the opposite,' she said, smiling. 'Elevator music is the equivalent of painting everything beige. It's just music to fill a gap. Ambient music is designed to be more like an aural sculpture. You can listen to it, you can ignore it, or you can let your mind shift between the two. There's going to be nothing in the music to offend or surprise the listener, but it shouldn't bore them either.'

'I'll give it a whirl,' he said doubtfully.

'You haven't got a choice. If you try to leave, I'll scream.' She squeezed his arm gently. 'If we're going to get you going out more, we need to ease you gently into the real world. So – no Wagner, no Mahler. Something soft and inoffensive, but still interesting, to start.'

Inoffensive, but still interesting. Okay, he'd have a go.

Before he could ask anything else, the lights dimmed in the auditorium and a group of musicians entered and crossed the stage, to a subdued but still warm round of applause. Without acknowledging the audience, the musicians sat, sorted out their music scores, paused for a moment, and then started to play.

And Lapslie was entranced.

The piano player led the piece, with the keyboards and vibraphones providing accompaniment, but the piano appeared to be playing the same few notes over and over again in different ways rather than an actual melody, while the accompaniment was a background of what appeared to be randomly played notes which melded together to form a rippling surface upon which the piano floated gently. It should have been boring, but it wasn't. Each moment was different from the previous ones, but linked to them. It wasn't so much a musical journey as a musical drift through a fascinating aural landscape. There was no destination in mind, as Lapslie would have expected with most music, no rush to get to the climax, just an appreciation of the moment. Of every moment.

He sneaked a glance at Charlotte. Her eyes were closed and her lips were curved into a secret smile. She was more beautiful than he had ever seen her, and he realised at that moment that, yes, he *did* love her. For years he had been at war with himself, trying to be what he thought Sonia and the rest of his family wanted him to be. Not only did Charlotte want him to be himself; she wanted him to find out what 'himself' actually was. And he wanted to let her.

His mind drifted back to the music. It seemed to be exactly where it had started, and yet at the same time it had moved on to other, mysterious places. In a strange way it wasn't music at all, but highly structured noise. Abstract music, paralleling abstract art. There was no development, but there was a sense that it was building, growing, developing organically.

When the music finally drifted to a close Lapslie found that he had lost all sense of time. It might have been playing for ten minutes or an hour. As the last notes faded away, and just before the audience applauded, he felt a sense of loss. Something beautiful had been present, and it had gone, and he couldn't even put a name to it.

'Let's get a drink,' Charlotte said. She seemed nervous.

He squeezed her hand, and smiled. 'That,' he said, 'was incredible. I've never heard anything like it.'

She gazed up at him. 'Are you sure? We could leave now . . .'

'No, let's stay. What happens next? More of the same?'

'Some more Brian Eno music. I think they're doing his set of variations of Pachelbel's "Canon in D". You'll like it.'

'You know, I think I will.'

They headed out of the auditorium to the bar. Lapslie, uncharacteristically, ordered a glass of red wine. Charlotte had the same.

They moved out onto the terrace, overlooking the Thames. The lights of the distant City of London glittered in the choppy waters. He sipped at his wine. It tasted of summer fruits, vanilla, oak.

Something dark drifted past in the water. The policeman part of Lapslie's brain wondered if it might be a body, but he pushed that to one side. Tonight wasn't the time for him to be a policeman. Tonight was an opportunity for him to see if he could be a complete human being.

He slipped an arm around Charlotte's waist. She nestled against his side and said, 'I'm looking forward to getting you back to my place later on.'

'DCI Lapslie?'

The voice broke into his contemplative state of mind. He recognised it before he turned around.

'Mr Stottart.'

'I thought it was you.' The man's face was flushed. Behind him, Lapslie spotted his daughter, Tamara, along with a woman of about Lapslie's age and a son of about nineteen or twenty. The girl was glaring at Lapslie. Her mother was looking embarrassed, and her brother was looking bored, as all teenage boys did.

Charlotte moved away from Lapslie slightly, straightening up. 'Hi,' she said. 'I don't think we've met. I'm Charlotte. Charlotte Meyer.'

'Steve Stottart. I'm in a therapy workshop with your husband.'

'Partner,' she corrected.

'At least, I thought that was the only contact we had. Turns out he's also been investigating my daughter behind my back. He thinks she's a murderer.'

Behind him, his daughter flushed and turned her head away. Her mother put an arm around her shoulder. She shrugged it off.

'Mr Stottart,' Lapslie said calmly, but with a warning tone in his voice, 'I'm off duty. I can't talk about anything to do with the case.'

'I put in a complaint,' Stottart said. He'd been drinking. It made his Mancunian accent seem thicker.

'I know,' Lapslie said. 'You have that right.'

'Damn straight I do. I hope they *crucify* you. Disrupting our lives like that: it's just gash. Tamara is distraught.'

The word flashed across his mind like a firework fired into the night. *Gash*. The voice on the sound file had said, 'No, that's gash. That's just gash.' Lapslie had presumed the voice was referring disparagingly to the woman who was blundering through the wire maze, slowly bleeding to death. Referring to her in terms of her genitalia. But Steve Stottart had used the word in a different context. Gash, as in wrong. Some kind of northern slang that Lapslie hadn't come across before. But what if the voice on the sound file had meant there was something wrong with the sound of the woman's *voice* – something 'gash'? The fact that the killer and Stephen Stottart had used the same unusual word wasn't evidence that he was involved, but it was indicative of a connection.

'*Dad!*' Tamara Stottart hissed, instantly breaking Lapslie's chain of thought.

'She's got *exams*! If she fails, it's all your fault!'

For some reason, the sheer pathetic nature of Stottart's accusation needled Lapslie. Exams, for God's sake! Lapslie had murders to deal with. Murders and kidnappings!

'Mr Stottart, I've not got time for this,' he snapped. 'Your daughter is a material witness in a murder and kidnapping investigation. She knows something, and both you and she are obstructing my investigation. If you want to raise a complaint, that's up to you, but I'm trying to stop four more murders.'

Stottart's lip curled, and he looked like he was going to say something else, but his wife grabbed hold of his arm and pulled him back. Lapslie turned away too, aware of a heated argument going on within the family.

'That was interesting,' Charlotte said drily. 'You didn't tell me you were under investigation.'

'I'm always under investigation. It comes with the territory.'

'Same if you're a doctor. There are always people who think you're like a plumber, and can fix anything within half an hour. They don't understand that some things can't be fixed, and it's nobody's fault. It just *is*.' She paused. 'Is that girl really a murder suspect?'

'She certainly knows something about a murder: I just don't know what it is. And I have strong suspicions about her father.'

The crowd on the terrace was beginning to thin out, and somewhere in the auditorium a bell rang. 'Let's go back in,' Charlotte suggested.

The remainder of the concert was as endlessly fascinating as the first half, with the keyboards now providing electronic vocals that shifted up and down in a ribbon of sound: never clashing, never discordant, but always moving along the boundary between structure and randomness. Lapslie found that he couldn't focus, however. He kept scanning the audience, looking to see where Stephen Stottart and his family were sitting. The confrontation had unnerved him. He wouldn't have thought that the concert was the kind of thing they would have liked, but a family trip out indicated something more than just casual interest.

At the end, as the performers stood for the applause, Lapslie said: 'Let's go before the encore, if there is one. We've got a bit of a drive ahead of us, and we're both working tomorrow.'

'And you've got a stalker in the audience you want to avoid,' Charlotte pointed out. 'Okay, let's go.'

They spent the walk along the Thames Embankment, past the London Eye and County Hall, with Charlotte telling Lapslie more about Brian Eno and about ambient music in general. She promised to take him to some more upcoming concerts of music by someone called Philip Glass. Apparently he wasn't ambient but minimalist, although Lapslie wasn't sure he could explain the difference to anyone.

Back at Charlotte's maisonette Lapslie was about to make his apologies and leave when she took his hand and, without a word, led him upstairs. They made love with a passion and yet a tenderness that eclipsed anything he'd previously experienced in his life. No direction, no aim, just a growing, developing intensity; an exploration of every moment in time and every square inch of each other's bodies.

Later, lying awake in the darkness with Charlotte's arm around him, he whispered to himself: '". . . And my heart beneath your hand, quieter than a dead man on a bed",' and then shivered.

He must have fallen asleep, although he never actually marked the moment when it happened, because some indeterminate time later he was jerked awake by a woman screaming.

For a moment he thought he was listening to the sound file again. In his half-conscious state he thrashed around, trying to find the controls to turn it off. At the same time he realised that the sound wasn't recorded, but real, he became aware of a light outside, flickering through the curtains.

Charlotte stirred beside him. 'What the hell is that?' she slurred.

Lapslie slid from under the duvet and ran to the window. Regardless of his nakedness, he pulled the curtain back.

Down on the grass outside Charlotte's flat, beside his Saab, a woman was on fire.

CHAPTER FOURTEEN

When Emma screeched up in front of the block of flats it looked like the circus had come to town. A large white tent had been set up, with guy ropes holding it stable, and various cars and vans had been parked in a circle around it. People were moving purposefully to and fro, obviously part of the environment, while other onlookers were held back by cordons from entering the area. But unlike the circus, the people who were working inside the barrier were police and crime scene investigators, not roustabouts, and the people gawping from outside were intrigued locals rather than potential customers.

Emma showed her warrant card to get through the cordon. She could smell the roast-pork odour of burnt human flesh from outside the tent. She had an atavistic urge to turn away now and run, but she overcame her revulsion and kept on going.

She had to flash her warrant card again to get inside

the tent. It had been erected over a patch of grass which had become muddy and flat now because of the traffic of so many feet. The white plastic was lit up by the rising sun outside, making it glow with a directionless effulgence. The air inside the tent was humid as the ground warmed up inside the tent, releasing water vapour which had nowhere to go. Rather than a circus, it now looked and felt more to Emma like somewhere a preacher might have addressed his flock at a revivalist meeting in the American Deep South. The various police constables inside were already sweating. God knew what the CSIs in their white coveralls and hoods and blue plastic gloves were feeling. They were even wearing facemasks, just to add insult to injury.

She saw Lapslie standing just off-centre, beside a huddle of activity. Now that the thought of a revivalist meeting had occurred to her, she saw the huddle as being like the group of supporters you might expect around someone being cured of lameness with a laying-on of hands by a charismatic preacher. At any moment she expected everyone to spring back with a cry of 'Hallelujah!'

Shrugging off the uncomfortable simile, she went across to join Lapslie. He glanced at her, and she was shocked at the evident strain on his face. His eyes looked wary and pained, like those of a hunted animal.

And beside him, at the focus of attention of the various CSIs and forensics experts, was a patch of scorched grass with a collection of charred branches and a burned tree trunk in the centre. Except that they weren't branches: they were limbs, and the tree trunk was a torso, with a cracked and blackened skull on top.

No revivalist preacher was going to bring this body back from the dead, no matter how charismatic they were.

'What happened?' she asked in a hushed voice. 'And why are we here? This isn't a part of our case, is it?'

'That block of flats is where my ... girlfriend lives,' Lapslie said quietly, obviously stumbling over the word 'girlfriend'. 'I saw flames. I looked out of the window and there was a woman down here. She was on fire.' His eyes were fixed now not on what was in front of him, but what was in the past. 'She was looking straight up at me. I swear she was looking straight up at Charlotte's window.'

'Coincidence,' Emma said forcefully. Lapslie looked like he was on the verge of coming apart. 'Sheer coincidence. It was some Asian girl forced into an arranged marriage who set herself on fire. It always is. We'll find out that her husband, or her family, live somewhere in this block, and she was staring up at *them*, not you.'

'She held her arms away from her body,' he whispered

as if he hadn't heard her. 'Like she was appealing to me.' He shuddered. 'I phoned for an ambulance. We got down here just as the crowd was gathering. Charlotte started treating her, but it was too late.'

'Where is Charlotte?'

'Gone to clean up and get properly dressed.'

A thought struck Emma. 'You didn't see anyone else here, did you? Someone running away? I mean, I'm presuming this was a suicide, not murder by arson.'

He shook his head, more to rid himself of the memories of what he'd seen than to answer her question. 'Just her,' he said eventually. 'Just her.'

'Sir?' One of the constables approached them. He was holding a handbag.

'Found this over in the bushes.'

Emma took it before Lapslie could react; not sure why, but aware in some dark recess of her mind where her instincts resided that it wouldn't be a good idea for him to look inside, that there was something in there that he shouldn't see. 'Thanks,' she said to the constable. She opened the handbag and glanced inside, angling it away from Lapslie. A pink Hello Kitty mobile phone. Hairbrush and make-up. Lots of bits of tissue paper. And a purse. She fished the purse out, feeling uneasy. A Hello Kitty mobile phone did not suggest they were dealing with a mature woman. More like a teenager.

She opened the purse and looked inside. The first thing she found was a student ID card.

Her heart thudded heavily in her chest. For a second, a long second, she debated putting the ID back in the purse, the purse back in the handbag, the handbag back in the bushes, and pretending that nothing had changed, but she knew that it had. In some ineffable way, the very atmosphere inside the tent had altered, become heavier. They were on a different road now. The atomic bomb could not be uninvented, and the handbag could not be unfound.

'It's Tamara Stottart,' she said levelly. 'Stephen Stottart's daughter. She's killed herself.'

She forced herself to look into Lapslie's face, and saw there, in his eyes, that he had already known. Part of him had already known.

'I saw her face,' he confirmed. 'I'd hoped I'd imagined it, still half-dreaming, but I *did* see her face.' He paused; swallowed. 'Maybe she saw Charlotte and me together at the hospital, realised Charlotte was working there and got her address from the hospital files, or something.'

'What do we do now?'

'We tell her father. Her family.'

'*No!*' The forcefulness of Emma's response shocked even her. 'I mean, not you. You're already under investigation for harassing her. The last thing you should do is go anywhere near them right now. You'll only make matters worse. I'll send a constable to do it. And leave the investigation here to someone else. We've got a killer to catch.'

She gestured to the constable to come back. 'Take a WPC with you,' she said to him. 'Go to the address on this ID. Ask them if their daughter is home. If she isn't tell them that we discovered the ID in a handbag beside a body, and ask them if it belongs to their daughter. For God's sake, make sure you check first that their daughter is missing – we don't want to find that she's been at a sleepover and this is some mugger who took her bag. Oh, and tell them that I will be there soon.'

As the constable retreated, the group of CSIs around the body edged away to allow someone to step back. Emma wasn't surprised to find that it was Jane Catherall, the pathologist.

'Doctor Catherall.'

'DS Bradbury.' Her face was grim. 'I do so hate death by fire. So messy, and so much evidence just burned away.'

Emma left space for Lapslie to ask a question, but he was silent so she said: 'What can you tell us?'

'The body is pretty well destroyed, which indicates to me the presence of an accelerant. The poor girl's clothes were probably soaked in something like petrol or paint thinner. Bodies, of their own volition, don't burn very well. No doubt Mr Burrows will be able to tell you what kind of accelerant was used.' She glanced back at the body. 'You will note the characteristic pugilistic pose: legs tucked up beneath the body, arms held tight in, hands curled into fists. It was thought for a long time that this was caused by the person curling up into a ball because of the pain, but it actually occurs after death when the muscles dehydrate and contract in the fire. As to cause of death—'

'She burned,' Emma interrupted. 'The DCI saw her.'

Jane's gaze moved to Lapslie. 'I'm sorry,' she said. 'That must have been terrible for you.'

'Worse for her,' Lapslie whispered.

Jane Catherall glanced back at Emma. 'As to cause of death, I'm not suggesting she was stabbed or shot and then set on fire to cover it up, although I have known that to happen. No, I was referring to the actual mechanism by which the fire killed her. Usually it's due to asphyxiation from breathing in smoke and carbon monoxide. I'll know more when I can get her back to the mortuary. Now forgive me – I have to get Dan mobilised with a trolley.'

She turned and walked away. Emma watched her go, fascinated as always by the way her crippled little frame could hold so much power and authority.

She turned back and opened her mouth, aware that she needed to say something to break Lapslie out of his bleak mood, but someone else was already rising up from the huddle around the body. It was, of course, Sean Burrows, the lead CSI. He was holding a device that looked like a small car vacuum cleaner.

'I heard what Jane said about accelerants,' he said in his thick Irish burr. 'This is one of the latest Vapour Trace Analysers. Not only can it tell me that an accelerant was present – which it was – but it can also give me a good indication which one.'

'Let me guess,' Emma said. 'Petrol? Or perhaps paint thinner?'

'No,' Burrows said triumphantly. 'Ether. It's an inflammable—'

'I know what it is,' Lapslie said. There was a tone in his voice, an edge that hadn't been there moments before. 'It's an inflammable gas which is normally used as an anaesthetic.'

'Like in the Baillie household!' Emma breathed.

'And in the other kidnappings,' Lapslie confirmed. 'We thought it might have been chloroform, but it might just as well have been ether in those cases as well. She *was* connected to the kidnappings and murders. She *did* send me that email! I know that doesn't make it any less tragic that she killed herself, but maybe I didn't push her to it. Maybe she knew something that pushed her to do it, or felt so guilty that she felt she had no other choice.' He glanced over at Emma, and there was fury in his eyes. 'I am going to get this bastard. I really am.'

'I'll head over to the Stottart house,' Emma said. 'The constables will have notified them by now. The nature of the poor girl's death gives us due reason to search the house without needing a search warrant.'

'Be scrupulously polite and reasonable,' Lapslie warned. 'There's something going on in that family. I forgot to tell you earlier that I saw them last night – the Stottart family – at a concert Charlotte and I were attending. It was as if they had sought me out to gloat over my IPCC investigation. Anyway, the father used the word "gash", Emma. Maybe it's a northern expression that everyone uses, maybe not, but with this IPCC investigation hanging over me we can't afford you getting a complaint against you as well. Be sympathetic, talk to them, but get inside her room and search everything.'

Emma nodded. 'Look, boss, there's nothing else you can do here. It's all process now. Go and check that your girlfriend is okay.'

He turned to go. She let him leave the tent, looked around one final time, then left herself.

She debated switching on her blues-and-twos as she

drove, but what was the point? Getting to the house any earlier wasn't going to bring the girl back to life, and the sound of sirens approaching would only heighten the family's pain.

She drove past large farms bereft of people but filled with machinery that, in the early morning sun, reared up menacingly over hedges and the fences, like giant mechanical insects frozen in the act of taking over the Earth.

The Stottart family lived in a small semi-detached house in Chipping Ongar, probably built in the 1950s or 1960s. The front garden was well maintained. Stephen Stottart drove a Vauxhall Vectra Estate, she noticed. Two other cars sat in the drive outside the house: a Fiat Uno that probably belonged to Mrs Stottart and a Mini Cooper, presumably the son's. Tamara, at fourteen, was too young to have had her own car.

Emma parked behind a police car that was already parked on the road. She took a deep breath before heading for the front door. A WPC opened it before she could knock. She'd probably been watching from the window.

'How are they?' Emma asked.

'Distraught,' the WPC confided quietly. 'The girl went to bed last night, but she must have sneaked out some time after midnight. Her bed's not been slept in. They

just can't understand what could have driven her to ...'
She tailed off, shrugging uncertainly.

'Okay. I'll have a quick word with them.' She walked
through the hallway, past a display case filled with
trophies and medals, and into the living room. Thick
carpets, she noticed. Very thick. And leather sofas. The
walls were covered with photographs of the children –
some posed portraits, some informal snaps; some with
their parents and some by themselves.

Stephen Stottart was sitting on the edge of the leather
sofa, poised as if he was going to dive off into the deep
pile of the carpet. His wife was sitting curled up in a
corner of the sofa. She was still wearing a dressing gown.
Her face was streaked and blotchy, and the skin around
her eyes was puffed up.

They both looked up as she entered; the flash of
hope in their gaze soon dying as she shook her head
slightly. Emma had experienced that kind of thing
before, in situations of extreme grief. It was as if there
were two parallel tracks of communication going on:
the body language which conveyed so much emotion
and the words which just allowed the slower exchange
of facts.

'I'm sorry to be here under such ... tragic circumstances,' she started.

'There's no doubt, is there?' Stephen Stottart asked.

His body already knew, but his mind needed to hear the words to help him accept it.

'We haven't made a positive identification,' Emma said carefully, 'but what I can say is that we have found the body of a young girl in close proximity to your daughter's handbag.'

'I need to see her,' he said, standing. 'I can identify her.'

Emma shook her head. 'Given the condition of the body, any identification will have to be made using dental records.' She glanced over at the WPC, who was stood in the doorway. She nodded. 'PC Evans has gone to the family dentist,' she said. 'He'll retrieve the records.'

'Okay.' She turned back to the family. 'Mr and Mrs Stottart, I need to look in your daughter's room. I need to find out if she left any notes behind, or any clue as to why she may have . . . taken her own life.'

Mrs Stottart's fragile façade broke, and she buried her face in her hands. Her husband nodded numbly. 'Anything . . .' he said, brokenly, and Emma knew that the sentiment wasn't so much 'Do anything you need to', but more of an agonised 'Anything that might prove that it's not my daughter out there.'

'Thank you.'

She left the living room and headed up the stairs. More family portraits, diagonally aligned. On the landing there was a choice of four doors. One had a lock on it – presumably the bathroom. One was plain; one marked with a poster of a horse and a male pop star of some kind, and one had a large yellow and black sticker that Emma recognised as being the international biohazard warning symbol. So – parents, daughter and son, in that order.

She pushed open the door of Tamara's room and went inside. Judging by the combination of posters, books and cuddly toys, she'd still been on that cusp between childhood and adolescence. A laptop sat on a desk beneath the window, and Emma went across, sat in the rather undersized chair in front of the desk and woke it up from hibernation.

She'd done courses on how to search a computer. What with the increasing size of hard drives, along with the prevalence of external storage devices and USB sticks, it was critical that police had a strategy to follow under these circumstances. She checked the emails first, but it looked as if Tamara had deleted everything from her inbox, and her sent items folder. That was a telling sign in itself. A quick check in the My Pictures section of the hard drive threw up a lot of photographs of her and her friends at parties and out around Essex, but nothing remotely worrying or suspicious.

Remembering the sound file that had been sent to

DCI Lapslie, Emma searched under the 'All Programs' tab, looking for some kind of sound-editing software, but there was nothing obvious. The geeks in the forensics lab could take a closer look, but Emma was familiar enough with programs like Sound Forge to know what she was looking for. And there was nothing. More out of duty than hope she did a search for any file with a '.wav' or '.mp3' extension, but the only ones she could find were music files downloaded from the internet.

She booted up the word processor, but the last five documents to have been edited were mostly homework, along with a note to a friend – a classmate of Tamara's – inviting her to a sleepover.

Everything in the room seemed to spring into heightened colour and brightness, as if the sun was suddenly shining directly into the room.

The note was addressed to Gillian Baillie.

Surely, Emma thought, the same Gillian Baillie who was currently the only member of her immediate family not to have been kidnapped.

Emma's mind was racing, trying to sort through the implications of what she'd discovered. The two girls knew each other. That had to be significant. If Lapslie was right – if Tamara was somehow connected to the disappearances and the deaths – then perhaps Gillian had been chosen because she *knew* Tamara.

Downstairs was a grieving father who might, if Lapslie was right, be an accessory to the kidnappings and murders, if not the actual perpetrator. He had an alibi for the time Catriona Dooley's body was dumped at the kids' play area, but that didn't mean he didn't have an accomplice who could do the heavy lifting for him.

Emma had to tread carefully. If he was just a grieving father then she didn't want to make things worse – especially as he was currently pushing through a complaint about her boss. And if he was a kidnapper and a murderer then she didn't want to alert him to her suspicions in case he made a run for it, or tried to cover his tracks. Four members of the Baillie family were still unaccounted for.

She pulled her phone out from her jacket pocket and pressed the memory key for DCI Lapslie's number. It rang for a few moments, then she heard his gruff voice:
'Lapslie.'

'Boss – it's Emma.'

'Where are you?'

'I'm still at the Stottart house,' she said. 'I've discovered something.'

'So have I,' he interrupted. 'The Baillie girl – the one who wasn't taken with the rest of the family—'

'Yes, that's what I'm trying to tell you!'

'She's *mute*!' he said.

Emma's brain juddered to a halt momentarily while it tried to switch tracks. 'What do you mean?' she asked eventually.

'The Child Welfare people have just been on to me. She hadn't spoken to anyone since she was found in the house. We all assumed that she was in shock, that she'd seen something that drove her brain into a state where she just had to withdraw or go mad, but that's not the case. Barnes's people found a whole pile of medical stuff: leaflets, sign language posters, all kinds of things. She's been mute since birth.'

'Okay,' Emma said cautiously, 'that's obviously a tragedy for her, but—'

'Don't you understand?' Lapslie snapped. *That's why she wasn't taken!* We already suspect that the kidnapper is taking people who are singers, and discarding the ones who fail some kind of bizarre audition. He deliberately focused on a family of singers, but he left behind the one who can't sing, who can't *possibly* sing.'

'It makes sense,' Emma agreed, 'but does it help us find them?'

'It confirms what we thought about the kidnapper,' Lapslie said, 'and that means we're closer to finding him. Now, what have you got?'

'The girl who was left behind, the mute girl. Her name is Gillian Baillie, isn't it?'

'Yes. Why?'

'The girl – Tamara Stottart. She was at school with a Gillian Baillie.'

Silence from the other end of the line. 'Was she indeed?' Lapslie said eventually. 'That gives us a link, then. That ties the Stottart family in with the disappearances and the murders. Pull them in for questioning. Get them down to Chelmsford. I'll meet you there, and—'

'Boss, they've just lost their daughter. You can't possibly question them now.'

Another long silence. Emma could hear Lapslie breathing.

'You're right,' he said. 'Damn. Okay, get whatever you can from her room and her computer. If you can search the rest of the house discreetly, then do it. Let me know what you find.'

'I will.'

She disconnected, wondering how she was going to search the house of a family who had just lost their daughter without agitating them even more than they were now. Stephen Stottart already believed that Lapslie had been hounding his daughter; it was only a matter of time before the paralysis of grief faded away and it occurred to him that her suicide might have been the inevitable result of that hounding. And then the shit would hit the fan, both for Lapslie and for their case.

Her eye was attracted by the shelves above Tamara's bed. As well as the standard teenage fiction there was a shelf and a half devoted entirely to CDs. From where she sat, Emma could see that some of them were rock and pop, but others – the majority, in fact – were classical CDs. A lot of them were pieces for violin, symphonies and concertos and chamber pieces, by composers ranging from Liszt and Bruch and Beethoven to names she had never heard of, like Philip Glass and Michael Nyman. She let her gaze scan the room, and found the violin case by the side of the bed. Tamara was a musician. Yet another fact to add to the growing collection that connected the case to some kind of twisted, perverse music.

Something different caught her eye. She turned slowly to face the door.

Someone was standing there.

He was eighteen or nineteen; built like a rugby player, with hair the same colour as Tamara's and with the same receding hairline as Stephen. He was wearing combat trousers and a hooded top, with red Converse plimsolls. He watched Emma with unreadable grey eyes.

'You're Tamara's brother,' Emma said.

'Gavin,' he said. His voice was edgy, underpinned with tension. 'She's dead, isn't she?'

Emma nodded. 'It's not confirmed for sure yet, but yes – we think Tamara is dead. We think it was suicide.'

'It was that policeman, wasn't it?' There was venom in his tone. 'The one who was hounding her? He drove her to it. She felt like he was watching her all the time. He even turned up at the concert hall last night when we were there. It was meant to be her birthday treat, but he ruined it for her. He's been following her everywhere.'

'That's not necessarily true,' Emma said carefully. 'The circumstances of your sister's death will be carefully investigated, and if anyone is to blame then there will be consequences.'

'But that won't bring her back.'

'Nothing will bring her back, Gavin.'

'She was a brilliant singer,' he said out of nowhere. 'I loved listening to her.'

'Do you sing?'

He shook his head. 'I can't hold a note. My dad says the music gene never got passed on to me. I'm good with my hands: you know, repairing cars and computers and stuff. But Tamara – she could sing, and she could play the violin. She was amazing. Dad and Mum both said she was going to be a professional musician when she grew up.'

Emma got to her feet. 'Look,' she said awkwardly, 'I have to go. But if there's anything you ever want to talk about—'

'I don't think so,' he said, and was gone.

Emma closed down the laptop and closed the door to the bedroom before giving it a quick but thorough once-over. Nothing that you wouldn't expect to find in any teenage girl's bedroom. If Tamara was tied into the disappearances and the murders, if indeed the whole family was connected, then there was no evidence for it there.

She remembered what Lapslie had suggested about searching the house, but a sudden thought struck her. She checked her watch. Damn! She was meant to be seeing the IPCC investigator at Canvey Island! For a split second she thought about phoning him up and crying off, telling him that an urgent case had come up, but it would just be putting off the inevitable, and if she could help to get this thing off Lapslie's back then it was the least she could do.

Heading back down the stairs she glanced at the door to Gavin's room. It was shut again. Presumably he'd shut himself back inside to be alone with his thoughts.

Emma indicated to the WPC that she was leaving, and headed out towards her car. Starting it, she drove off towards Canvey Island.

Ten minutes into the journey she felt a bumping from beneath the car, and felt the steering pulling to the left. Damn it! Of all the times to get a flat tyre, it had to be now! She pulled over to the side of the road, cursing. Was she going to have to try and change it herself, or should she call the recovery people and wait an hour until they turned up?

She brought the car in to the side of the road and turned the engine off. She got out and went around to the passenger side. The tyre was definitely sagging. Not gone yet, but on the way.

A hand was clamped over her mouth. A body pressed against her from behind: lithe, strong, wiry. The hand was holding a cloth. By the time she registered the strong smell, and the wetness against her lips, it was too late, She had breathed it in, and she was falling into darkness.

CHAPTER FIFTEEN

'So where *is* she?' Lapslie snapped. His patience wasn't just wearing thin: it was threadbare.

'Not sure, Sir,' the voice on the other end of the phone said. 'She was meant to be here this morning for a meeting with the IPCC. She phoned ahead to book an interview suite. The man from the IPCC turned up, but he wasn't happy when she didn't arrive. Very curt, he was. We tried phoning her mobile, but it kept on going to voicemail.'

'I know,' Lapslie said. 'It's doing the same to me.' His breath hissed out between his teeth. 'Can you do something for me? Check the system for any car crashes that have been reported. She's driving a Vauxhall Tigra.' He gave the licence number. 'It might not be registered to her,' he added, remembering that Dom McGinley had bought it for her, 'but that's what she's driving.'

'Will do, Sir. I'll ring you back.'

Lapslie slipped the phone back into his pocket and gazed around the Chelmsford Police HQ car park. He'd arranged to meet Emma there that afternoon so they could drive out to Tolla Limited and take a look around at the field site, and it wasn't like her to be late. Emma Bradbury was a lot of things – sarcastic, edgy, intensely private and prone to living life on the edge – but she wasn't unreliable. He'd known her turn up for work so crippled by a hangover that she had to head off every ten minutes to throw up, but he didn't say anything and neither did she, and she still managed a good day's work. He remembered when she broke her wrist chasing a murder suspect and still got all the reports typed into the police computer system before heading off to hospital to have it set. She had a high pain threshold and a low tolerance for bullshit, and that's why he liked working with her.

'What have you done with my woman?' a voice growled from behind him. He turned, knowing already who he was going to see.

Dom McGinley's body blocked the light like a black bear standing on its hind legs. And, Lapslie had to remind himself, he was just as prone to violence.

McGinley was wearing black jeans and a black leather jacket. Underneath the jacket was a tailored shirt in purple and violet stripes. His chest-hair tufted up through the open neck of the shirt. On the one hand that shirt was in the worst taste Lapslie had seen for years; on the other hand the lapel, the French cuffs and the lack of a pocket suggested it was a classy brand: T. M. Levin, perhaps, or Charles Tyrwhitt. McGinley was a living, walking contradiction in terms.

'You like the shirt?' McGinley growled.

'I was just remembering,' Lapslie replied mildly, 'that when the Clerkenwell Crime Syndicate used to dish out beatings, back in the seventies, they used to send their victims away with a fresh shirt on the basis that they'd got blood all over the one they'd been wearing. Didn't bother getting them medical treatment for the broken bones and internal bleeding, but at least they worried about their sartorial condition.'

McGinley grunted. 'If you heard that the Clerkenwell Crime Syndicate were going to give you a new shirt, you knew what it meant,' he said. 'The phrase entered the language. *Our* language. Gave a boost to the tailoring profession in the East End, let's face it. There's five shirt-makers I know of who would have gone out of business if not for them. So – where's my bird?'

'I don't know,' Lapslie admitted. 'I assumed she was with you.'

'She didn't come back last night. I thought she was probably staying over in Canvey Island again, but I tried her mobile, and I tried the hotel. The mobile didn't answer and the hotel didn't have a booking for her.' His face had the texture of a brick wall that had been exposed to the elements, but there was an unexpected concern in his eyes. Lapslie had never seen that expression before, and frankly McGinley's face looked unaccustomed to it.

Lapslie opened his mouth to say that he was sure she would turn up somewhere, but his mobile rang. He pulled it from his pocket. 'Lapslie.'

'Sir, it's Sergeant Murrell at Canvey Island. You asked about Emma Bradbury's car?'

'I did.' Lapslie's heart felt like it was calcifying in his chest. He could hear the tone of voice beneath Murrell's professionalism.

'It was reported abandoned last night. The local police put a "Police Aware" sticker on the windscreen, but they couldn't trace the owner.'

'Crashed?' Lapslie asked urgently, aware that McGinley's entire body had tensed beside him. His body was so dark and so heavy that light seemed to curve into him and get lost.

'No damage reported, apart from a flat tyre.'

'No sign of . . . of a body?'

'No sign at all.'

'Any signs of a struggle?'

'Nothing, Sir. Apart from the car itself, there's nothing to say that she'd ever been there.'

'Okay.' Lapslie's mind was racing. 'Get a CSI team out there straight away. I want that car and the surrounding area gone through with a fine-toothed comb. If there's a flake of dandruff on the ground that might belong to her abductor, I want it picked up and processed. If he spat anywhere, I want the spittle checked for DNA and blood type. I want *everything*.'

'Sir . . .' Murrell's voice was apologetic. 'Perhaps she just walked off to find a garage when she realised she had a flat, found they were closed and booked herself into a hotel or a B&B nearby. There's actually no evidence of foul play.'

'Doesn't matter,' Lapslie snapped. 'The man who took Catriona Dooley and all the others, the man who kidnapped the entire Baillie family three days ago – he's got her. Let me know if you get anything.'

Stopping the call, he turned to McGinley. The man was as still and as massive as a mountain, but Lapslie could sense the imminent landslide.

'She's been taken by the killer we're hunting,' he said. 'I need to report this to Rouse. You . . . do what you need to do. Ask questions. Find out who has her.'

'The victims,' McGinley said. 'Give me their names. I'll see if anyone's heard anything.'

'Catriona Dooley, Lorraine Gregory, Alison Traff, David Cave and the Baillie family: Mark, Sara, Corwin and Duncan.'

'Catriona Dooley?' McGinley mused. 'Out Maldon way?'

Lapslie nodded.

'I used to work with her dad,' McGinley mused. 'Fucking good bloke.' He turned to go, then turned back towards Lapslie. 'As her boss, I hold you responsible,' he said, his voice low. 'Whatever happens to her, I will make sure it happens to *you*. Whether that's an incentive, a punishment or an act of revenge depends on what condition you find her in.'

'Just when I thought we were friends,' Lapslie murmured.

'I'm like the last of the dinosaurs,' McGinley said, turning and walking away. 'All my friends are dead, and I'm surrounded by the descendants of rats and shrews.'

Lapslie looked up at the bulk of the Police HQ. Part of him wanted to get in his car and drive to where Emma's Tigra had been abandoned, but he knew it wouldn't do any good. The CSIs would do their work whether he was there or not, and he had to notify the senior management that one of their officers had been kidnapped, and was on a path that led to murder.

He entered the building and went straight up to DCS Rouse's office.

'He's busy,' said his PA as Lapslie stormed past.

'Isn't he always?' Lapslie called over his shoulder.

Opening the door, he found Rouse sitting at the meeting table with a tall, cadaverous man wearing a pinstripe suit that hung off him like the clothes of a scarecrow. His hair was black, and brushed straight back off a bulbous forehead.

'Ah,' Rouse said without missing a beat, 'Mark. This is Mr Grimshawe, from the Independent Police Complaints Commission. He was just telling me that Sergeant Bradbury didn't show up for her interview yesterday. Mr Grimshawe is quite perturbed.'

'Emma's gone missing,' Lapslie said, still holding the door handle. 'Her car's been found abandoned. I think she's been taken by the person we believe is responsible for this wave of kidnappings and killings.'

Rouse's eyes narrowed. Lapslie would have liked to think he was considering how best to mobilise his resources to get one of his people back intact, but he knew that the DCS was more likely to be thinking about the public relations fallout. To be fair, Lapslie thought, perhaps he could think about both things at once. He was a senior police officer, after all.

'You've initiated an investigation,' Rouse said, more of a statement than a question. 'So there are two parallel strands of activity. The investigation into her disappearance may throw up a lead, or the investigation into the previous disappearances and murders might provide a pointer. Either way, the situation is covered.'

'I should get back,' Lapslie said. 'With Emma gone I need to make sure that both investigations have appropriate leadership.'

'Actually,' Rouse said, glancing at Grimshawe, 'that's what we were talking about. Following the apparent suicide of the Stottart girl, I'm removing you from the case.'

Time seemed to slow down and stop in the vicinity of Rouse's office. Although Lapslie could hear Patricia, the PA, using the photocopier outside, he could also see motes of dust swirling in slow motion in the beam of early morning sunlight that speared across Rouse's office from the window to the far wall. Rouse and Grimshawe seemed frozen, fixed in time, staring at him. Even his heart appeared to have become suspended.

'Removing me?' he repeated, checking the words as he said them, turning them over in his mind and looking for ambiguities or alternative meanings. And finding none.

'Yes, Mark. I can't have you involved in an investigation where you are potentially implicated in the death of one of the persons of interest. I'm sure you understand.'

'Of course,' he said blankly. Grimshawe's face grinned at him like a Halloween skull. 'Who are you putting in charge?'

'Detective Inspector Dain Morritt. You remember him?'

'I do indeed.'

'He's a good copper, Mark.'

'And I'm comforted to know that when Emma's dead and mutilated body is found,' Lapslie said without changing his tone of voice, 'we can be sure that all proper procedures were followed during the investigation.'

'*Mark* . . .' There was a warning note in Rouse's voice.

'I presume the IPCC investigation will continue as before, Sir?'

'It will. And Mr Grimshawe is keen to talk to you.'

'I'm sure he is, Sir.' Rouse's face was unreadable. Even back when they were both constables, he had been the best poker player in the station house. What did Rouse want him to do? What did he *expect* him to do? He could resign, and avoid the entire IPCC investigation, but if he did that he had no chance of getting to Emma through official channels. He'd be out on his own, with only Dom McGinley to fall back on. But if he stayed he'd be remote from the investigation, unable to influence it. Except that he'd still have his warrant card, and he could still phone up Jane Catherall and Sean Burrows and have them talk to him.

'I'm afraid I have a hospital appointment today,' he said eventually, looking at the man from the IPCC. 'I'll call you later to set up an appointment.'

Before either Rouse or Grimshawe could react, he'd closed the door and was walking rapidly away.

As he walked, waiting all the time for Rouse to yell down the corridor at him to come back, he kept running through what little evidence they had. Apart from some dubious profiling and the genetically modified pollen found at the church, there was nothing. The pollen was the place to start. In Emma's absence, he still needed to go and see the Tolla field site.

His mobile rang. He pulled it from his jacket on the move, heading for the lifts that would take him out of the building.

'Lapslie.'

'Mark? It's Jane Catherall.'

'Jane, I can't talk at the moment. It's Emma. She's gone missing. I think the killer has her.'

Strangely, telling Murrell and McGinley and Rouse about it earlier hadn't affected him, but telling Jane, who was the closest thing to a friend he had next to Charlotte, suddenly brought it home. He felt his throat close up and his eyes prickle, and had to force back a choke.

'I know,' she said soberly. 'Sean Burrows phoned me.

He's going over her car now. He said to tell you that he hadn't found anything more than was at the other crime scenes.'

'Okay. Thanks.'

'But that wasn't why I phoned you. I've been conducting the autopsy on Tamara Stottart, and there's something you should see.'

'I'm off the case, Jane. Rouse has pulled me off.'

'And what are you going to do?' she asked urgently. 'Go home? Put your feet up? Have a glass of wine and listen to a CD? No, you're going to go after the man who has Emma captive, aren't you?'

He smiled, despite the situation and despite himself. 'How did you know?'

She made a *tch* sound. 'Don't you realise, you stupid man – that's why you get such incredible loyalty from the people around you? We know – we all know – that if any one of us was in trouble then you would do whatever it takes to get us out. *That*'s why we stand by you.' She paused. 'It's not your personal charm and charisma, you know.'

He pushed down on the wave of gratitude and warmth that threatened to swamp him, in the same way that he had pushed down on the sob that had threatened to overwhelm him earlier. 'Do you want me to come over?'

'As soon as you can, please.'

His mobile beeped at him as Jane Catherall's call disconnected, telling him that someone else had tried to get in touch while he was on the phone and had left a voicemail message. He checked the 'Missed Calls' tab. It was Rouse, probably demanding he come back. He'd check it later, once he was far enough away.

The drive to the mortuary didn't occupy his mind anywhere near enough. He knew the route so well that his thoughts were free to wander, and inevitably they kept coming back to Emma, kidnapped and at the mercy of an insane murderer. He remembered what had been done to the other victims – Lorraine Gregory, Alison Traff, David Cave and Catriona Dooley. The first one slowly pulled apart, the second one stuck through with skewers again and again, the third one with his skin stripped off and the fourth cut to pieces with wires. What was in store for Emma? And how long could she last?

His hands suddenly spasmed on the steering wheel, nearly sending him into the path of an oncoming truck. He swerved out of the way, getting a *blast* from the truck driver's horn. He could feel a tightness in his chest, a panicky sensation of breathlessness. His hands were shaking. His heart was hammering. What if he were too late? *What if she died?*

Pulling up at the mortuary, he had to spend a minute

with his eyes closed, getting his breathing under control. He would get Emma back. He had to.

The ever-reliable Dan let him in and escorted him to Jane Catherall's laboratory. She was dressed in a white lab coat, and was standing over a metal autopsy table with a gutter and a thick metal rim running around the edge. His stomach turned over when he saw what was on the table. It was Tamara Stottart's extensively burned body.

On the grass in front of Charlotte's flat, the body had appeared to be almost completely carbonised, at least on the surface. Now, seeing it under the stark lighting of Jane Catherall's mortuary, Lapslie could see that there were areas on the backs of her legs and the insides of her forearms that were blistered rather than burned, and that the cuts Jane had made during the course of her autopsy had revealed vivid red flesh just beneath the blackened areas.

'Ah, Mark. I won't keep you more than a few moments. Come over here.'

Reluctantly, he complied. He could feel an acidic burning at the back of his throat as his stomach contents rebelled at the sight and the smell of the girl's body.

'Obvious fourth degree burns covering at least seventy-five per cent of the surface area,' Jane murmured. 'As expected, the histological tests indicate that the cause of death was respiratory failure, and I have discovered no other wounds on the body that might have caused her death, but look here.'

She indicated the inside of Tamara's left forearm. Lapslie leaned closer. It looked as if there were cuts along the skin. The heat and the blistering had reddened them, making them more visible.

'Self-harm?' Lapslie asked.

'I don't think so. Look at the other arm.'

Lapslie moved around the table. The right forearm had similar marks.

'So she self-harmed symmetrically. You're losing me.'

'You're not thinking properly,' Jane said critically. 'Typically, self-harmers tend to concentrate on the arm opposite to the one with which they are dominant. Right-handed girls – and they are usually girls, by the way – will cut into their left arms, and left-handed girls will cut into their right arms. The scarring here is symmetrical, indicating to me that the cuts were inflicted by somebody else.'

Lapslie straightened up, his mind a whirl of thoughts. 'She was tortured?'

'She was brutalised, at the very least, and over a long period of time, if the scarring is to be believed. There is evidence of scars over scars which themselves lie over scars.'

'So even if she did commit suicide, it could well have been more to escape the torture being inflicted on her than because she thought I was harassing her.'

'That would be a reasonable assumption, based on the evidence.'

'And that torture is likely to have been inflicted by a family member?'

'Statistically,' Jane agreed, 'most physical abuse occurs within the family.'

'Stephen Stottart,' Lapslie muttered. 'It keeps coming back to him.' He reached out to squeeze Jane Catherall's shoulder. 'Thanks, Jane.'

'Bring her back. Just . . . bring her back.'

He nodded. 'I will.'

He drove away from the mortuary, setting his satnav for the postcode of the area where Tolla had its field sites for genetically modified wheat. If the pollen had been transferred from there to the clothing or the shoes of whoever had killed Catriona Dooley – Lapslie's brain managed to think 'Stephen Stottart' at the same time as it was thinking 'whoever had killed Catriona Dooley' – then he needed to find out how far the pollen could drift. And Emma hadn't managed to do that before she had been abducted, although she had at least established that Tolla was the only company experimenting with GM wheat in Essex.

The site was a few miles outside Billericay, along a straight, single-track, tarmac lane that led off a main road with no sign to say where it went. On either side the ground was uncultivated, running to long grass. He passed a handful of tents a few hundred yards down, but couldn't see anyone in them. Strange place for a campsite, he thought.

Far enough away from the road that it wasn't obvious, a fence separated the Tolla site from the rest of the world. A gate set into the fence bisected the road. A small Portakabin had been concreted into the ground beside the gate, and as Lapslie pulled up a security guard stepped out.

'Private property,' he said, scanning Lapslie's dashboard for a car pass. 'No entry, Sir.'

'Police,' Lapslie said, flashing his warrant card. 'I need to see whoever is in charge.'

'Wait one moment.'

The guard retreated back into his cabin. Lapslie could hear a one-sided conversation as he phoned through for instructions. After a minute or so he came back. 'Mr Standish will see you by the main car park. Straight down the road, and you'll see the car park to your left, just by the main enclosures.'

'Enclosures?'

'You'll see.' He vanished back inside the cabin. A few seconds later, the gate rolled open.

Lapslie continued down the road. Ahead he could see what appeared to be huge white balloons, half-inflated, lying on the ground. It was only as he got closer, and saw the car park which had been built off to one side of the road, that he realised that these were the 'enclosures' he had been told about: massive plastic tents built above what he presumed were the fields where the GM wheat was being grown.

The car park was half-filled with cars, but only one of them had a man standing beside it. He was wearing a three-piece suit, rather surrealistically given the circumstances. His hair was close-cropped and his face had a weatherbeaten, outdoors look to it.

'Dave Standish,' he said, walking across and extending his hand as Lapslie got out of his car. 'Site security. May I see your warrant card? Apologies, but we have to be sure of who we're dealing with around here.'

Taking Lapslie's card, he scrutinised it thoroughly while still talking. 'I suppose this is about the protest camp. Well, I say "camp". As far as I can see there's never more than ten people there at any one time.'

'It's not about the camp,' Lapslie said.

'Oh.' He seemed taken aback. 'Then it must be about Steve's kid. Not sure there's anything we can tell you.'

Lapslie felt the back of his neck tingle. 'Steve's kid?'

'Steve Stottart. His daughter died. I assumed you wanted to talk about it.' He shrugged. 'We heard it was suicide, but I guess there must be suspicious circumstances, otherwise you wouldn't be here.'

'Stephen Stottart works *here*?'

Standish frowned. 'He's one of our biologists, but he's not in today. Obviously. He's looking after his family. We understand that.'

Lapslie shook his head, trying to get his thoughts straight. He wasn't expecting to find such a direct connection. 'Where exactly does Mr Stottart—'

'*Doctor* Stottart.'

'— Doctor Stottart work?'

Standish pointed towards the furthest of the white plastic enclosures. 'Eco-Dome Eight. That's where his particular strain of wheat is being grown.'

'I need to see inside.'

Standish shook his head. 'No can do. There's all kinds of confidentiality issues here. If our competitors got to know what we were doing, it could be disastrous for Tolla Limited.'

'I'm in the middle of a murder investigation,' Lapslie snapped. 'If I have to come back with a search warrant, I will. I'll also come back with a convoy of fifty police cars and Crime Scene Investigation vans, and I'll make sure that your main gate is left open for so long that the entire protest camp can just walk through without anyone noticing.'

Standish smiled tightly. 'Well, if you put it that way,' he said. 'Let me show you to Eco-Dome Eight.'

They walked past the other Eco-Domes, each one labelled with a big number on the front, to Number Eight. Standish led Lapslie to an airlock attached to the side.

'We'll both have to put on protective coveralls,' he said.

'Why – what's so dangerous about the GM wheat?'

'We're not protecting us from it, we're protecting it from us,' Standish said.

Lapslie's mobile beeped, indicating there was a text message for him. He opened the message, hoping against hope that it would be something saying that Emma had been recovered safely.

It wasn't. The message was from an unknown number. All it said was: '*Look for a gift in your glove box. Use it. From a well-wisher.*'

Odd. Some kind of junk text, or a sister message to the email he'd been sent that had started this whole thing off? He saved it, just in case, making a mental note to check the glove box of his car later, just in case. There were some crazy people around. He'd arrested quite a few of them.

Five minutes later they were both dressed in hooded white paper coveralls strangely like the ones Sean Burrows and his people always wore at crime scenes. Elasticated cuffs at the wrists and ankles and around the edge of the hood maintained integrity. Standish also insisted on gloves and on plastic bags over their shoes.

'I don't know what you expect to find,' he grumbled as he led Lapslie through the second part of the airlock and into the Eco-Dome proper.

The inside was like a massive high-tech greenhouse. The plastic material of the Dome which had been white from the outside was almost transparent from the inside, and Lapslie could see the tracery of struts and stanchions that held it up. Rows of wheat led away from him in perspective lines, divided up into sections that were labelled with signs and surrounded with atmospheric sensors. The soil in which they were growing looked strange: orange rather than brown, more like sand or gravel.

Standish led the way down a central aisle. 'Doctor Stottart is evaluating the growth rates of numerous different varieties of GM wheat,' he confided over his shoulder. 'There's something like fourteen or fifteen main diseases that are endemic to wheat, which means a lot of pesticide has to be used to keep it healthy. Our aim is to reduce the use of those pesticides by creating breeds of wheat which are resistant to most, if not all, of those diseases. The soil here is artificial. It's been sterilised of all bacteria and fungi, and the Eco-Domes are kept free of all insect life.' He stopped by a batch of wheat that was growing particularly straight and strong. 'As you can see, some of the varieties do better than others. That's what Doctor Stottart is evaluating.'

'He's doing more than that,' Lapslie said darkly. The soil beneath the wheat was lumpy in a way that Lapslie was familiar with from so many previous cases. He bent and plunged his hand into it.

'Hey!' Standish cried. 'You'll contaminate it!'

Lapslie pulled his hand out. Grasped in it was another hand: the skin splitting apart and mottled in green and black.

'Too late,' Lapslie replied. 'It's already contaminated.'

CHAPTER SIXTEEN

Emma's head felt as if it was half-full of some heavy liquid, like mercury. Every time she moved, the liquid sloshed slowly from side to side, rocking her head back and forth against her will and making her feel nauseous; it still shifted around for minutes even when she held her head still. Even when she didn't move, the liquid weighed her head down, forcing it towards her chest and making it hard to breathe properly.

Her head ached as well. It ached like the worst hangover she'd ever had. Like a port and whisky hangover. Spikes of pain were drilling into her temples, and there was a sharp ache just behind her eyes. Her mouth was full of saliva, and every time she swallowed her salivary glands pumped more in, accompanied by sharp pangs.

She tried to work out where she was. It wasn't in bed, that much was for sure. If she was in bed then she would be lying down, not sitting up with her head bowed forward. Had she fallen asleep in her car? It's wouldn't be the first time, but her back didn't feel like it was nestling into curved leather seats. It felt more like it was pressed up against a padded board.

And she couldn't move her hands. They were resting on a cold, plastic surface. She could wriggle her fingers, but she couldn't move her hands.

Maybe she was in hospital. The thought brought with it a momentary giddy relief. If she was in hospital it would explain why she was sitting up: she was probably propped up so that the nurses could monitor her. She'd seen other people like that, usually when they'd just come out of surgery, or were in intensive care. The reason she couldn't move her arms was obviously that they were attached to the bed so that she couldn't turn over and pull out whatever intravenous drip was in her arm. She was feeling like shit because she'd had an accident of some kind. Maybe a car had hit her while she was trying to fix the tyre on her own car! She was injured, but she wasn't quadriplegic because she could wriggle her fingers.

A sudden panicky thought occurred to her, and she tried wriggling her toes. Yes, they moved too! Her legs didn't seem to want to cooperate, but that would come back with time.

An uncomfortable idea wriggled up into her conscious

mind like a worm emerging from dank earth. People with amputations often said they thought they could still feel their missing limbs. What if she only *thought* she was moving her fingers and toes? What if they weren't moving at all? What if they weren't even there?

Time to open her eyes. She didn't want to, afraid of what she might see, but she did it anyway.

She wasn't in bed. That was the first thing. And if she wasn't in bed then she probably wasn't in hospital. Was that a good thing or a bad thing? Through smeary eyes she thought she could see her hands resting on the arms of a chair: blue vinyl over soft padding which had been wrapped around a metal frame. She blinked a couple of times to clear her vision. Yes, her hands were indeed resting on what looked like the arms of a metal chair.

And they were fixed there with plastic cable-ties which had been tightened around her wrists and forearms.

Emma was beginning to get a bad feeling about this.

Somewhere, through the sick throbbing in her head, she remembered a hand clamping around her face and a sharp, medicinal smell in her nostrils and catching at her throat as she breathed it in. Experimentally, she sniffed. She could still just about detect the residue of that chemical, whatever it was, on her skin, or possibly on her clothes from where it had dripped and soaked in.

Her clothes! Quickly she looked down. Yes, she was

still dressed. Thank Christ! Whoever had done this to her, they'd left her dressed. Somehow, that was important.

She closed her eyes as that heavy mercury in her head swirled around, feeling her head nodding as the mercury pushed forwards and backwards, like an inexorable tide. Gradually it ebbed back to stillness, and she opened her eyes again.

She could see her knees, but not her legs. Judging by what had happened to her arms, they were probably tied to the chair as well. It was hard enough to break plastic cable ties at the best of times, when you had purchase and leverage. Trying to snap them by flexing her muscles was going to be impossible.

Which wasn't going to stop her from trying, but she'd wait until she knew more about the situation, and panic seemed more of an attractive option. For now, her best course of action was to wait and watch and listen.

Something caught her attention. Beside each leg she could see a curved section of grey rubber. It took her a good few minutes to work out that they were tyres. At the end of the day, her only consolation was that the angle was unusual. She hadn't expected to be looking down on tyres. But these were not from a car.

She was in a wheelchair. The knowledge took a little while to filter through her drug-slowed mind. A wheelchair.

Back to the hospital idea again?

No, she was fastened to the wheelchair. She wasn't in a hospital. She'd been abducted. Imprisoned.

That smell was still just about discernible. Ether – wasn't that what had been used as an accelerant on Tamara Stottart? If it was then Emma was lucky to be alive. A slight miscalculation with the amount of ether on the cloth that had been pressed against her face, or the length of time she had been forced to breathe the fumes, and she'd be brain damaged or dead. Assuming she wasn't already brain damaged and just didn't know it.

The fog was beginning to clear from her mind, and she didn't think she was going to throw up. Not immediately, at any rate. The best thing she could do was make an evaluation of her environment. See if there was any opportunity for escape.

Without moving her head Emma lifted her gaze until she was looking out from beneath her eyelashes. Her eyelids and eyebrows were massed like a dark cloud above her. The movement sent fresh spikes of hot agony back through her eye sockets, but she swallowed hard and tried not to cry out.

She was in a shadowed room with breeze-block walls that had been painted white – an attempt at covering up the unpalatable truth, similar, as far as Emma was concerned, to spraying perfume on a corpse. She regretted the analogy as soon as it passed through her mind. She didn't want to be thinking about corpses. Not here. Not now.

The room seemed to extend for some distance left and right, but her eyeline was cut off by two mobile room dividers, the kind Emma was familiar with from open-plan police offices. They had been placed about six feet to either side of her wheelchair, extending from the breeze-block wall out to about two-thirds the width of the room. This left an open space running down the building on the wall opposite where she was parked – a little like a corridor. The dividers were probably at least six feet high; more than enough to stop her from seeing down the length of the room, even if she'd been standing up.

There was nobody in sight, so she raised her head and looked around. No point in still pretending she was unconscious.

The floor was covered in old linoleum marked in green and black triangles. It was cracked in places, and the edges were curling up, and there were brown stains splattered across it that made her feel like she wanted to simultaneously curl up and empty her bowels.

Frankly, if she was going to have to die, there were more attractive places to do it.

'Either this lino goes or I do,' she muttered to herself, trying to keep her spirits up.

'Hello?' A man's voice from her left.

She kept silent.

'Hello? Are you awake?'

'We saw you being brought in,' another voice said. This time it was a woman. She was also on Emma's right, but sounded further away.

Analysing their tone of voice, Emma decided that they sounded scared. Maybe it was a come-on, a trick on the part of her abductor, but she might as well play along. Take nothing for granted; learn what you can.

'My name is Emma Bradbury,' she said, loudly and clearly. 'I'm a sergeant in Essex Police.'

'You're with the *police*?' the man said, surprised. 'But you're tied up.'

'Yeah, funny old thing,' Emma said quietly; then, more loudly, added, 'We were looking for you, but I hadn't planned on finding you quite like this. You *are* Mark and Sara Baillie, aren't you?'

'Yes. Oh God, yes.' The woman sounded relieved. Relieved and yet terrified. 'Where are we? Why are we here?'

'Not sure,' Emma said. 'I was hoping you might know.'

'We woke up here,' Mark Baillie said. 'We're tied to wheelchairs, just like you.'

'What happened?' Emma asked.

'We don't know!' That was Sara again. Her voice sounded raw, as if she'd been crying. Or screaming. 'We were in bed. Asleep. I remember smelling something funny, and then it was like I was falling down a dark hole in the ground. When I woke up, I was here. And so was Mark.'

'What about our children?' Mark asked urgently. 'Are they all right? Have you seen them?'

Emma's mind raced. The boys weren't here? They certainly hadn't been left in the house. That meant one of several things, none of which she wanted to share with Mark and Sara. Either the boys had breathed in too much ether and were dead, or they were being kept somewhere else, by themselves, or whoever had kidnapped them was already . . . already what? Torturing them as an audition for some insane choir? What was all this about? And what was she going to tell the parents?

'I wasn't at the crime scene – at your house, I mean,' she lied. 'I'm not sure where they are right now but . . . I'm sure they're fine.' Quickly, she moved on. 'Did you see the person who wheeled me in? What did he look like?'

'Male,' Mark said, 'quite muscular. He was wearing something over his face.'

'Has he said anything to you?'

'Nothing.' Judging by her voice, Sara was on the verge of emotional collapse.

'He brings us stuff to eat and drink,' Mark said. 'Soup in a thermos. He holds it up while we drink it. And water, every few hours.'

'Like he's keeping us fresh for ... something,' Sara added dully. Then: 'Oh my God, where are Corwin and Duncan?'

'It's going to be okay, Sara,' Mark said. Emma could hear him suppressing his own hysteria so he could comfort his wife, if only from behind a barrier. 'It's going to be okay, love.'

It's not, Emma thought bleakly. It's really not.

'Does he ever let you loose?' she asked. 'I mean ... to go to the bathroom. That kind of thing?'

There was a long pause, broken by Mark saying 'No,' in a flat tone of voice that suggested he didn't want the subject pursued any more.

'Ah,' Emma said. Something else to look forward to: pissing and crapping herself as if she were a baby. This day was just getting better and better.

'Look on the bright side, Emma,' she murmured. 'At least there's soup.'

'What?' Mark again.

'Don't worry. Talking to myself.' She paused. 'So he's not ... *done* anything to you?'

'Like *what*?' said Sara, her voice getting shriller. 'Like torture? Like rape? Oh Christ, is he going to rape me and make Mark watch?'

'No,' Emma said. 'He's not going to do that. I can fairly confidently promise you that sexual assault isn't why we're here.'

'He's done this before?' Mark was quick on the uptake. 'When? What does he *do*? How often has this happened? Why haven't you caught him yet?'

'All good questions,' Emma said. 'I wish I had answers for you, but I don't. I'm tied up here as well. Whatever happens, happens to me as well as you.'

Silence, for a long while.

A door slammed open somewhere off to Emma's left. She could hear footsteps clicking on the linoleum. A shadow appeared, cast by a light behind the approaching figure.

He stopped just the other side of the room divider. She could hear him breathing. Mark and Sara were so silent it was deafening. She couldn't blame them. They didn't want to attract attention to themselves.

'Come on in,' she said, trying to keep her voice level. 'I want to see your face.'

He walked forward, past the end of the divider, and turned to face her.

Emma nearly screamed.

He was wearing some kind of mask, she realised belatedly, a black metal thing made of various sections riveted together, with holes for the eyes and dominated by an exaggeratedly pointed and hooked nose. A medieval executioner's mask.

'Brave,' he whispered, voice muffled by the mask. She tried desperately to recognise it, but failed. Was it Stephen Stottart? She couldn't tell.

'Braver than you. At least I can show my face.'

'You don't get the choice, girl.' There was venom in the tone of voice. Hatred. She still couldn't tell who it was, or even if she'd heard it before.

'My name is Emma Bradbury,' she said again. 'I'm a detective with Essex Police. Release me right *now*.'

Any hope that her status as a police officer would make him cower trickled away as he laughed. 'I've killed so many people,' he whispered hoarsely through the laughs. 'Why do you think killing a policewoman would give me a moment's unease?'

And that was the moment she knew she was probably going to die. Nobody knew where she was, nobody knew who *he* was, and there was no rescue plan in motion. No reprieve. No hope.

He walked towards her, and she flinched despite herself, but he walked round behind the wheelchair and pushed it forward.

'Let's take a little tour,' he whispered, still chuckling.

He took her left, back the way he had come, away from Mark and Sara Baillie, who were still being as silent as possible. He pushed her past a wooden stairway that led up to a trapdoor in the ceiling. Emma looked to her right as they passed a series of empty cubicles, like the one she'd woken up in, each with its own wheelchair sitting over by the wall, each with brown stains on the floor. Maybe blood; maybe shit. The thought of either was enough to terrify her.

Past the last cubicle the room opened out into a much wider space. Weak light filtered in through high, narrow windows. The space was filled with objects under covers. Each object was about the size of a person; some lower, some higher. They looked as if they might have been statues, covered with dustsheets. Each one was lit by a spotlight above it. Wires had been attached to the ceiling, running from the spotlights to a junction box on the wall.

'Some of these I found, some I bought,' he said, pushing Emma up to the first shrouded object. 'And some I made myself.'

He pulled the sheet off with a flourish. Underneath was a table, a simple folding table, with an object resting on top. The object looked like a pear made of metal and covered with ornate scrollwork. Four nearly invisible seams ran down its length, spaced equally around the circumference. On top, where the stalk would be, was a metal hoop.

'It's called the Pear of Anguish,' he breathed. 'Or the *Poire d'Angoisser*, if you prefer. Very popular in medieval times. It's inserted into the mouth, or the rectum or the vagina. Wherever there's an opening. There's a screw running all the way down the inside, and when that loop on top is turned, the four segments – you can see the four segments, can't you? – they open up. Each one is hinged at the top, and they just get forced further and further apart by the screw. Believe me, they can open up much further than the human body can without bursting.' He paused. 'I don't put it in the throat,' he added in a hushed voice. 'That would ruin the effect I'm trying to achieve. I need people to be able to scream.'

'Why?' Emma said through teeth that were trying to clamp themselves together, but he was pushing her on to another shrouded treasure.

'This one,' he whispered, 'is called the Scavenger's Gyres, or sometimes Skeffington's Daughter – named for Sir Leonard Skeffington, who was the Lieutenant of the Tower of London in the time of Henry the Eighth.' He tugged the sheet away. This time the object underneath was a wooden board holding a strange metal device about half the height of a person and made up of loops and rods of metal with sections that looked like they could slide along each other. It looked innocuous, like some oversized kitchen implement, and yet something about it made Emma's blood freeze. It actually seemed to radiate a sense of evil. 'Your neck and wrists and calves are locked into those hoops, and then the whole thing is gradually compressed. Your whole body is forced into a tighter and tighter space until the skin of your fingers and your toes splits open to let the blood spurt out and it gushes out of your mouth and nose and rectum. The pressure just gets too much, and the blood has to escape.'

'Great,' she said, forcing the words out. 'You never thought of just collecting stamps?'

He pushed her on to a third cloaked object. When he whipped the cloth off, she saw a large, flat sheet of metal about half the height of a person, supported on a metal base. The top edge had been sharpened to a razor's edge.

'The Spanish Donkey,' the voice whispered from beneath the metal mask. 'Your legs are placed to either side of the sheet, and weights attached to your ankles. The weights pull your body down, letting the metal sheet slice upwards. The heaviness of the weights can be used to control how quickly, or slowly, you slide down it. How far do you think it might go before you would die? Do you think you could feel it, all the way up inside you? Your womb? Your intestines? Your lungs? What noises do you think you might make?' He giggled. 'Shall we find out?'

'Let's not and say we did.' She felt hot, and breathless. The walls were closing in on her like a vice.

He whirled her around to another dust-sheeted object. This one was bulky, like a small car. He tugged the sheet off, but it snagged on something sharp and tore as he pulled it.

The thing underneath was like a single bed made out of rough wood with a revolving drum in the middle, its axis going from one side of the 'bed' to the other, but rather than being smooth the drum was covered in rusty metal barbs, like fish-hooks. At one end of the 'bed' was a wooden barrier with a large hole in it. A hole about the size of a head, Emma noted sickly. At the other end was a similar barrier with two holes; one for each foot she guessed. The axis of the drum ended up in a handle, just to make it easy for rotating.

'Let me guess,' she said. 'I get to lie down across the drum, with my head and legs secured, and someone gets to turn the handle. My stomach is slowly ripped to shreds.'

'The Spanish Drum,' the voice whispered proudly. 'Favourite of the Spanish Inquisition.' He gestured off to one side. 'I've even got an Iron Maiden over there. Opinions differ over whether the Iron Maiden was ever used in anger, or was just a bit of gothic decoration, but the idea is sound. It's a big metal coffin where the lid is hinged and the inside of the door is covered in spikes which can be gradually pushed further and further towards the middle.'

'Torture devices,' she said angrily. 'Great. Well done. We have Tasers in the police, for stunning violent criminals with an electrical charge, but Amnesty International wants to get them reclassified as torture devices. You can torture a person with a ballpoint pen, if you want to. You can probably torture them with a sheet of paper. *Anything* can be used as a means of torture. The question is, *why*? Why do you want to torture people? For Christ's sake, why do you want to torture *me*?'

She closed her eyes, waiting but not sure what for.

When she opened her eyes, she was looking down at her captor's feet.

At the red Converse plimsolls he was wearing.

'Gavin,' she breathed, despite the voice in her head warning her to say nothing, give nothing away. 'Gavin Stottart.'

The sound of the metal mask being pulled off made her open her eyes. Maybe, she thought, it would be better if she didn't look, but it was probably too late for that now.

The face staring back at her was that of a nineteen-year-old, the same boy – man? – she'd seen in Stephen Stottart's house the day before. His eyes were blue, and sad. So sad.

'*Why?*' she asked, putting all the urgency she could into the word.

'My father has synaesthesia, you know that?' he said, not bothering to whisper now that he knew that *she* knew who he was.

'I know. He's in the same therapy group as my boss.'

'I inherited it.'

'Gavin, there's lots of people with synaesthesia. They're not all murderers.'

'You don't understand,' he said. 'I've also got some-thing called achromatia. I can only see in shades of grey. Only shades of grey. No colours at all. Can you imagine that?'

'I can't,' she said, trying to put some emotiveness into her voice, trying to make a connection, trying to make him see her as a *person*. 'But Gavin, if you don't know what a colour is, you don't know what you're missing. That's not a reason to kill people.'

'Killing people isn't the point,' he said. 'As I was growing up, I used to hurt my sister. Chinese burns, that sort of thing. All kids do it, don't they? But sometimes, sometimes when she screamed, *I could see colours.*' His eyes were far away. 'It was like seeing paradise! I'd never dreamed that things could be that beautiful. I just . . . I can't describe it. I knew I would do *anything* to see those colours again. I couldn't live without them.'

'So what – you abducted people? And you tortured them to make them scream for you?'

He looked away, unable to meet her gaze. 'You don't understand. It's like a drug. I *need* to see those colours. Those glorious, incredible colours. The trouble is, not everyone makes the right noises. Some people, it's like I see jagged shapes; vicious, sharp things, dark and muddy. Other people it's like everything is smooth and round and soft, and glowing in such incredible warm shades. It makes me feel – complete. Real.'

'Lorraine Gregory? *She* was real, Gavin.'

'She couldn't give me what I wanted. What I needed. I tried. God knows, I tried. The things I did to her body to get her to scream as loud and as long as she could, but all I got was tinges. Hints of colour. Not the real thing.'

'Alison Traff?'

He smiled. 'Close. There was something there. I kept shoving meat skewers through her skin. The noises she made – I don't know what you'd call them, maybe red, maybe blue, maybe some colour that nobody apart from me has ever seen, but she was good. I tried to keep her alive, I really did. I fed her and everything, but I think she got an infection. One day I came in, and she'd just died.'

'David Cave?'

'Very different. The colours were much darker with him. Much more serious. I wanted something brighter.'

'Catriona Dooley, then? Was she the right one?'

He shook his head. 'The sounds she made were all wrong. All mixed up. The colours were running together and getting murky. I had to get rid of her. None of them were what I needed.'

'And now you have Mark and Sara Baillie. Do you think you're going to get something different from them? You're wrong, Gavin. You're on the wrong track. Pain is not the way to get the colours you want.'

'It is,' he insisted. 'I've just not found the right kind of pain yet.' He gestured around with a wave of his arm. 'But with these things . . . the medieval torturers knew what they were doing. They took the causing of pain to a fine art. They could keep people alive for days. Weeks! Based on what they did, and what I know, I think it can do it. I think a duet, rather than a solo, is what I need. Two voices – one male, one female, screaming together. I think that'll take me to paradise.'

'And if it doesn't?' Emma asked. 'Where next? How far do you go, Gavin?'

'I don't know,' he admitted. He switched his gaze back to her, and smiled. 'Maybe a trio ...' he said thoughtfully.

CHAPTER SEVENTEEN

'The locations change, but the faces remain the same,' Jane Catherall said grimly.

Lapslie could only nod in agreement. In front of them the Tolla site spread away towards the horizon; Eco-Dome after Eco-Dome, each containing who knew how many varieties of genetically enhanced wheat. And behind them, one particular Eco-Dome which contained more than just wheat. It contained two dead bodies.

'What can you tell me?' he asked.

'They're children,' she said. 'Just children. Two boys.'

'The Baillie sons.' He felt his heart calcify just a little more than it already had.

'I can't tell yet,' Jane pointed out. 'I will have to compare dental and medical records before I can form a proper judgement. But I can tell you they died within the past thirty-six hours, and they were buried comparatively recently. Rigor mortis has fully set in.'

'I'm not exactly in a position to tell their parents they're dead,' he said. 'I just . . . Never mind.' He paused, not wanting to ask the next question, but forced the words out. 'What was done to them?'

'Nothing.'

He cast a questioning glance in her direction. 'Nothing? No torture?'

'No torture. Because it's you, I'm going to go out on a limb and say either asphyxiation or poisoning. Not strangulation. There are no other marks on the body.'

'Ether poisoning?'

She nodded reluctantly. 'I wish I could tell you that their blood is bright red, or their lips are purple, and that means it's ether poisoning, but I can't. There *are* no obvious physiological markers. I'll have to test their livers to know for sure. But given the timescale, and given that we know ether was used to abduct them and their parents, one could speculate that the abductor used just enough for the parents but too much for the kids, and he had to dispose of the bodies.'

Lapslie looked around. 'Dammit, we'll have to search every one of these Eco-Domes to see if there are any more bodies. I'm going to have to have people crawling over this place for months.'

His phone rang. He checked the display.

'It might be important,' Jane pointed out.

'It's Rouse,' he said. 'He'll have heard that I've just discovered two more bodies even though I'm off the investigation.'

'What can he do?' she asked. 'Take you off again?'

He smiled thinly. She was right. He was close to rock bottom now.

'Find her, Mark,' Jane said softly. 'Find her.'

And she turned to go back inside the Eco-Dome, to the two children who now claimed her sole attention.

Lapslie grabbed hold of the security guy, Standish, as he passed by talking worriedly on his BlackBerry. 'I need your security records,' he said. 'I need to know when Stephen Stottart was last on this site.'

Standish waved his BlackBerry. 'I had them downloaded into here,' he said. 'I guessed you'd want to see them.' He glanced at the display and scrolled down with the thumbwheel. 'Here,' he said, handing it over. 'These are the records of who's swiped their cards in and out over the past three days. Like I told you, Steve Stottart's not been in.'

Lapslie slid his gaze down the list. Lots of names, none of them meaning anything.

Apart from one.

'Look – he's just *here*. He came in yesterday.'

Standish grabbed the BlackBerry back and scanned it. 'No, that's not Steve. That's Gavin.'

'Gavin?'

'Gavin Stottart. His son.'

Lapslie felt like the world had just tipped sideways on him. 'His *son*? His son works *here*?'

Standish nodded. 'It's a casual job. We prefer to employ relations of our staff – it keeps everything in-house, and it reduces our carbon footprint because they can give each other lifts in to the site. Gavin Stottart works in the quality assurance area. He has to drive out to the remote sample sites every few days and collect the pollen traps. He has keys so he can get into sites – they're usually owned by someone else, but they allow us to site our traps on their property.'

'What are the traps for?'

'We need to know if any of our pollen escapes from the Eco-Domes. It's part of the legal agreement that allows us to operate, but it's good business practice as well. Of course, the protesters claim that because we have these remote sample sites it implies that we're already admitting the pollen might escape, but—'

'Focus!' Lapslie snarled. 'Two dead kids. Missing sergeant. Not interested in protesters or legislation.'

'Okay. Okay.' He was flustered. 'We have sample boxes spaced out around the site here, up to thirty miles away.'

'Based where?'

'Typically we rent some space from an existing landowner. All we need is a box on a pole. It's—'

'Do you have a list of your sample sites on that little CrackBerry thing?' Lapslie interrupted.

'I think so.' He clicked and scrolled away. 'Yes, here.'

He handed the device over again. This time there was a map on the high-resolution colour display, covered with red dots. Lapslie spent a few seconds mapping the locations onto what he already knew. 'A kids' play area in Canvey Island,' he said. 'A deconsecrated church in Bishop's Stortford. A car garage. A bakery. A holistic therapy centre.'

'That's right!' Standish frowned. 'But how do you know? That map just has dots on. How do you know what's at the sites?'

'Because I know what else is at the sites. Crime scenes and dead bodies.'

He cursed himself for being so stupid. It wasn't Stephen Stottart. It never had been. And it hadn't been his daughter either. They were both just innocent parties caught up in the machine. It had been the son all along – Gavin. Lapslie didn't know how, and he didn't know why, but at least he knew who.

'I'm taking this thing,' he said, slipping the BlackBerry into his pocket.

'You can't!'

'I can. It's ... oh, I don't know. Evidence, or something.'

He ran over to his car just as Jane Catherall was leaving the Eco-Dome. Dan was pushing a stretcher trolley behind her. There were two body bags on the stretcher. They'd been folded over because their contents were so small, and so that both of them could be fitted on the same stretcher.

Lapslie felt his breath catch in his throat. He'd been pushing it to the back of his mind, but he had two kids, roughly the same age.

No. No time for that.

'Jane, with me!' he shouted. 'I need your help.'

To her credit she didn't complain. Turning to Dan, she said something that Lapslie assumed was along the lines of 'Take these bodies to the mortuary and wait for me,' and then she scurried across the ground as fast as her spindly, polio-emaciated legs would carry her.

'A day trip,' she said, strapping herself in. 'How wonderful.'

'I need you to do some analysis,' he said, handing her the BlackBerry and starting the car. 'You've seen the files of the other torture cases, and you know about the locations in the Catriona Dooley case. Filter out all of those locations, and tell me what's left.'

'And where are we going while I'm doing that?'

'Stephen Stottart's house.'

The drive took less than fifteen minutes, and Lapslie nearly caused five major incidents on the way. He screeched to a halt outside the Stottart house with the sound of sirens in the background, heading his way.

'Here,' he said, tossing his warrant card into Jane Catherall's lap. 'Tell them I'm on official business.'

He strode up the path to the front door. It looked as if the police presence from the day before had been withdrawn. He rang the doorbell.

Stephen Stottart opened the door. He was haggard, pale, worn. He looked to Lapslie like he was gradually fading out of life, becoming a ghost in small steps.

'You,' he said, but there was no venom in his voice. There was no venom left. 'How dare you come here.'

'Mr Stottart, I need to see your son. Is he in?'

'You bastard!' he spat. 'Haven't you done enough damage? What's the matter – can't persecute Tamara any more so you're turning your attention to our *son* now?'

Lapslie sighed. There was no easy way to do this. 'Mr Stottart, under the terms of the Police and Criminal Evidence Act 1984, Section 17, I have reason to believe that you are harbouring a known fugitive. I therefore have a right to enter this house and search it.'

'You can't! My wife's upstairs, asleep!'

'I'm sorry, but I have to insist.'

'You bastard!' Stottart cried. He lashed out at Lapslie, but Lapslie stepped past the blow and Stottart's fist struck the doorframe. Lapslie left him behind and headed for the stairs, and Gavin's bedroom.

'I'm going to phone my solicitor!' Stottart cried after him. 'I'm going to phone the IPCC! They'll *crucify* you!'

'They can join the queue,' Lapslie muttered. He chose the door with the biohazard sticker on it, realising that it was Gavin's idea of an ironic joke considering where he and his father worked; evidence of his twisted sense of humour.

The bed was rumpled, unmade. Books and CD covers were scattered around. A large gaming computer was sat beneath a table by the window. On the table was a widescreen high-definition LCD monitor surrounded by a Creative Labs 5.1 surround sound audio system, including a sub-woofer the size of a beer-cooler. Evidence that Gavin cared about the quality of the sounds he listened to.

Lapslie booted the machine up and scanned through the hard drive's contents. A folder labelled 'Colours' caught his eye, more because of the discrepancy between its name and the more system-related names around it than for any other reason.

He was right. It was full of sound files. Hundreds of

them. Thousands. Each was labelled with a name like: 'blue054' or 'green-purple121', or sometimes 'warm-fuzzy339' or 'sharp-twitchy983'. Sensory impressions. Something connected with synaesthesia, perhaps?

He clicked on one of the sound files at random. Microsoft Media Player booted up. A pair of headphones that Lapslie hadn't noticed – Sennheiser, of course – crackled. He slipped them on.

He was listening to a woman screaming herself hoarse. Begging to be killed.

He clicked on another file, sickened.

A man, this time, but screaming in a high-pitched tone of disbelief and sheer agony.

Another file.

Sobbing, punctuated by occasional cries of pain. Lapslie imagined sharp skewers being plunged into soft flesh and then pulled out.

The door to the room burst open. Stephen Stottart was standing there, shaking with fury.

'Get out, you bastard! Get *out*!'

Lapslie pulled the headphone jack out of the socket on the computer. The system defaulted back to the speakers, and the sound of a woman being tortured filled the room with a pressure that Lapslie could almost feel pushing in on his skin.

'What—?' Stottart asked, dumfounded.

'Your son's hobby,' Lapslie shouted over the noise. 'You should ask him about it. If you want to know why your daughter killed herself, this is why. I think she was using his machine. I think she found these files.'

'She wanted to download some music from the internet,' Stottart breathed. 'Her network adaptor was playing up. I said she could use Gavin's machine. He wasn't around. But . . .'

'Didn't you see those cuts on your daughter's arms?' Lapslie knew he was taunting Stottart now, but he couldn't help himself. The man must have known. Somehow, he must have known that *something* was wrong. How could he not? 'Didn't you ever ask her how they got there?'

'She said . . . she said she cut herself. She said all her friends did it. We were . . . taking her to a counsellor. She stopped . . .'

'It was Gavin,' Lapslie said, sliding the words in like a knife. 'And when she wouldn't let him cut her any more, he moved on. To others. And when she discovered the sound files, she sent one to me. She'd probably looked up "policeman" and "synaesthesia" on the internet and found some reference to me – God knows I've attracted enough journalistic interest over the past year. She must have thought I was the only person who would understand. And when I didn't, when it looked like I was going to be taken off the case, she couldn't face it any more, and she set herself on fire. In front of me, Stephen! *In front of me!*'

Stottart slumped to his knees, eyes wide and mouth open in a silent anguished scream. Lapslie stepped past him as Stottart fell to the carpet, went out onto the landing, leaving the sound file still playing behind him. Mrs Stottart was just coming out of her bedroom, hair awry and eyes wild. She saw Lapslie and started screaming.

Lapslie walked away, leaving a shattered house behind him.

'Tell me you have something,' he asked as he slid back behind the steering wheel of his car.

'I think I do,' Jane Catherall replied. 'I presume you are looking for a location large enough to hold several people in, including dear Emma, and remote enough that screams would not be heard by anyone nearby. The best bet is a boat house located along the coast, out past Felixstowe, on the way to Aldeburgh. It belongs to a yacht club, but the club itself has gone bankrupt and the house is disused. I'll direct you.'

'Right.' Lapslie gunned the engine into life. 'Let's go.'

'Mark – ' she said warningly, 'Felixstowe is in Suffolk, not Essex. We're going into another Force area. Shouldn't you . . . well, *tell* someone? Ask permission?'

'There's lots of things I should do,' Lapslie growled. 'That one is low on the list.'

He drove at frantic speeds up through Essex and into Suffolk, his mind tumbling with images of Emma being sliced open, hung from meat hooks, impaled, disembowelled. Sweat trickled down his ribs and stuck the back of his shirt to the leather car seat. He kept feeling that he couldn't breathe in enough air, that something was sitting inside his chest and taking up all the room.

'Aldeburgh,' Jane mused at one point in the wild ride. 'Benjamin Britten used to live there, you know.'

'Fascinating,' he snapped back. 'If you can access the internet on that thing, can you see if you can get into Gavin Stottart's medical files. I think he's synaesthesic.'

'You can't just access confidential medical records via the internet,' she chided.

'Then phone a friend! I don't care how you do it!'

He was heading out past Ipswich and towards Woodbridge when Jane said, 'I think I've got something. I called in a favour from a colleague, and he emailed me a summary.'

'Go on.'

'Gavin Stottart suffers from achromatia, or achromia as it's sometimes known. It's a neurological deficit that causes a type of sensory deprivation in which the brain can't process colour. He literally only sees in shades of grey.'

'Okay,' Lapslie said, slewing the car around a round-about and cutting up another car. 'More.'

'According to his notes, it's linked to a form of synaes-thesia – ah, you were right! – in which sudden loud noises overload the part of his brain that processes visual signals and cause his vision to completely "grey out". He literally goes blind!'

'Thanks.'

Five minutes later, they were pulling up in front of the defunct yacht club's disused boat house. It was an ugly building in an ugly location: painted breeze blocks set against scrubby grasses and shingle, a single storey at the side adjoining the car park area, but it was built on a slope leading down towards a grey beach where listless waves deposited grey scum on the stones, and the side closest to the beach was two storeys. Gulls cried forlornly in the distance. Tiny black shapes crawled along the horizon: long and low, with built-up super-structures at one end. Ocean-going tankers.

Lapslie was just about to get out of the car when he remembered something. The text message from earlier. He suddenly had an idea what it meant.

He reached across Jane's knees and opened the glove compartment.

There, inside, was a gun. An automatic. A SIG Sauer Mosquito, if he didn't miss his guess.

A little present from Dom McGinley.

Part of Lapslie's brain was screaming, 'Don't touch it, don't get your fingerprints on it, there's probably ten separate murders linked to that gun,' but another part, the dominant part, said, 'Oh fuck it,' and reached out to take the weapon.

'Oh my,' Jane said. 'Normally I disapprove of weapons such as that, having seen their effects at close range, but in this case – lay on, Macduff.'

Lapslie smiled. It felt like a death's-head grin, like something that could have been carved on a pumpkin. 'Call it in,' he said. 'Call it in to DCS Rouse directly. Tell him everything.'

He walked forward, towards the door of the boat house.

If he'd been on duty, if he'd been on his own patch, if he'd not been removed from the case, he would have stood back and declared loudly that he was with the police. Instead, he reached out and opened the door.

The darkness inside seemed to glow of its own accord. He slipped inside and closed the door behind him.

Shadows, and the faint rusty tang of blood. A sense that there was open space to his left and right, and some obstructions ahead. He waited until his eyes adjusted to the meagre illumination.

The building stretched out to either side of him. The roof was exposed, with metal rafters criss-crossing the space. He was in a large, open space that was probably used as a bar or a social area, judging by the chairs and tables scattered around. No sign of Emma. No sign of anyone.

Off to one side he saw a trapdoor. Bloodstains surrounded it: splashes and splatters and droplets, some old and some fresh.

He moved over quietly and raised the trapdoor.

Voices in the distance; ladder-like stairs heading down. He descended, gun ready.

The ladder led down into a dark corridor. Barriers of some kind reached up to a point over his head, separating the space into a series of cell-like enclosures.

The voices were coming from his right, so he went left; SIG Mosquito raised so that the barrel lay alongside his cheek.

The first few cells he came to had brown stains on the concrete floor, and wheelchairs sitting in the middle of the stains like surreal sculptures. *Objets trouvés* – wasn't that the phrase? Found art.

The next cell was empty, but scuff marks in the dirt on the concrete floor indicated that a wheelchair had been wheeled away.

A man was strapped into another of the wheelchairs

in the next cell. His eyes widened when he saw Lapslie. He was just about to say something when Lapslie touched the slide of the gun to his lips, indicating silence. The man nodded. His skin was grey with fatigue or shock, and his hair was dishevelled.

'Mark Baillie?' Lapslie mouthed.

The man nodded.

'Mrs Baillie?'

He jerked his head to his left; Lapslie's right.

'Is the man who kidnapped you here?' Lapslie mouthed.

The man frowned.

'Is the *man* who *kidnapped* you *here*?' Lapslie mouthed again, emphasising the words.

Comprehension dawned. The man nodded, then jerked his head in the other direction – the one that led off to the right from the door where Lapslie had come in.

'Emma Bradbury?' Lapslie questioned silently.

The man nodded.

'Alive?'

Something about his face changed. Lapslie couldn't read the expression. Was it regret? A warning? Or just an indication that he didn't know?

Lapslie moved on, past Mark Baillie, to the next cell. Sara Baillie was in the same situation as her husband: fastened to a wheelchair. Her head was resting on her chest. Lapslie hoped she was unconscious, rather than dead, but either way he was glad that she wasn't in a position to make a surprised noise when she saw him.

The next cell was the last one before the wall. In it, proudly displayed in the centre, was a wheelchair with a third occupant.

This one was dead.

She was slumped in a wheelchair, head lolling unnaturally over the hard, vinyl-covered back. Her face and arms were marble-white with streaks marking where her veins were buried beneath the skin, and the bindings which tied her down were cutting into the swollen flesh. Putrefaction had swollen her lips, mouth and tongue to grotesque proportions. Her blood-soaked jeans were ripped at the knee, and the knees themselves looked like someone had drilled their way inside: dark holes, edged with dried blood and torn tissue.

Whoever she was, she was beyond help now.

Slowly, quietly, he moved back down the building, past Sara Baillie, past Mark Baillie, past the cell where he suspected Emma had been held captive, past the empty cells and past the door where he had entered the building. The weight of the gun was making his wrists ache.

Moving in the other direction, along the wall of the building, he entered a vision of hell.

That part of the building was a large area filled with misshapen objects under sheets. In the centre, strapped in a wheelchair, Emma Bradbury was shaking from side to side, trying to free herself. The wheelchair rocked from side to side, but it didn't fall over. Even if it had, she had nowhere to go.

A microphone on a stand had been set up a few feet in front of her. A cable led away from the microphone to a mixing desk.

Gavin Stottart stood in front of Emma. He had something in his hand; something big. Lapslie recognised him from the Festival Hall, where he had been standing behind his father. Now, alone, he seemed larger, more in control.

He brought his hands around in front of him. He was holding a conical clown's hat in one hand, bizarrely coloured in candy-coloured red and white stripes. In the other he had a saucepan. Whatever was inside steamed, and smelled like road works.

'I'd thought about infecting you with necrotising fasciitis,' he was saying in a very quiet, distressingly sane voice. 'It's surprisingly easy. All I have to do is take a swab from inside my throat, make a cut in your stomach and stick the swab in the cut. The bacteria will just . . . eat away at your skin. It's so fast you can watch it happening, watch your fat and muscle just . . . disappearing. The pain is apparently phenomenal. But it's too fast, and once it's started it can't be controlled, so I chose something else for you. It's called 'pitch-capping'. It was developed by the British Army in Ireland in the eighteenth century. It's a pretty simple concept. I pour melted tar into the hat, like so.' and he tipped the saucepan up, pouring the tar into the hat in a black, glutinous stream. The hat sagged under the weight and the heat. 'And then I put the hat on your head. The tar will settle into your hair. The burns will be – oh, indescribably painful. I'll be recording the sounds you make all the time. Every scream, every cry, every whimper. It will all be captured. And then, when the tar has solidified, I'll pull the hat off. Apparently, according to the historical records, it'll pull your scalp off with it, and I'll be recording that as well. I'll be interested in seeing whether the noises you make then will be different. And the beautiful thing is, you'll probably survive, and then we can try something else. Maybe the Iron Maiden.'

He reached out with the hat towards Emma's head, intending to turn it over quickly and slam it on before any of the tar could escape.

Lapslie fired at the hand holding the hat.

The blast shocked the boy. He whirled around, dropping the hat. Tar splattered down his crotch and his legs. He clapped his hands to his eyes. 'Jesus *Christ*!' he shouted, but the heat of the tar suddenly seared through the cloth of his trousers and he screamed, high and shrill and long.

Emma glanced over at Lapslie with terror in her eyes.

Bizarrely, Gavin began to laugh. 'Oh God, the colours!' he said, and then screamed again as the black, molten mass of his trousers clung to every curve of his skin. 'Oh God, the incredible colours. This is it. This is what I was looking for. This is *perfect!*'

He fell backwards, panting and whimpering with the agonising pain.

Lapslie moved across to free Emma with a pocket knife. She clung to his arm as he pulled her from the chair.

'Thanks, boss,' she breathed. 'I was . . . I—'

'I know,' he said reassuringly. 'I know.'

A sound made him turn around.

Gavin Stottart had pulled himself up onto the mixing desk. His hands were covered with black, steaming tar, and his was smearing it on the sliders as he tried desperately to capture the sound that he had been seeking all his life – the sound of his own screams.

CHAPTER EIGHTEEN

The sea was a sheet of rippled glass extending from the concrete of the flood barrier out to the infinite horizon. There was no mist this time, and Emma could see black objects floating on the water, far away, that might have been birds or might have been boats. It was difficult to tell. She appeared to have lost her perspective somewhere along the way.

The birdwatchers were still there, still with their telescopes and their binoculars. They were still wearing the same anoraks and holding the same thermos flasks. She could swear they were even waiting for the same bird to appear. She hoped it was worth it.

One bird among many, looking to the casual observer just like all the rest. Wasn't that just like police work? You came up with a profile, identified a suspect, arrested him as a criminal, but to anyone else he just looked like one of the flock. Nothing special at all.

She could hear someone climbing the concrete slope behind her. She had a little bet with herself that it was Lapslie, come to see if she was ready to return to work. It wouldn't be Dom, that was for sure. He was content to wait for her to come back to him. That was his style.

A gull cried out overhead, and she flinched. These days, anything that sounded like someone in pain made her heart beat fast within her chest and her mouth go dry.

A figure joined her and stared out across the water. She turned her head, and was mildly surprised to find it wasn't Lapslie or Dom, or anyone else she might have expected. It was Professor Peter Wilkinson from Essex University – the man she had asked about genetically engineered wheat, all that time ago. He was slimmer and taller than she had remembered. His North Face jacket whipped around him in the North Sea wind.

'They said I might find you here,' he said, still staring out into the distance. When she didn't reply, he went on: 'Various people told me you were in various places. I tried them all. This was my last option.'

'It's like the end of the world, here,' she said quietly. 'Which is kind of what I want.'

'I want to help,' he said. 'I know some of what

happened from the newspapers, and some from what people have told me. You don't need to tell me anything, but I do want to help.'

'Why?' she asked.

'Because I like you,' he said simply.

She thought about Dom McGinley, and about what he might think, might say, might do, and then she thought, what the hell? This is the end of the world. I can do what I like here. No consequences.

'Okay,' she said. 'I think what would help right now is hot chocolate piled high with whipped cream, followed by ice cream.'

A pained expression crossed his face. 'I wasn't expecting to go that far,' he said, and then smiled.

She smiled too. Perhaps it *was* all going to be all right.

Perhaps.

AUTHOR'S NOTE

The drug thorazitol, used to treat Mark Lapslie's synaesthesia, was invented for this novel. No such drug exists in reality.

ACKNOWLEDGEMENTS

Thanks to: Andrew Lane, for research, ideas and editorial assistance; Cat and Marc Dimmock, for encouragement and comments at a critical stage of low willpower; and to the indefatigable Robert Kirby, for champagne cocktails and much else. Continued thanks to John Catherall and Dain Morritt, for the use of their names. And a wave to Alec Charles, for adding academic credibility.

ACKNOWLEDGMENTS